"WEREWOLVES AND ROMANCE, WHO COULD ASK FOR MORE?"

—*ParaNormal Romance*

PRAISE FOR MARYJANICE DAVIDSON'S
WYNDHAM WEREWOLF TALES

Derik's Bane

"Putting her own offbeat twist on werewolf mythology, Davidson delivers another hilarious howler. Her gift for dishing up wacky scenarios, witty dialogue, and sexy romance is unmatched."

—*Romantic Times*

"A unique, well-written romantic fantasy with a Camelot twist."

—*Midwest Book Review*

"This new addition to the Wyndham Werewolf Tales by Ms. Davidson was a treat to read . . . I was sorry the story had to end."

—*The Best Reviews*

"One of the most unique werewolves ever described. Have you read about another one who not only loves to cook, but has a 'Free Martha Stewart' T-shirt and is obsessed with meeting Rachael Ray? . . . Thumbs-up . . . Priceless."   —*Reading Amidst the Chaos*

"Love's Prisoner"
(from *Secrets Volume 6*)

"This is by far the sexiest and most romantic story in this collection . . . My Grade: A."   —*All About Romance*

"An arousing triumph."   —Harriet Klausner

"Erotica at its best."   —*Affaire de Coeur*

continued . . .

"Jared's Wolf"
(from *Secrets Volume 8*)

"Four stars!" *—Romantic Times*

"[A] phenomenal story." *—Romance Reviews Today*

PRAISE FOR MARYJANICE DAVIDSON'S NOVELS FEATURING
BETSY TAYLOR, VAMPIRE QUEEN

Undead and Unwelcome

"Packs a chic coffin." *—The Denver Post*

"Twists and turns to keep the readers hooked and longing for the next part." *—ParaNormal Romance*

"A memorable visit with the Wyndham werewolves that fans should enjoy." *—Darque Reviews*

"Outrageously wacky." *—Romantic Times*

Undead and Uneasy

"A winner. Like sitting down to a cup of O-negative with a friend . . . Told with the irreverent humor Ms. Davidson's fans have come to expect." *—Fresh Fiction*

"Fans of Davidson's reluctant vampire queen will be thrilled . . . breezy dialogue, kick-ass action, and endearing characters."
—Booklist

"A charming read whose creator never fails to make me smile . . . MaryJanice Davidson has the terrific ability to create characters that appeal, entertain, and endear themselves to readers."
—A Romance Review

continued . . .

Undead and Unappreciated

"The best vampire chick lit of the year . . . Davidson's prose zings from wisecrack to wisecrack." —*Detroit Free Press*

"Readers who love the sassy . . . Queen of the Undead will enjoy this latest installment." —*Booklist*

Undead and Unemployed

"One of the funniest, most satisfying series to come along lately. If you're fans of Sookie Stackhouse and Anita Blake, don't miss Betsy Taylor. She rocks." —*The Best Reviews*

"I don't care what mood you are in, if you open this book you are practically guaranteed to laugh . . . Top-notch humor and a fascinating perspective of the vampire world." —*ParaNormal Romance*

Undead and Unwed

"Delightful, wicked fun!"
—Christine Feehan, #1 *New York Times* bestselling author

"Chick lit meets vampire action in this creative, sophisticated, sexy, and wonderfully witty book." —Catherine Spangler

Anthologies

CRAVINGS
(with Laurell K. Hamilton, Rebecca York, Eileen Wilks)

BITE
(with Laurell K. Hamilton, Charlaine Harris, Angela Knight, Vickie Taylor)

KICK ASS
(with Maggie Shayne, Angela Knight, Jacey Ford)

MEN AT WORK
(with Janelle Denison, Nina Bangs)

DEAD AND LOVING IT

SURF'S UP
(with Janelle Denison, Nina Bangs)

MYSTERIA
(with P. C. Cast, Gena Showalter, Susan Grant)

OVER THE MOON
(with Angela Knight, Virginia Kantra, Sunny)

DEMON'S DELIGHT
(with Emma Holly, Vickie Taylor, Catherine Spangler)

DEAD OVER HEELS

MYSTERIA LANE
(with P. C. Cast, Gena Showalter, Susan Grant)

Derik's Bane

MaryJanice Davidson

B

BERKLEY SENSATION, NEW YORK

THE BERKLEY PUBLISHING GROUP
Published by the Penguin Group
Penguin Group (USA) Inc.
375 Hudson Street, New York, New York 10014, USA
Penguin Group (Canada), 90 Eglinton Avenue East, Suite 700, Toronto, Ontario M4P 2Y3, Canada
(a division of Pearson Penguin Canada Inc.)
Penguin Books Ltd., 80 Strand, London WC2R 0RL, England
Penguin Group Ireland, 25 St. Stephen's Green, Dublin 2, Ireland (a division of Penguin Books Ltd.)
Penguin Group (Australia), 250 Camberwell Road, Camberwell, Victoria 3124, Australia
(a division of Pearson Australia Group Pty. Ltd.)
Penguin Books India Pvt. Ltd., 11 Community Centre, Panchsheel Park, New Delhi—110 017, India
Penguin Group (NZ), 67 Apollo Drive, Rosedale, Auckland 0632, New Zealand
(a division of Pearson New Zealand Ltd.)
Penguin Books (South Africa) (Pty.) Ltd., 24 Sturdee Avenue, Rosebank, Johannesburg 2196,
South Africa

Penguin Books Ltd., Registered Offices: 80 Strand, London WC2R 0RL, England

"Monster Love" was originally published in e-book format and also appeared in the anthology *Dead and Loving It.*

PRINTING HISTORY
Berkley Sensation mass-market edition / January 2005
Berkley Sensation trade paperback edition / August 2011

Library of Congress Cataloging-in-Publication Data

Davidson, MaryJanice.
  Derik's bane / MaryJanice Davidson.
    p. cm.
  ISBN 978-0-425-24507-1
  1. Werewolves—Fiction. I. Title.
  PS3604.A949D47 2011
  813'.6—dc22

                                                                        2011016475

PRINTED IN THE UNITED STATES OF AMERICA

10 9 8 7 6 5 4 3 2 1

For Giselle McKenzie,
who has been waiting for this book for years.
And my husband, who hasn't.

~• ACKNOWLEDGMENTS •~

Thanks as always to my family, who willingly shares me with the computer, and my husband, who shares the computer with me, not so willingly. Thanks also to the fans of *Love's Prisoner* and *Jared's Wolf*, who write me every week asking for Derik's story. Here it is.

~• CONTENTS •~

"What, were you raised by wolves?"

—SARA GUNN, R.N., PH.D.,
SORCERESS

"Uh . . ."

—DERIK GARDNER,
AMATEUR COOK, WEREWOLF, WYNDHAM AFFILIATION

DERIK'S BANE

PART ONE

Sara and Derik

Prologue

The Past

The man had short brown hair, neatly trimmed. His eyes were that mold-colored shade between gray and brown, a color everyone has seen at one time or another in the back of their fridge. His skin was the color of cheap milk chocolate, and his height was supremely average.

He was dressed in a suit several shades lighter than his skin tone, a white button-down shirt, and a gray tie with brown stripes. He had a plain gold wedding band on the third finger of his left hand, although he wasn't married. He wore black wire-rimmed glasses, although his eyesight was 20/20, and his shoes had never been shined. He looked like an accountant.

He wasn't an accountant.

The man gazed through the glass at DOE, JANE, born seventy-two minutes ago. DOE, JANE was a sweetly chubby infant with a wild shock of dark red hair. DOE, JANE was apparently born surprised, because her hair stood straight up from her skull, and her small reddish brows arched above her blue, blue eyes. She opened her small, wet mouth and let out a yell the man who wasn't an accountant could hear even through the glass.

"Well?" the nurse asked. She was a floater, here at the hospital—so thought those in charge of such things—because of understaffing. In truth, her presence at the delivery of DOE, JANE had been foretold six centuries ago. As had the violent death of DOE, JANE's father just minutes before the child crowned. As had, of course, DOE, JANE herself. "Is it . . . are they right? Is that—?"

"She who will redeem us, and our king," the man replied. "Yes. She is Morgan Le Fay, among us again, and this time she will do what she could not before. This time . . ." The man smiled, showing a great many white teeth. Too many, it seemed, for his average, unassuming mouth. "This time, ours will be done."

The nurse smiled back. By contrast, her smile wasn't frightening in the least—she had the grin of a beauty contestant. But her eyes were dead.

They watched DOE, JANE through the glass for a long time.

One

The Present

Michael Wyndham stepped out of his bedroom, walked down the hall, and saw his best friend, Derik Gardner, on the main floor, headed for the front door. He grabbed the banister and vaulted, dropped fifteen feet, and landed with a solid thud he felt all the way through his knees. "Hey, Derik!" he called cheerfully. "Wait a sec!"

From his bedroom he heard his wife mutter, "I *hate* when he does that . . . gives me a flippin' heart attack every time," and couldn't help grinning. Wyndham Manor had been his home all his life, and the only time he walked up or down those stairs was when he was carrying his daughter, Lara. He didn't know how ordinary humans could stand walking around in their fragile little shells. He'd tried to talk to his wife about this on a few occasions, but her eyes always went flinty, and her gun hand flexed, and the phrase "hairy fascist bastard" came up, and things got awkward. Werewolves were tough, incredibly tough, but compared to Homo sapiens, who wasn't?

It was a ridiculously perfect day outside, and he couldn't blame Derik for wanting to head out as quickly as possible. Still, there was something troubling his old friend, and Michael was determined to get to the bottom of it.

"Hold up," Michael said, reaching for Derik's shoulder. "I want to—"

"I don't care what you want," Derik replied without turning. He grabbed Michael's hand and flung it away, so sharply Michael lost his balance for a second. "I'm going out."

Michael tried to laugh it off, ignoring the way the hairs on the back of his neck tried to stand up. "Touch-ee! Hey, I just want to—"

"I'm going *out!*" Derik moved, cat-quick, and then Michael was flying through the air with the greatest of ease, only to slam into the door to the coat closet hard enough to splinter it down the middle.

Michael lay on his back a moment like a stunned beetle. Then he flipped to his feet, ignoring the slashing pain down his back. "My friend," he said, "you are so right. Except you're going out on the tip of my boot, pardon me while I kick your ass." This in a tone of mild banter, but Michael was crossing the room in swift strides, barely noticing that his friend Moira, who had just come in from the kitchen, squeaked and jumped out of the way.

Best friend or no, nobody—*nobody*—knocked the alpha male around in his own . . . damned . . . house. The other Pack members lived there by his grace and favor, thanks very much, and while the forty-room house had more than enough room for them all, certain things were simply . . . not . . . done.

"Don't start with me," Derik warned. The morning sunlight was slanting through the skylight, shining so brightly it looked like Derik's hair was about to burst into flames. His friend's mouth—usually relaxed in a wiseass grin—was a tight slash. His grass-green eyes were narrow. He looked—Michael had trouble believing it—ugly and dangerous. Rogue. "Just stay off."

"You started it, at the risk of sounding junior high, and you're going to show throat and apologize, or you'll be counting your broken ribs all the way to the emergency room."

"Come near me again, and we'll see who's counting ribs."

"Derik. Last chance."

"Cut it out!" It was Moira, shrieking from a safe distance. "Don't do this in his own house, you idiot! He won't stand down, and you two morons—schmucks—losers will hurt each other!"

"Shut up," Derik said to the woman he (usually) lovingly regarded as a sister. "And get lost . . . this isn't for you."

"I'm getting the hose," she warned, "and then *you* can pay to have the floors resealed."

"Moira, out," Michael said without looking around. She was a fiercely intelligent female werewolf who could knock over an elm if she needed to, but she was no match for two males squaring off. The day was headed down the shit hole already; he wouldn't see Moira hurt on top of it. "And Derik, she's right, let's take this outside—ooooof!"

He didn't duck, though he could see the blow coming. He should have ducked, but . . . he still couldn't believe what was happening. His best friend—Mr. Nice Guy himself!—was challenging his authority. Derik, always the one to jolly people out of a fight. Derik, who had Michael's back in every fight, who had saved his wife's life, who loved Lara like she was his own.

The blow—hard enough to shatter an ordinary man's jaw—knocked him back a full three steps. And that was that. Allowances had been made, but now the gloves were off. Moira was still shrieking, and he could sense other people filling the room, but it faded to an unimportant drone.

Derik gave up trying for the door and slowly turned. It was like watching an evil moon come over the horizon. He glared, full in the face: a dead-on challenge for dominance. Michael grabbed for his throat, Derik blocked, they grappled. A red cloud of rage swam across Michael's vision; he didn't see his boyhood friend, he saw a rival. A challenger.

Derik wasn't giving an inch, was shoving back just as hard, warning growls ripping from his throat, growls that only fed Michael's rage

(rival! rival for your mate, your cub! show throat or die!)

made him yearn to twist Derik's head off, made him want to pound, tear, hurt—

Suddenly, startlingly, a small form was between them. Was shoving, hard. Sheer surprise broke them apart.

"Daddy! Quit it!" Lara stood between them, arms akimbo. "Just . . . don't do that!"

His daughter was standing protectively in front of Derik. Not that Derik cared, or even noticed; his gaze was locked on Michael's: hot and uncompromising.

Jeannie, frozen at the foot of the stairs, let out a yelp and lunged toward her daughter, but Moira moved with the speed of an adder and flung her arms around the taller woman. This earned her a bellow of rage. "Moira, what the hell? Let go!"

"You can't interfere," was the small blonde's quiet reply. "None of us can." Although Jeannie was quite a bit taller and heavier, the smaller woman had no trouble holding Jeannie back. Jeannie was the alpha female, but human—the first human alpha the Pack had known in three hundred years. Moira would follow almost any command Jeannie might make . . . but wouldn't let the woman endanger herself, or interfere with Pack law that was as old as the family of Man.

Oblivious to the drama on the stairs, Derik started forward again, but Lara planted her feet. "Quit it, Derik!" She swung her small foot into Derik's shin, which he barely noticed. "And Daddy, you quit, too. Leave him alone. He's just sad and feeling stuck. He doesn't want to hurt you."

Michael ignored her. He was glaring at his rival and reaching for Derik again, when his daughter's voice cut through the tension like a laser scalpel. "I said *leave him alone.*"

That got his attention; he looked down at her in a hurry. He expected tears, red-faced anger, but Lara's face was, if anything, too pale. Her eyes were huge, so light brown they were nearly gold. Her dark hair was pulled back in two curly pigtails.

He realized anew how tall she was for her age, and how she was her mother's daughter. And her father's. Her gaze was direct, adult. And not a little disconcerting.

"What?" Shock nearly made him stammer. Behind him, nobody moved. It seemed nobody even breathed. And Derik was standing down, backing off, heading for the door. Michael, in light of these highly interesting new events, let him go. He employed his best Annoyed Daddy tone. "*What* did you say, Lara?"

She didn't flinch. "You heard me. But you won't hear me say it again."

He was furious, appalled. This wasn't—he had to—she couldn't—But pride was rising, blotting out the fury. Oh, his Lara! Intelligent, gorgeous—and utterly without fear! Would he have ever *dared* face down his father?

It occurred to him that the future Pack leader was giving him an order. Now what to do about it?

A long silence passed, much longer in retrospect. This would be a moment his daughter would remember if she lived to be a thousand. He could break her . . . or he could start training a born leader.

He bowed stiffly. He didn't show the back of his neck; it was the polite bow to an equal. "A wiser head has prevailed. Thank you, Lara." He turned on his heel and walked toward the stairs, catching Jeannie's hand on the way up, leaving the others behind. Moira had released her grip on his wife, was staring, openmouthed, at Lara. They were all staring. He didn't think it had ever been so quiet in the main hall.

Michael was intent on reaching his bedroom where he could think about all that had just happened, and gain his wife's counsel. He didn't quite dare go after Derik just yet—best to take time for their blood to cool. Christ! It wasn't even eight o'clock in the morning!

"Mikey—what—cripes—"

And Lara. His daughter, who jumped between two werewolves with their blood up. Who faced him down and demanded he leave off. His daughter, defending her dearest friend. His daughter, who had just turned four. They had known she was ferociously intelligent, but to have such a strong sense of what was right and what was—

Jeannie cut through his thoughts with a typically wry understatement. "This *can't* be good. But I'm sure you can explain it to me. Use hand puppets. And me without my So You Married a Werewolf guide . . ."

Then he was closing their bedroom door and thinking about his place in the Pack, and his daughter's, and how he hoped he wouldn't have to kill his best friend before the sun set.

Two

Derik heard the footsteps and slowed. He'd made it almost all the way to the beach but, unless he felt like swimming to London, it was time to stop and think with his head instead of his temper.

Whoever was approaching was downwind, so he didn't know for sure, but he braced himself for Michael. He'd have to apologize, or there would be real trouble. And he *would* apologize. He would. He owed it to his friend, and worse, he'd behaved badly. So he would apologize. Yes. Absolutely.

But it would taste like shit in his mouth.

Derik stared out to sea and shook his head at this sorry-ass turn of events. He and Mike had grown up together. Their mothers had often put them in the same crib to nap. They had experienced their first Change the same month of the same year; he remembered

Mike had been as thrilled, as terrified, as drunk on the moon as he had been. They had chased together, hunted together, killed together. Had defended the Pack together.

He had no problem with Michael; he loved the big dope.

He just didn't love Michael being the boss. Not anymore.

Derik made a fist and hit himself on the thigh. This was his problem, not Michael's, and he had to figure out how to fix it, pronto. He owed the big guy respect, not just brotherly love. And show it he would, no matter how the words wanted to choke him. He wasn't some—some monkey, fighting for the sake of it. He was a werewolf, member of the Wyndham Pack, and fully grown besides. Squabbling was beneath him. So was picking fights.

He turned, forcing a smile . . . and the clod of dirt hit him right in the middle of the forehead. It exploded, and dust sprayed everywhere.

"Idiot! Putz! Dumb ass!"

"Jeez, Moira," he complained, secretly glad showing throat had been put off a bit, "you could have put my eye out."

"I was *aiming* for your eye, you stupid asshole!"

"Now, Moira, you know you shouldn't use such vague terms," he teased. "You gotta speak in black and white, honey, really let people know what's on your mind."

She wasn't having it; the scowl didn't crack. She marched the rest of the way up to him—looking cute as hell in khaki shorts and a lavender T-shirt—and kicked him smartly in the shin. It hurt, too; Moira had toenails like a sloth. "How could you risk your life like that? We nearly had a fight for dominance in the main hall in front of all your friends. In front of Lara! You're lucky Michael didn't tear your head off. You're lucky Jeannie didn't shoot you!"

He didn't want to, but couldn't help it: He felt his lips draw back from his teeth. "I could have taken him."

Moira threw up her hands. "What is *wrong* with you? You've been like a hungry bear all summer. This is a good time for us, Derik—Michael's brought peace, Gerald's gone, we caught the monster who'd been killing those poor girls . . . there's never been a better time to be a werewolf. So why are you trying so hard to screw things up?"

He looked at her, this fine woman, as dear to him as Michael was. *Oh, yeah?* a treacherous inner voice whispered. *Dear to you, huh? You've got a funny way of showing it, jerkoff.*

He didn't have an answer for her. "I don't know what's wrong," he said dully. "I just want to fight, all the time. Everything that comes out of Michael's mouth is pissing me off. I love him, but I could choke him right now just to watch his eyeballs bulge."

Moira's own eyeballs bulged a bit at that, but she recovered quickly. Her eyes—so fine a blue they were nearly lavender—went narrow and thoughtful. She began to pace, looking not unlike a petite blonde general.

"Okay, well, let's figure this out." He smiled in spite of himself. Moira the math genius. Every problem could be broken down to an equation and, thus, solved. Well, hell, she'd figured out where Bin Laden was hiding, hadn't she? Luckily for the world, one of the cabinet members was a werewolf. Moira had sent an e-mail, and forty-eight hours later, hello, spider hole. "Are you in love with Jeannie?"

"Wha— no!"

"Okay, calm down. It's an explanation, you know . . . if you wanted another man's mate."

"Well, I don't. I mean, I *like* her and all, but she's Michael's. Just like he's hers. You can't really picture either of them with anyone else, can you?"

Moira stopped pacing and smiled at him. "No, you're right about that. All right, then," she continued matter-of-factly, "are you in love with me?"

"Ewww, no!"

Unfortunately, she kept going. "Are you upset because I've taken a mate and am having sex with him pretty much every chance I—"

"Aagghh, Moira, please, my eardrums are gonna implode!"

She arched her brows. "'Eww'?"

"Honey, you're too cute to be believed, but I have never— *never*, yuck!—thought of you that way. Never. Ugh! Did I say never?"

"All right, you don't have to induce vomiting to get your point across."

"If it'll get your mind off that track . . ." he warned, fully prepared to shove a finger down his throat.

"Well, it's another theory, that's all."

"A bad, terrible, awful, yucky theory. Baby, we grew up together. You're like the sister I never wanted." He flopped down onto the sand to watch her pace. "Don't take this the wrong way or anything, but if you put your tongue in my mouth, I'd probably barf."

"Mutual, wise guy. Actually, I was sure you were picking a fight because you've got the urge to settle down with a mate, and you're surrounded by mated couples, and . . . well, I know how you feel, is all." She paused, looking pensive. "I was so lonesome before Jared came."

"Moira mated with a monkey, Moira mated with a monkey," Derik sang.

"Shut up, don't call him that! God, I really hate that term."

"I dare you to use it in front of Jeannie," he teased.

"Do I look like I want to spend the rest of the day in an iron lung? Never mind the humans in our lives . . . my point is, I couldn't stand to be around Michael or Jeannie, because seeing their happiness made me feel worse. I figured that was your problem, too."

"Well, it's not. Don't get me wrong, cutie, I'd love to find the right girl and knock her up—"

"And cherish and love her," Moira added dryly.

"—but I've got time. Hell, I'm not even thirty yet."

"Well, we could see if Michael—"

"Leave him out of this."

She chewed on her lower lip for a moment, then adopted an overly innocent expression that put him instantly on guard. The last time she'd looked like that, she had encouraged Lara to cut up his cashmere sweater to make soft puppets. "We should talk to Michael, you know. He's our leader. He'll tell us what to do."

He ground his teeth in irritation. "Moira, whatever the problem is, *I will figure it out*. I don't need Michael shoving his snout in where it's not wanted."

"But he'll fix everything. He'll tell you how to solve your problem, and you'll listen to him, and you'll be better."

"I said I can handle this *by myself*!"

"You don't want his help?"

He bounced to his feet so swiftly, to a human it would have looked like he teleported. "Jesus, do I have to write it on my forehead? Whatever it is, it's my problem, not his, so he should just *leave me be*!"

"Ah," she said quietly. "So that's it. Also, back up before I bite off your chin."

He did, realizing he and Moira were nose-to-nose. As nose-to-nose as they could be, anyway—he was a foot taller. "Sorry. I should probably take a walk, sweetie, I'm not good company right now."

"I wonder when it happened?"

"When *what* happened?" he practically snarled.

"When you became alpha."

"Don't be ridiculous," he said automatically, but inwardly he could feel himself nodding.

"Oh," she said, watching him, "and you knew, of course. Sure. You knew, but you ignored it, because you don't want to hurt anyone, and you don't want to leave us. Why would you? You've lived here all your life—we all have. This is home."

He stared at her. Moira, so pretty and cute and helpless-looking . . . Moira, the most intuitive person he'd ever met. "Sometimes you're scary, you know?"

She smirked. "Of course." Her smile dropped away. "I'm only annoyed I didn't figure it out sooner. But Derik . . . as you know perfectly well, one Pack cannot support two alphas. It just can't.

That's why there are fights for dominance. That's why you have to leave. Now. Today."

"But Moira, I—"

"Now. *Today*. Before this gets worse and you do something we'll all regret, forever." She softened her brisk tone and gently touched his brow. "Because if you or Michael died . . . none of us could bear it."

She didn't add what they both knew. If Michael killed Derik, she would leave. And if Derik killed Michael, she would kill him— try, anyway—and leave. Would the Pack hold? Sure. It had been around for centuries and had been through much worse than the squabbles of alpha males. Would the Pack be a place of love and light any longer?

No.

He didn't dare say a word. She was speaking exact truths, her specialty, and though he could hardly stand to hear the words, he'd ignored the problem long enough. But if he spoke, he'd probably burst into tears like a kid and embarrass them both. He hadn't cried since his mother died, but these thoughts had been heavy on his heart for the last few months.

"Derik, the wolf in you wants the Pack. But the man in you would never forgive himself if he took it."

Still he said nothing, but she stepped closer, and he rested his forehead on her shoulder. They stood that way, motionless on the beach, for a long time.

Three

"Aaaaaagggggg—"

"I'm really sorry—"

"—ggggggggggghhhhhhhhh—"

"—but the transmission's completely shot—"

"—ggggggggggghhhhhhhhh—"

"—and we'll have to keep the car for at least a week—"

"—ggggggggggghhhhhhhhh—"

"—while we work on it—"

"—ggggggggggghhhhhhhhh—"

"—it'll cost a little more than the estimate I gave you . . . Christ, lady, take a breath, will ya?"

Sara Gunn sagged against something large and greasy—not the mechanic—and concentrated on not passing out. New transmission! Eighty zillion dollars to fix, and meanwhile no car for at least a week! Now the mechanic would gouge out her eyes and make her catch up on her laundry, and the day would be complete.

"We coulda caught it earlier if you had more than two oil changes a year," the mechanic ("Dave" was emblazoned on his shirt pocket) said with mild reproach. "Ask me how to save on your next tire rotation!" was on his T-shirt in migraine-inducing yellow. Sara disliked lectures from men who wore instructions on their clothing.

"I hate bringing my car to the garage," she muttered. She could feel the clammy sweat of panic beginning to bead between her shoulder blades.

"How come?"

"Because I always get expensive news!" she snapped. "Look. I'm sorry. I know it's not your fault. It was a shock, and I don't handle surprises well."

"How could you be surprised? Your car's an automatic, but it doesn't change gears unless you hold the accelerator down for at least ten seconds—"

"Well, it started okay, so I didn't think much of it."

"And the cruise control locks up on you all the time—didn't you say the car forced you through a school zone at seventy miles an hour?"

"Hey, it was Sunday at ten o'clock at night, all right? It's not like there were kids around." He frowned at her and she flushed. "Well, that's why I brought it in."

"M' point is, you got no cause to be shocked that it's an expensive problem. You're exactly like a gal who finds a lump in her tit but won't go to the tit doc and then gets pissed when he tells her she has cancer," Dave pronounced. "I see it all the time."

"First of all, that's the worst analogy I've ever heard. Second, I'm not paying you to lecture me."

"Actually, you ain't paid me at all," he pointed out with a grin. She could be cute, if you liked them rangy and curvy and red-haired, which he surely did. "Nope, not a cent."

"Well, I'm going to, okay? Hell, your kids will go to Harvard thanks to my stupid transmission." On "stupid," she kicked her rear left tire.

"Ha! Harvard. I coulda gone," he confided, "but I didn't want to live on the other coast."

"Trust me, it was overrated." Sara sighed and ran her fingers through her too-long bangs. If hair that grew past your chin could be considered bangs. "Well, as long as you're doing the transmission thing, see what you can do about the clock. It goes off when I turn on my headlights."

"It does?"

"Yes. But as soon as I turn my lights off, it comes right back on, except then it's wrong, and I have to adjust the time until the next time I turn on my headlights. Also, I lost the car lighter—"

"How could you lose—?"

"I just looked down one day and it was gone, all right? Why don't you get a spotlight and shine it into my eyes? Anyway, every once in a while sparks will shoot out from the lighter, which is kind of distracting."

"I guess *so*."

"My horn doesn't work, either."

"Now, how did that happen?"

She ignored the question. "Also, my radio only gets the local pop station. Which wouldn't be so bad, but they play about six Lenny Kravitz songs each hour." She sighed again. "I used to like Lenny Kravitz."

Dave blinked slowly, like a lizard. "Why haven't you bought a new car?"

"It was my mom's car," she said simply. "She loved the wretched thing."

"Oh." He gnawed his lower lip a moment. Everybody in town knew what had happened to Mrs. Gunn. Nobody talked about it. He'd have felt sorry for her even if she wasn't such a dolly. And Sara *was* cute, with those crystal blue eyes and the flyaway mass of red curls. Her skin was perfectly white, like fresh cream . . . not a freckle in sight. He figured if she ever set foot on a tropical beach, she'd go up in flames.

"Look, Dr. Gunn, I'm sorry to be the bringer of bad news to you and stuff, but I'll get your car in as quick as I can. Shouldn't take more than a few days."

"A few days of purgatory!" she shouted, startling him. That was another thing about Dr. Gunn. You'd be having a perfectly normal conversation with the woman, when she'd start screaming. It was true about the temperament of redheads, and that was a fact.

"Meantime, I got a loaner I can let you have for"—at least forty a day, or his boss would kill him. Okay, thirty. Twenty-five ninety-five and that was his final offer—"for nothing. On account of you getting such a bad shock and all."

She smiled and he nearly fell back into the tire pile. She was cute when she was ranting and fussing and being a pain. She was completely gorgeous when she smiled. Her dimples popped into view, and her eyes crinkled at the corners and made you wonder what her mouth would taste like.

He smiled back.

What are you doing, Davey old pal? You got as much chance with Dr. Sara Gunn as you've got to grow tits and fly away.

"That'd be great, Dave," she said with real warmth. "I'm sorry about the tantrum."

"It's not the first one I've seen. You gotta temper on you like a rabid polecat." He said this with total admiration.

"Uh . . . thank you."

"Maybe after your car is fixed, we could have dinner?"

"Of course! And it'll be my treat, for the free loaner." She smiled at him again. The way she smiled at her students, her colleagues, love-struck mechanics. Dr. Gunn was brainy, high-strung, occasionally shrill, and had no freakin' clue she was a stone knockout.

"Thanks," he sighed. *Ehh. Worth a shot.* "I'll call you when I get an idea how long it'll take."

"Thanks again."

He ended up giving her the nicest loaner he had, a silver 2004 Dodge Stratus. His boss would strangle him like a rooster when he found out what he'd done.

Screw it.

Four

"You have to save the world."

Derik fought to keep his jaw from dropping. "Me?"

"Yes, brain-drain, you. In fact, could you get started on that right away?"

Moira clapped her hands. "A quest! Just what you needed, oh, it's perfect, perfect!"

"A quest? Do I look like a Hobbit to you? *I* have to save the world? From what?"

Antonia smirked. "From who, actually."

"From whom, actually," Moira corrected.

Antonia glared at her. Moira stared back, eyebrows arched, and after a moment the taller woman dropped her gaze. Antonia was one of those rare human/werewolf hybrids, but nobody liked her much. Born of a human father and a were mother, she couldn't

Change, though she had the preternatural strength and speed common to their kind.

Being unable to Change had been a tremendous burden on her as a child . . . the Pack expected much from its hybrids. Her parents tried—and failed—to hide their despair. Hers had not been an easy adolescence, as much from the tremendous pressure she put on herself, as anything ever said, or intimated. "The only thing I have going for me," she often said with bitter insight, "is my looks. And around here, gorgeous bims are a dime a dozen."

This was true. No one was sure if it was breeding or genetics or great good fortune or the omnivore diet, but werewolves, in addition to being exceptionally strong and exceptionally fast, were exceptionally easy on the eyes. Antonia had enormous dark eyes and creamy skin, long legs and the figure of a swimsuit model, but it didn't set her apart.

Nobody had a clue what Antonia was until she woke up the morning of her seventeenth birthday, made herself toast and poached eggs, then fell over in a dead faint. When she regained consciousness, she brushed the egg out of her hair and told her astonished parents, "Michael's going to get someone pregnant today, will be married by summertime and a father before Easter. Oh," she added thoughtfully, "the baby will be a girl, and the epidural won't work for the mom-to-be. Hee!"

To everyone's amazement, she had been right. It was the first of dozens of predictions, some mild ("Moira's going to get stuck with another audit . . . ha!"), some major ("Stay the hell out of New York on September 11, 2001."). She was never wrong. She was never even off a little bit. No one had seen anything like it. No one was even sure what it meant—could werewolves harness mental power as well as physical? It was a mystery to all.

And overnight, Antonia had gone from Pack Nobody to Pack Demigod. Piss her off, and nothing might happen . . . or she might foresee your death and fail to warn you, out of spite.

Now here she was, holding court in the solarium, explaining that the world was going to end unless Derik made it to 6 Fairy Lane, Monterey, California, as soon as possible.

"You guys know who Morgan Le Fay is?"

Moira nodded. Derik blinked. "Guess I'll play dumb blonde," he said, avoiding Moira's poke. "No idea."

"She was the half sister of King Arthur," Antonia explained. "She had an incestuous affair with her brother and was responsible, indirectly, for his death. She was also a powerful sorceress."

"Uh-huh. That's fascinating, hon. I like story time as much as the next fella, but this is relevant because . . . ?"

"I got a line on her."

"A line on her," Moira repeated. "Toni, what in God's name are you talking about?"

"An-TON-ee-uh. And Morgan Le Fay is in Monterey Bay."

"You're a poet, and you don't know it," Derik joked, and was unsurprised to see both women ignore him.

"She's reincarnated and goes by the name of Dr. Sara Gunn. You have to get over there and take care of her. If you don't, a week from now none of us will be here."

Dead silence, broken by Moira's faint, "Oh, Antonia . . . for real?"

"No, I made it all up because I want the attention," she snapped. "Yes! The world's gonna end, and we're all fucked, unless the Pack's answer to The Rock gets his ass in gear."

Another brief silence, and then Moira said, "I think—I think I'd better go get Michael and Jeannie."

For once, Derik didn't argue.

~ ◦ ◦ ◦ ~

Michael cleared his throat from the doorway. "You're going, then?"

Derik straightened up from his packing. He'd tossed a few things into a carry-on and was ready to leave. More than ready. He was taking the Wyndham jet to San Jose, California, and from there he'd pick up a rental car to the Monterey Peninsula. He'd already said good-bye to Moira and Jeannie.

"Yeah, I'm going now. In fact, I'd better get a move on."

"Well. Be careful. Don't let her get the drop on you."

"The reincarnation of the most powerful sorceress in the history of literature, fated to destroy the world in the next few days? No chance," he bragged, and was relieved to see a ghost of a grin on Michael's face. "Leave it to me. This'll be just like the time I agreed to cater your mating ceremony. Except with less flour."

"I am leaving it to you," Michael said seriously. "You knew Jeannie was pregnant again, right?"

He nodded. They all knew.

"Well, for God's sake, don't tell her you knew before I told you,"

Michael said hastily. "I had the worst time pretending to be surprised when she finally got around to breaking the news. And, of course, she knew I wasn't surprised, and then the shit hit the fan."

"It's not your fault you can smell it on her," he said, puzzled.

"You'd think. Anyway . . . my point is . . . everything I have, and am, is in your hands. It's too bad—" *We haven't been getting along* was the obvious end to that statement, but his friend was too tactful to say it.

"Yeah. Don't worry, chief."

Michael smiled again. "I'm not. Well, I am, a little—it's how I'm made. But, hell, if anyone can save the world, you can. I'd bet my life on it." He paused. "I *am* betting my life on it."

Derik was too gratified to speak for a moment. He remembered his earlier words—his earlier actions—and felt his face burn with shame. So he wanted his own Pack—or at least, wanted to be his own man. Did that mean he had to treat his best friend like something to be scraped off the bottom of his shoe?

"Uh . . . thanks . . . but before I go . . ." He slung his bag over one shoulder, crossed the room, and started to hunch lower, prepared to show throat.

Michael grasped his shoulder and jerked him back up. "Don't do that," he said quietly. "For one thing, you're off to save the world, so as far as I'm concerned, the slate's clean between us. For another, Moira says you could be alpha. Since I'm pretty sure she's never been wrong about anything—"

"It's annoying," Derik agreed.

"—it's best for you to get out of the habit of showing throat as soon as possible."

Derik paused. "So . . . we almost had to cha-cha today, but because I'm gonna save the world, you're gonna let that go?"

"That's just the kind of swell guy I am," Michael said solemnly, and both men cracked up, their laughter sounding more like howls than anything else.

Five

The Monterey Peninsula

He knew it made him shallow. He knew he was probably too old for such nonsense. He knew he should be focused on saving the world. But he couldn't help it.

Derik loved convertibles. And this one was sublime—electric, eye-watering blue, with leather seats and a superb sound system. Robert Palmer's "Addicted to Love" was tearing his head off, because, joy of joys, he'd found a local all-eighties rock radio station. The weather was gorgeous—low 70s and sunny—and his proximity to the ocean meant that thousands and thousands of tantalizing scents were on the air.

He took a gulp and dizzily tried to process. Derik's nose was an instrument of frightening precision, but even it could be confused and overwhelmed. Shit, that was half the fun of a convertible! Right now he was smelling seaspraylilacshottarmacdeerpoop-

raccoonsseagullfeathers—whoops! Now he was getting a tantalizing whiff of fishoceangrasslawnmowerexhaustpossumfriedchicken
and—thank you, Jesus!—girlsweat and Dune perfume.

*I am in California, land of babes and cool cars and movies-of-the-week,
but I can't think about that until I save the world.*

At the thought of what was riding on this little day trip, his
heart lurched. He had always thought of himself as a mellow kind
of fellow (recent events notwithstanding), and if someone had told
him he'd be responsible for saving the world—not the Pack, or
even his closest friends, but the *world*, the *entire world* . . . well, his
mind just couldn't get around it. It would try, and then it would
veer away and think about something stupid, like how great it was
to find an eighties radio station so far from home.

Saying good-bye to Lara did it. Brought it home for him, however briefly. He loved that little stinker like she was his own pup.
He'd die for her in a New York minute. He'd wring the neck of
anybody who hurt her and snap the spine of anyone who made her
cry. But if he fucked up—if this Morgan gal got away from him—
Lara would never make it to first grade. Never go on a date, never
experience her first Change. Never grow up to be his boss, the
way her daddy was.

Shit, he'd almost burst out crying just saying good-bye to her.

Quickest done, quickest back home. Not that he was so terribly
anxious to go back home—the mansion held its own unique set of
problems. Derik figured you knew your life was screwed up when
you were almost glad you could use saving the world as a
distraction.

Well. He and Mike would work shit out. They had to. Otherwise—otherwise, he just would never go home again, even though that probably wasn't the best way to handle things.

He didn't trust himself around Mike, that was all. If he lost his temper and things got way out of hand, the deed would be done, and Mike would be dead, and he'd be Pack leader, and Jeannie would be a widow, and Lara would be without a daddy, and then he'd probably go off in a corner and blow his brains out. Better to be a *(coward)* loner than risk that. Way better.

~ . . .~

Sara Gunn thrust her foot into the second pair of panty hose of the morning and, incredibly, had the same thing happen. There was a zizzzzzzzz! sound, and then her big toenail ripped a runner through her last pair of panty hose.

"Right," she grumbled. "Why is it that when I'm running late, everything goes wrong? More important, why am I talking to myself?" She jerked the nylon torture chamber off her foot and flung it over her shoulder to the floor. "Okay, then . . . it's gorgeous out. A perfect day to go bare-legged." She ran a hand down her left leg. A little raspy, but hardly Yosemite Sam whiskers. *Note to self: Shave legs more often when low on panty hose.*

She heard the doorbell, that annoying dum-DUM-dum-dum . . . dum-DUM-dum . . . dum-DUM-dum-dum-DUM! Dah-dum-dah-dum-dum. She cursed her late mother's infatuation with Alex Trebek and *Jeopardy*. Every time she had a visitor, she felt like phrasing everything in the form of a question.

I will never see twenty-five again . . . or twenty-eight, for that matter, and I never quite managed to move out of my mother's house. Nice one, Gunn. Not pathetic at all!

She slipped her feet into a pair of low-heeled pumps and squinted distractedly at the mirror. Hair: presentable, if not exactly glamorous, caught up in one of those big black clips that looked like a medieval torture device. Skin: too pale; no time for makeup. Eyes: big and blue and bloodshot—damn that *Deep Space Nine* marathon, anyway. Suit: cream linen, which meant she'd be a wrinkled mess in another hour. Legs: bare. Feet: narrow and stuffed into shoes so pointy, she could see the crack between her first and second toe.

"Too bad, my girl!" she told herself. "Next time don't hit the snooze button so many times."

Dum-DUM-dum-dum . . . dum-DUM-dum . . . dum-DUM-dum-dum-DUM! Dah-dum-dah-dum-dum.

"Be right there!" She hurried out of her bedroom, glanced through the kitchen, and breathed a sigh of relief at the sight of the loaner car. Finally! David, her mechanic, had at last had a chance to send over a loaner car for her use. A flashy loaner car, at that. Well, beggars can't be . . . et cetera. The other loaner had conked out after an hour—was it her fault she couldn't drive a stick?

She flung the door open. "Thank goodness you're—whoa."

She stared at the man standing on her front porch. He was, to be blunt, delicious. He was to Homo sapiens what a hot fudge sundae was to vanilla ice cream: a complete and total improvement on the original. A full head taller than she was, he practically filled the door frame. His blond hair was the color of sunlight, of ripe wheat, of—of something really gorgeous. He had swimmers' shoulders and she could actually see the definition of his stomach muscles through the green T-shirt he wore. The shirt had the puzzling logo "Martha Rocks" in bright white letters. He was wearing khaki shorts, revealing heavily muscled legs tapering into absurdly large feet, sockless in a pair of battered loafers. His hands, she noticed, were also quite large, with squared off fingers and blunt, short nails.

He was lightly tanned and had the look of a man equally at home camping in the woods, lounging poolside, or hunched over a computer. His eyes were the brilliant green of wet leaves, and they sparkled with turbulence and lusty good humor. His mouth was wide and mobile and looked made for smiling.

He was smiling at *her*.

Get a grip, she ordered herself. She was annoyed to find her pulse was racing. *It is unbelievably juvenile to be panting at this man, when all he's done is ring your bell twice and stand there. He hasn't even opened his mouth and you're practically a puddle on your own doorstep. He—oh, oh! He's talking!*

"—wrong house."

"What did you say?"

"I said, I must have the wrong house." His smile widened, as his gaze raked her from head to foot, taking in her bare legs, scuffed shoes, rumpled suit, and messy hair. His teeth were perfectly straight, almost blindingly white, and looked sharp. The guy probably ate his steak raw. He could make a fortune doing Chiclets commercials. "I'm sorry to bother you."

"No, you've got the right house. I've been waiting for the loaner." She nodded at the flashy little blue convertible. "The other profs are going to accuse me of entering my midlife crisis a little early, but what can you do? Come in. How are you getting back to the garage?"

He stepped inside, and as she reached past him to shut the screen door, she was reminded all over again—as if she needed it!—just how large he was. She was not a petite woman by any means—in fact, she ought to lay off the chocolate croissants—but he made her feel absolutely tiny. She caught a sniff of him and nearly purred. He smelled like soap and male. Big, clean male.

He glanced around her kitchen. "Listen, I don't want to put you out, but can you tell me which house is number 6 Fairy Lane?"

"It's this one," she said with bare impatience. Gorgeous, but not terribly bright. Well, nobody was perfect. "I told you, you're in the right place. I'm running late for rounds, so if you could just arrange to have someone pick you up—"

"Yeah, I'll do that. 'Cuz there's obviously been a mistake."

"Tell me about it," she said, looking at him with longing. In a perfect world, he would be her pool boy. Instead, she was late for work and he had to hitch a ride back to his place of business. "Well, thanks for dropping off the car—see you."

He followed her onto the porch. "It was nice meeting you. Sorry about the misunderstanding." But, interestingly, instead of being regretful, he sounded weirdly relieved.

Odd! But, she had no time to ponder it. "Bye!"

She got the car going with no trouble—she'd heard the phrase "the engine purred like a kitten" before but had no real experience with it until now—and pulled out of the driveway. She waved to the man who should have been her pool boy, who was looking as though he'd had a touch of sun, and dropped the pedal.

Six

Derik went to the nearest safe house, the one down the block from the aquarium. An adorable cub answered the door, a boy about eight years old with big dark eyes and black hair.

"Hi," Derik said. "Are your folks home?"

"Sure. What's your name?"

"Derik."

"Okay. Come on in."

Derik followed the boy into a kitchen that smelled like cookie dough and found the lady of the house up to her elbows in butterscotch chips. "Well, hi there," she said, her greeting a soft Midwestern twang. "My name's Marjie Wolfton; this is my son, Terry. Do you need some help?"

"Just a private phone. I'm—uh—sort of on a mission to—um—

never mind." He just couldn't bring himself to say "save the world." It was too bizarre.

Marjie, however, seemed to know all about it. Either that, or she was used to strange werewolves showing up at her door. "Yes, of course. Terry, show Derik the den."

"Okay." The boy snatched a fistful of dough and disappeared down a hallway. Derik followed him into the den, which had a hardwood floor, windows set into the ceiling, a computer, a phone, and a television.

"Are you from Massachusetts?" Terry asked.

"Uh-huh." He was going to have to call Antonia and figure out this mess. No way was that distracted cutie Morgan Le Fay. *No* way. "How'd you know? Am I dropping my Rs?"

The boy ignored the question. "And you live with Michael Wyndham? The Pack leader?"

Derik looked at the boy, really looked. That was pure hero worship, if he wasn't mistaken. And since he used to think of Michael's father in the exact same way, Derik completely understood where the kid was coming from. Men who took a Pack . . . ran a Pack . . . they were just . . . different. More *there*. And they could make you like them. It was a talent, the way some people could raise just one eyebrow. It was hard to explain.

"Yeah, I live out there with those guys. Michael's my best friend." Was? Is? *Save the world first,* he reminded himself. *Then you can worry about it.* "He's a really great guy, and his wife is supercool. You should try to get out to see him sometime."

"I'm going when I'm twenty." The age of consent, for werewolves. Eighteen was too damned young; everybody knew that. "I'm going to see if he needs a bodyguard, or maybe Lara will." The boy hugged himself and smiled. "I can't wait! I bet it's so cool, living in a mansion with all the boss weres."

"It's pretty great," Derik admitted. And it had been, until he'd fucked it up. Until he'd gotten the idea in his head that he could be a boss were. Dumb ass. "I'll put in a good word for you, if you want."

"Would you?" The boy's eyes, already big, went huge. "That'd be great. Thanks a lot."

"What do your folks think about your ambition?"

"Oh." The boy waved his parents away in the careless manner of preadolescents. "Mom wants me to stay out here and go to USC. Dad says I should aspire to more than being a 'spear carrier,' that's what he calls it. But I don't care. They're doing what *they* like. Now it's my turn. I mean, it will be."

"Well, while you're waiting to turn twenty, you could take a year or two of college, see if it suits you."

Terry shrugged.

"Terry! Get out of there and let the man have some privacy."

Terry sniffed the air. "Also, cookies are almost ready," he muttered.

"And cookies are almost ready! So get out here!"

Derik cracked up when the boy rolled his eyes and walked out, closing the door behind him. Jesus, had he ever been that young?

Sure he had; he and Michael and Moira had practically been littermates. Man, the shit they used to pull . . . it's a wonder Michael's mom hadn't drowned them all.

He picked up the phone and punched in the main number of the mansion.

"Wyndham residence," Jeannie answered, sounding harassed.

"Hey, Jeannie, it's me, D—"

"Lara! No! Don't you dare jump from there—don't you dare! Hello?"

"Uh, yeah, Jean, it's me, D—"

"Lara! I don't care if your dad does it all the time. Your dad's an idiot! And if you think I'm wasting my afternoon by driving you to the E.R.—hello?"

"It's Derik!" he hollered. "Can you patch me through to Antonia's house, please?"

"Jeez, stop with the yelling. Sure I will. How's it going? Save the world yet?"

"I'm gonna, just as soon as I finish my butterscotch chip cookie," he said dryly.

"All righty. Patching you—Lara!—through now." There was a smooth, humming silence, then another ringing telephone.

"That *is* Morgan Le Fay," Antonia said by way of greeting. "She's an unspeakably evil creature and must be stopped from destroying the world. So get your ass back there and take care of her."

"What? Antonia? How'd you know it was—"

"I don't know about you," she said, "but I don't have a lot of time for dumb questions. Also, you're boring the tits right off of me."

"Come on, you should *see* this girl! There's no way she's the one. She's a goof, and she's *so* cute. Not to mention really clueless. I think you got your wires crossed, or whatever, on this one."

"Impossible. It's her. And you know what they say about the devil and pleasing faces. Now get back there and do your job."

"This sucks," he said to the empty line, and hung up.

"Cookie?" Marjie asked brightly when he stomped into the kitchen.

He took six.

~ • • ~

Sara Gunn, the unspeakably evil creature, noticed the van as she was parking her loaner, but shrugged it off—Monterey wasn't *that* big a town, and lots of people went to and from the hospital. Monterey Bay General was a teaching hospital, the largest in two hundred miles, and the parking lot was the size of a small college campus.

She hurried through the main lobby, afraid to look at her watch to see how late she was. Dr. Cummings hated it when staff was late for grand rounds, though God knows he'd kept them waiting often enough. And even though she was *Dr.* Gunn, her doctorate was in nursing, so to old-school jerkoffs like Cummings, she was just a glorified maid with an extra diploma. Most days it slid off her like water off a duck, but days like today, when she knew she was in for a reaming and resented the hell out of it, she—

"Sara Gunn!"

She had been just about to step into the elevator when she heard her name and jerked her foot back. She turned, and her brain processed the half-dozen men dressed in—could it be?—flowing red robes. They had monks at the hospital now? Monks dressed in red? Like big lipsticks?

Armed monks?

An avid movie fan, Sara recognized nine-millimeter Beretta pistols when she saw them and was so startled, she froze in place. It was the context, of course. Sure. Seeing men in robes (big lipsticks!), toting guns, in the hospital, *her* hospital, was just . . . weird. If she had any sense, she'd be screaming her head off and hitting the floor, like several of the people around her, but she just stared, and now she was staring down the barrel of more than one pistol, and how many people could say *that* in life, that not only did they have one gun pointed at them, they had several, it was just too—

The one nearest her tripped on the newly mopped floor, knocking over the bright yellow CAUTION sign. He hit hard, too hard; she heard the wet snap as his neck broke.

She heard a muffled explosion from her left and flinched, but the pistol had misfired and the barrel imploded; the would-be gunman was screaming through a faceful of blood, screaming and staggering around and dripping. He'd lost all interest in her, and she could actually hear his blood pattering to the floor, which now needed to be mopped again.

The clip fell out of the third one's gun, something Sara had never seen before—a day for firsts! She didn't realize clips *could* fall out of guns, just slide out and clunk to the floor without anyone touching it, but this one had, and the robed man had taken to his heels, and then the lobby tipped crazily, as someone kicked her feet out from under her.

"Cross of Christ," Dr. Cummings grumped. He was lying on the floor beside her, and she realized he was the one who had knocked her down. His white beard, hair, and eyebrows were their usual chaotic mess; the eyebrows in particular resembled a pair of large, struggling, albino caterpillars. He looked like a pissed-off Colonel Sanders. "Leave the hospital for fifteen minutes, and the whole damned place falls apart. Last time I ever try to get coffee before rounds."

"Sorry I'm late," she said to the tile.

"Do you know why they're trying to kill you?"

"I have no idea. They—they knew my name." She realized she was existing in a ball of shock-induced calm. Well, that was all right. It was better than the screaming meemies. "But they're not having much luck, is the thing, and lucky for me."

She heard a terrific explosion, magnified in the lobby, and then heard it again, and saw the last two men fall, and saw the policeman standing by the Information Desk, gun out, very pale.

"Lucky for you," Dr. Cummings said, "there was a cop here."

"Uh-huh."

"Really lucky," he said, giving her a strange look.

"I'm going to go throw up now, I think."

"No you aren't. We're late for rounds." He seized her by the elbow—for a man in his late fifties, he was as strong as a PCP addict—and hauled her to her feet, then pushed her into the elevator. "You can puke later."

"I'll make a note of it in my Palm Pilot," she said, but already the urge was passing. Damn Dr. Cummings! Or bless him. She could never decide which.

Seven

The pool boy was still there when she got home. He was sitting on her front steps, chin cupped in hand, obviously waiting for her.

Sara brought the convertible to a smoking halt, bolted out the door, and ran to him. She had no idea why he was still there—Couldn't get a ride? Had news about her car?—and she didn't care. After the morning she'd had, she needed to talk to someone, and Dr. Cummings wasn't what you'd call a warm and nurturing person. This walking Ken doll would do just fine.

"You wouldn't believe it, you *wouldn't* believe it!" she cried as he stood. She seized a fistful of his shirt and shook it. He stared down at her. "A bunch of robed weirdos came to the hospital today and tried to kill me! There were guns all over the place!"

"I believe it," he said, nodding glumly.

"*And* I was late for grand rounds! And then I had to talk to the police for, like, ever. And I have no idea why you're here, but I have to tell you, I'm going in for a drink before I do anything, but you can have your car back, and maybe I'll have two drinks, I—I—oh, crap." She was fumbling with her keys and finally got her kitchen door unlocked.

Wordlessly, he followed her inside. She was momentarily uneasy, then dismissed it. Lightning wasn't going to strike twice today, and, besides, she knew this guy. Sort of. At least, her mechanic knew him. She was pretty sure.

"You wouldn't believe it, you wouldn't *believe* it," she babbled again, pawing through her freezer for the bottle of Grey Goose vodka. A screwdriver—light on the O.J.—was just what she needed. Possibly more than one. Possibly half a dozen. "What a crazy day! Even saying 'crazy day' doesn't do it justice—"

"Wait." At his command, she fell (uncharacteristically) silent. "You're Sara Gunn?"

"What? Of course I am. You know who I am. Yes. Am I out of ice? Oh, who cares. I'll drink it neat, if I have to . . . is vodka good with vanilla ice cream?"

"Sara Gunn of 6 Fairy Lane?"

"Yes. We've been *over* this." He was so beautiful, and so, so dumb. It wasn't fair. Like she needed *this*, today of all days. "Now, d'you want a drink? Because I'm having one. Or do you need a ride? Am I supposed to keep the blue one? It's a nice car and all, but not really my style. Although frankly, the day I've had, I don't give a shit either way." Belatedly, she remembered her manners.

"I'll call the garage for you and have someone come pick you up. Okeydokey?"

He scowled at her, his gorgeous green eyes narrowing until they looked like pissed-off lasers. "D'you think you can ramp down the condescension a little bit, Miss Gunn? I get enough of that from my friend Moira."

"Doctor Gunn," she said automatically, even as she blushed. "Sorry," she added. "It's just that you seemed . . . confused. Even more than me. And that's saying something." She reached for the phone. "I'll call the garage."

He took the phone out of her hand, moving so quickly she didn't realize he'd taken it, until she saw he was holding the cordless.

Odd. Odd! One second he'd been standing by the kitchen door, the next he was *right in front of her*. It was like watching a home movie, speeded up. Had she started drinking already?

He made a fist, still holding the phone, and then small pieces of plastic were raining down on her tile.

"I'm really, really sorry about this," he said dully. "It won't hurt. Just stand still."

"*What* won't hurt?"

His hands reached for her throat.

Eight

At the last second, she wriggled out of his grip like a greased fish and kicked his shin pretty hard for a human. It actually hurt. "What is *wrong* with you?" she screeched. Her eyes were starry and wild. She reeked of tension and stress and fury. "Has everyone in this town gone completely nutso bonkers today?"

"Sort of." He took another swipe at her—if he could get his hands around her neck, he could end it in about half a second for her—she'd be in Heaven before she heard the snap. She ducked, and his hands closed on air. "It doesn't really matter. I'm so sorry. But I have to do this. You're—I guess you're pretty dangerous. Sorry," he added lamely.

"Jerkoff, you have no idea! Now get the hell out of my house!" She snatched a statuette from the shelf by her head, and he ducked, but not fast enough—the five-inch-high Precious Moments figurine hit his forehead just above his right eye and exploded. By the time he shook the chips out of his hair and wiped the blood off his brow, she had darted down the hallway.

Grimly, he plodded after her. He didn't much like killing—heck, he'd only killed two people in his entire life, and they'd both been rogue werewolves. That had been a totally different thing, not even in the same universe as what he was attempting now. He'd been defending the Pack then, and that was entirely different from snapping this poor girl's neck.

This is defending the Pack, too, buddy. You'd better believe it. Now get your head in the game!

He tried. He really did. He understood intellectually that this sort of thing went against his even-tempered grain. He also understood that this woman was a threat to his family, his entire way of life. Intellectually. But he wasn't angry at her, he wasn't scared of her, she wasn't fucking somebody dangerous, he wasn't defending territory, he wasn't feeling any of the things he needed to feel in order to be okay with breaking a person's neck.

Not to mention, Sara Gunn was a stone cutie. He really liked her, even on such short acquaintance. He liked her sass, he liked her scatterbrained good humor, and he *loved* the way she smelled: like roses wrapped in cotton. Since she was a doctor, he figured she was the comely female embodiment of the absentminded professor, which was cute all in itself. Another time and place, and he'd be tempted to charm her into getting a nice hotel room for the day and . . .

He caught up with her in the hallway, but she tripped as he

reached for her neck, and he missed again. Well, of course he did. His heart was so completely not in this, it would have been funny if it wasn't so fucking depressing.

She kicked out at him from the floor and scrambled away. He reached again, and this time *he* tripped, falling hard enough to rattle his teeth.

Christ, will you get on*? Stop drawing this out! Bad enough you have to kill her, you've got to play cat and mouse first? Scare her worse than she is? Asshole.*

Except she wasn't so much scared as infuriated. Oh, he could smell the fear, an undercurrent beneath her rage, but she was primarily pissed. He really liked her for it. Any other woman— person!—would have been gibbering in the corner and begging for their life.

He climbed to his feet—only to be hit in the face with a box of tampons. The white missiles exploded out of the box and rained down on the floor.

"Get . . . *lost!*" she shrieked, hurling a perfume bottle at him. This time he did duck, and the bottle shattered behind him. Instantly the hallway reeked of lavender, and he sneezed.

"Out!"

"I can't," he said, then sneezed again. "You know, if you just stand still a minute, it'll be over in—"

"Fuck you!"

"Right. Well, that's understandable. I mean, I wouldn't stand still for this, either. It's okay," he added soothingly, if inanely. What, exactly, was okay? Nothing. Not a single goddamned thing.

He followed her into a bedroom and was momentarily startled at the sheer mess—it looked like someone had been killed in there. Then he realized that she was just a slob. There were clothes on almost every surface, and he couldn't tell what color the carpet was because of all the junk on the floor.

There were plenty of things to throw, too, and her aim was frightening—he was fast, but in her terror and anger, she was just a bit faster, raining missiles on him and shrieking like a fire alarm. He ducked about every two out of three, but that still left him vulnerable to: a jar of Noxema, an empty vase that smelled like stale water and dead flowers, a DVD case (*Vertigo*), a remote control, an empty box of Godiva chocolates, a box of computer discs, a hardcover copy of Stephen King's *The Stand*—cripes, how much did *that* weigh?

Have you noticed you haven't been able to kill her? Sure, you're phoning it in, but come on—you're a werewolf in your prime. So how come she's not a corpse?

His inner voice sounded weirdly like Michael, which made him inclined to ignore it. Normally. But he realized—on the top of his mind this time, not just the bottom—that it was true. He hadn't been able to kill her. Every time he got close, she tripped, or he did, or she scored with another missile. His head was throbbing, and it was hard to think.

Still, she should have been toast about three minutes ago.

Okay, that was it. No more fooling around. She was treed on top of her dresser, which was bare of things to throw at the moment—she'd run out of ammo, finally. Instead of cowering, she crouched on it like a cat, one with several swipes left in its paws.

"You son of a bitch," she rasped, hoarse from all the screaming hysterics. "I haven't done a single thing to deserve this—"

"Well, not yet," he said.

"—and now look at this mess! Worse than usual! My house is a wreck, there's a tear in my skirt, there's dead bodies all over my workplace, and my crazy blond stud of a mechanic's helper is trying to kill me! Son of a bitch!"

"It's been a bad day for both of us," he admitted. Then, "Blond stud?" He was absurdly flattered.

"Fuck you! I want you to get lost and *leave me the hell alone*!"

She had screamed that last part, shrieked it, roared it. Her fury was intense, overwhelming—he couldn't get the smell of burning cedar out of his nose—it was practically choking him.

Suddenly, startlingly, the pain in his head intensified—cripes, it felt like his skull was splitting!—and he started to get dizzy for the first time in his life. It was extremely unpleasant. But before he could complain, or explain, everything got dark around the edges, and the room tilted, and then he didn't know anything, anything at all.

Nine

More exhilarated than frightened, Sara finished taping Psycho Jerkoff to her kitchen chair with her last roll of electrician's tape (a must for any single woman's toolbox). Then she stood back, looked at him for a long minute, and went to get her bag.

She supposed she should find a phone and call 911, but she wasn't too worried about what's-his-face getting out of that chair. In fact, she wondered if he'd ever get up again . . . he was the color of kitchen plaster, and his body had a loose, boneless feel she didn't like at all.

She found her bag, shook the dirt off it, stepped over the spilled planter, and returned to the kitchen. She briefly wished for a cell phone—she kept losing the fucking things, and she was paying for it now—and bent to Psycho Jerkoff. She peeled up one of his eyelids and grimaced—blown pupil. *Really* blown . . . the thing looked like a burst pumpkin, all brownish orange leaks. The sclera was shot with red threads, and his breathing was gasping, agonal.

What had she done to him? Was it like the rapist who was waiting—

But she wouldn't think about that now. What happened back then wasn't relevant to this poor fucker . . . he was dying before her eyes. He had tried to kill her, but that didn't mean she wanted him to go toes-up in her kitchen. Poor dumb ass. Even his eye was—

Actually, it looked a little better. Less red, and the pupil seemed to be . . . shrinking? Shrinking and pulling back, and the red was pulling back, too, disappearing, and then his perfectly whole pupil was *fixed on her*, and he shifted his weight, and she stumbled backward so fast she tripped over another chair and went sprawling.

Ten

(decorative ornament)

"Well," Derik said, waking up. "That was embarrassing."

She scuttled back from him, startled. He blinked down at her. What was she doing on the floor?

"What are you doing on the—"

"That was *fast*," she said, almost gasped. "One minute you were out cold, and the next—"

"I'm a quick healer." He started to get up, then realized he couldn't. He was—for crying out loud! "You've taped me," he observed. "Taped me to one of your kitchen chairs. That's a new one."

"Electrician's tape," she said, gesturing to the depleted rolls on the counter. "A must for every household. Now go back to sleep so I can call the cops, you psychotic freak."

He wriggled. He could get loose, but it would take some time.

She was fiendish in her cleverness! Tape was *tough*, and he sure couldn't untie it.

"You might not believe this," he said, "but I'm sort of glad." And he was! He hadn't been able to kill her. She was alive, and pissed, and he was actually kind of happy about it, and relieved. It was strange, and probably stupid, but right now he didn't care. "Sorry about the mess in your house."

"Oh, shut up. Listen, you were really screwed up. How, how did you get better?" she burst out. It was as if she'd been dying to ask the question. "You had a blown pupil—do you know what that means?"

"Well," he said, "it doesn't sound very nice."

"You got that right. It's indicative of an aneurysm, get it? Brain bleed? Nothing good, in other words. But you got better while I watched. Which is impossible."

"About as impossible as you still walking around alive. And I told you, I'm a quick healer. Got anything to eat around here?"

"I'm supposed to feed you now? After you tried to kill me?"

"I'm hungry," he whined.

"Tell it to the judge." She reached for the phone, found it gone, then spotted the pieces of the handset all over the floor. "Damn it! I forgot about that. You're buying me a new phone, buster. And a new everything else we broke!" She knew, just *knew*, she would regret lending her bedroom phone to one of her former patients. Rose was a sweetie, but lending never meant lending, it always meant giving, and that was just—

"Sure, okay. Hey, listen, I've got to tell you something." Man oh man, Antonia would *not* be pleased. Neither would Michael. Fuck it. "I was sent on a mission to kill you."

"I gathered," she said dryly, "judging from all the murder attempts."

"No, I mean, my family sent me here. Specifically, to you. Because you're fated to destroy the world. And it's my job to stop you. Except I couldn't."

"And *you're* fated for a Thorazine drip, as soon as the nice men in the white coats come." But she looked troubled, as if she was hearing a voice in a distant room, one that agreed with him completely. "And I—I might have been wrong about your eyes. In fact, after the day I've had, a misdiagnosis wouldn't surprise me at all."

"Sure," he sneered back. "Because you make them *all* the time." This was a guess, but he figured Dr. Sara Gunn didn't get where she was by being a fuckup.

"Never mind. Now: What the hell did I do with my old phone?" she mused aloud, running her fingers through her red, red hair. It kept wanting to flop in her face, and she kept tossing it back with jerks of her head. It was the brightest thing in the room; he could hardly take his eyes off it. Off her. "Did I throw it out? I don't think I did . . . I never throw anything out, if I can help it . . . soon as you throw it out you need it again . . . stupid thing."

"Listen to me. I'm not crazy, though I totally understand why you think I might be."

"Do ya?" she asked with faux brightness.

"I couldn't kill you. Get it? Never mind that I think my so-called sacred mission bites the bag; I was trying to kill you, and I couldn't do it. Don't you think that's a little bit weird?"

"No, I think *you're* a little bit weird." But she frowned.

"Hasn't stuff like this happened to you before? Weird days? Strangers popping up out of nowhere trying to do you harm? I can't believe my family's the only one who knows about you."

"This is California," she said, looking more than troubled; looking vaguely alarmed. "Weird stuff happens all the time out here. And it's not even an election year."

"Yeah, California, not the Twilight Zone." He wriggled more and the tape pulled at his arm hairs. "Ow!"

"Well, sit still."

"And starve to death? Forget it."

"Oh, for Pete's sake. How long have you gone without a meal?"

"Two hours."

"An eternity, I'm sure."

"Fast metabolism. Come on, you have to have *something* around here."

"Buddy, you have got some nerve." She sounded almost . . . admiring? But she still looked pissed. Not that he could blame her. "Weird stuff . . . you probably said that because you were in on it."

"In on what?"

"Oh, like you don't know!"

"I *don't* know," he said patiently. "What are you talking about?"

"You don't know about the team of red-robed weirdos who tried to kill me at work." She said this with total skepticism.

"No, but I can't say I'm surprised. See, you're the bad guy."

"*I'm* the bad guy?"

"Yup. In fact, you're fated to destroy the world."

She touched her chest, looking flabbergasted. "*I* am?"

"Yup. That's why I was sent to make you take a dirt nap, so to speak. And I bet the crack team of weirdos was sent to do the same thing. So you should do three things: Feed me, untie me, and get the hell out of this house."

She stared at him.

"Don't think you have to do it in that order, either," he added, wriggling again. Fucking tape! Why couldn't she use plain old rope, like his ex-girlfriend?

"That's it," she finally said. "I'm calling the police. Right now." But she didn't move, and he could smell that she didn't mean it. She was too confused and curious.

"Okay, Morgan. Fetch the fuzz."

"What did you call me?"

"Morgan. It's your other name."

"I think I would know if I had another name."

"Obviously, you don't."

"Oh, piss off!" she snapped, which almost made him laugh. "I've had about enough of this 'mysterious stranger trying to kill me and then being all cryptic' garbage. Spit it out."

"Okay. You're the reincarnation of Morgan Le Fay."

She threw up her hands. "Oh, please! That's the best you could do?"

He shrugged, as much as he could mummified in tape as he was. "It's the truth. You're a bad witch, back to wreck the world. Sorry."

"First of all, Morgan Le Fay wasn't necessarily bad. Second—"

"How do you know that?"

"I did some papers on her in college. Second—"

"Uh-huh. Of all the people in the world, living and dead, you picked her. I bet your minor in college had something to do with her."

"Lots of people minor in European history. And as for picking Le Fay for a research topic—me and about a zillion other people through the ages," she said, but again looked vaguely troubled, as if listening to something he couldn't hear. Which with his hearing was impossible, frankly. "Tell me, the place where you live . . . are there a lot of doctors there? And little cups of pills?"

"Very funny, Morgan."

"Don't call me that," she said automatically, but with no real heat.

"Look, at least consider the possibility. I mean, why would I come here? I live in Massachusetts, for Christ's sake, but I come all the way across the country just to wreck *your* house?"

"That's the theory I was going with, yes," she admitted.

"Pretty shaky," he told her. "And today not only am I here, but another group of killers? Would-be killers, I mean? And what happened to them? How come you're not dead? You avoided me *and* them?"

"We haven't established that you're not one of them," she pointed out. "And they ran into some bad luck."

"Yeah, I'll bet. I'll bet that happens a lot around you."

"Well . . ." Her brow knitted, and she looked severely cute as she pondered. Her blue eyes narrowed and her forehead wrinkled. "I've always been lucky . . . but I don't think that proves anything."

"Since we're going to talk for a while—which I'm totally fine with, so don't sweat it—do you have an apple, or maybe you could fix me a PB&J, or something?"

"Again with the food! You've got a lot of nerve, anybody ever tell you that?"

"Pretty much every day, back home. So, do you?"

"I don't believe this," she muttered but, praise God, she turned to the counter, plucked an apple out of the bowl, grabbed a knife out of the rack, and rapidly cut the fruit into bite-sized pieces. She stomped over to him and stuffed three chunks into his mouth.

"Fgggs," he said.

"You're welcome. So somebody sent you here to kill me because I'm the reincarnation of Morgan Le Fay, that's what you're telling me." He didn't answer because it wasn't an actual question. "And other people are also out to get me, because of this." He nodded, still chewing. "So I shouldn't call the cops, I should leave."

"With me," he said, swallowing.

"Oh, that's *rich.*"

"I figure there's more to this than meets the eye, y'know? So we should take off and see if we can see what's what."

She was cutting up another apple in rapid, angry motions, and he eyed the knife a little nervously; if she got pissed enough to plant it in his eye, he'd probably never howl at the moon again. He was a fast healer, but there was some brain damage that couldn't be fixed, no matter how close the full moon was.

"See what's what," she repeated. "Yeah, sure. Let's get right on that." She jammed a few more pieces into his mouth and, although eating cut-up apples had never seemed particularly erotic to him before, the smell of her and the touch of her skin on his lips was starting to, um, cause him a little problem. Okay, a big problem.

He shifted in the chair and wished he could cross his legs. "Look, you get kind of weirded out whenever I suggest that there's maybe more to you than meets the eye," he said around a mouthful of apple. "So why don't you tell me? What happened before today? How come you're so lucky?"

"I don't *know.* I just am. I always have been. My mom used to call me her lucky break."

"Oh yeah? Where is she now?"

"She's dead."

"Oh. Sorry. Mine, too."

"Gosh, we've got all kinds of things in common," she said, rolling her eyes and shoving another chunk of apple between his lips.

"Meant to be, I guess," he said, chomping.

"Okay, so, I won the lottery. A couple of times," she said grudgingly.

"You *what?*" He knew she wasn't lying, but it was still surprising. "More than once?"

"I tend to get . . . windfalls . . . whenever I'm short of money. And once I needed a few thousand to pay for the last quarter of school, and I won the lottery, and it was exactly the amount I needed. And I got a refund one year when I needed some extra money to—but everybody gets tax refunds."

"Yeah, but I've never even met one person who won the lottery, never mind won it twice."

"Four times," she muttered.

"Oh, for fuck's sake! And you're giving me shit like I'm crazy?"

"It doesn't mean anything," she insisted.

"Okay, Morgan—"

"Quit that!"

"—maybe you can explain how, at the exact moment you needed to get me out of the way, I get a freakin' *brain aneurysm*, how about that?"

"A happy coincidence?" she guessed.

"For Christ's sake."

"Actually," she said, clearing her throat, "there was a serial rapist in this area a couple years ago. And, um, he got in somehow while I was at school, but when I came home I found him dead in my kitchen."

"Brutally stabbed?"

"No, um, the autopsy showed he had a congenital heart defect, a minor one that shouldn't have given him any trouble, but for some reason, while he was waiting here to—to—well, he had an M.I. and died."

"What's an M.I.?"

"Myocardial infarction. Heart attack," she said impatiently.

He gaped at her. "Holy shit, I'm lucky to be alive!"

"Well, you really kind of are." She poked another piece of apple in his mouth. "Let the record show I still think you're nuts. Also, once when I overslept and missed the bus, it crashed, and half the people aboard were killed."

"Jesus Christ!" It was all he could say. This was worse—and cooler—than he had ever dreamed. "That's it, that's your magic. You're phenomenally fucking lucky. *All* the time."

"There's no such thing as magic." But that species of hellish doubt was on her face again. "Everybody's lucky."

"Sara, for God's sake. Listen to yourself."

"The team at the hospital . . ."

"Don't tell me, let me guess. They were like the Three Stooges—or however many of them there were. Knocking heads, falling down, having heart attacks on the spot . . . and you walked away without a scratch."

"That might be true . . ."

"We should go clubbing some night."

She laughed unwillingly. "Sure we should. I'm sure the police will let you out in no time."

"Oh, come on! After all this, you're still calling the cops on me? We should get out of here!"

"You *did* try to kill me," she reminded him—like he needed it! He'd never live it down. Derik Gardner, badass werewolf, totally unable to kill a nurse. A nurse with a doctorate, but still. "And I've only got your word that you're not going to try again."

"Well, my word's good," he grumped. Of course, she couldn't *know* that. Not like another Pack member would know it. It made everything harder. Which was kind of cool. Yet aggravating.

"And like I said, there's more to this than what we can smell. I think—"

"Than what we can *smell*?"

"Never mind. Look, let's do some digging, okay?"

"Okay!" she said with fake enthusiasm. "Do you want to be Nancy Drew or a Hardy Boy?"

He ignored the sarcasm . . . he'd had years of practice with Moira. "Let's find out what exactly you're supposed to do. I mean, you don't want to destroy the world, right?"

"This is the most surreal conversation I've ever had," she commented. "And no. Duh."

"So how come anybody who can see the future—I assume that's how the bad guys knew to come after you—says you're gonna do just that? Huh? Don't you think that's weird? Huh?"

"That's not the only thing I think is weird."

"Then hold on to your hat, sunshine."

She eyed him warily. "What? I'm not really up to more surreal revelations . . ."

"I'm a werewolf."

"Damn it! What did I just *say*?"

Eleven

"I'm a werewolf," the gorgeous nut job said again. He shifted in the chair and winced. She suspected he was sore . . . certainly there was plenty of dried blood on his forehead and speckled all over his shirt. She felt sorry for him and stomped on the emotion. "Soon to be a hairless one, but there you go."

"Whine much? Try getting a bikini wax."

"I'll pass."

"Look, one thing at a time, all right?" Sara tried not to show how rattled she was. She suspected she was fighting a losing battle. As if her day hadn't been upsetting enough, she was actually turned on by hand-feeding Hunka Hunka Burning Looney. She could feel the stubble on his chin when she popped more apple slices into his mouth, could feel the warmth of his face, smell the apple sweetness of his breath, could

(I could do anything to him, anything at all.)

feel his . . . his . . .

(He couldn't stop me. He's tied up. I could sit on his lap and do . . . do anything . . .)

Aw, nuts. His lips were moving. More nonsense about

(the true you)

Morgan Le Fay, no doubt.

"What?" she asked.

"I *said*, one of my Pack members told me what you were going to do, and my—my boss, I guess you'd call him, he sent me here to take care of you. And not in a good way, FYI."

"Sounds like a real prince," she muttered, trying not to stare at his mouth.

Derik shrugged. "More like a king, actually, and he's okay. He's my best friend, so I had to leave before I killed him."

"Oh yeah?"

"Yeah. I mean, I couldn't imagine anything worse than killing a friend."

"That's pretty bad," she admitted, wondering when she'd checked her sanity at the door. This was definitely the most surreal conversation she'd had in . . . ever. "It's probably just as well you left town to kill me instead."

"To try to kill you," he corrected. Then he grinned, showing many teeth. It was so startling—a white flash, and cripes, those chompers looked *sharp*—that she nearly took a step back. "And I like you, too, by the way," he added, which made no sense, but who cared? "You are, in case nobody's told you, extremely cute. Are you a natural redhead? You are, aren't you?"

"Never mind," she said severely. "I'm going in the back room now, to call the police. You're extremely confused, if gorgeous, and I . . . have had . . . enough."

"Oh, me, too," he assured her. "I don't think I've been less comfortable in my life. So if you don't mind . . . and even if you do . . ." Then he did something like an all-over shrug, and she heard tearing tape, and then he—he was standing up!

One more time: He was standing up!

"Gah," she said, or something like it. How had he—how had he torn through all that—and the arm of the chair was broken, too, which was weird, and—

He was grabbing her! Well, reaching for her. Taking her by the arms

"Gah!"

and pulling her into a snug embrace

"Gah!"

and bending his head toward hers

"Ga—mmph!"

and then his mouth was on hers, moving deliciously across hers, and she was grabbing his shoulders to, um, push him away, okay, she was going with that, yeah, pushing him away, except now she was up on her tiptoes, the better to fit against him, and he smelled delicious, he smelled like the woods in springtime, and his mouth, oh God, his mouth was warm, and his breath was redolent of apples and . . . and . . .

He'd broken the kiss and was standing three feet away from her. She'd never seen him move. She'd blinked, and he was done. Her mind tried to process his speed and couldn't do it. Just . . . couldn't.

"Sorry," he said cheerfully. "Wanted to do *that* for oh, about the last four hours. Now it's out of my system. Okay, maybe not. So! What's next, sunshine?"

"Gah?" she asked, raising a trembling hand to her mouth.

"I think we should put our, um, heads together and figure out what's what."

"You're *not* a werewolf," she said, because it was the only thing she could think of.

He sighed and walked into her living room, squatted, picked up her couch, stood, and held it in one hand, in much the same way she would hold a tray. Fortunately, she had vaulted ceilings.

"You're not gonna make me juggle it, are you?" He tossed her couch a foot in the air, caught it, tossed it again. "I don't think I have enough room."

"So you work out," she said through numb lips. "That doesn't mean you—you—you know."

"Get fuzzy and bark at the moon one night a month?"

"Well . . ."

"Look, I believed *you're* a hideously dangerous sorceress fated to destroy the world."

"Don't do me any favors," she snapped. "And put that thing down."

"Say it," he sang. He wasn't even out of breath!

"Just put it down, and we'll talk some more, okay?"

"Saaaaaaaay it . . ."

"Fine, fine! You're a werewolf, and I'm a demented sorceress. Now let go of my couch," she begged.

"Okay." He carefully put it back where he'd found it. "So, now what?"

"Well, I'm not going to destroy the world, I'll tell you that right now." She crossed her arms in front of her chest. It was easier to be brave—sound brave, anyway—when he was all the way across the room.

"Works for me. How about another kiss? No? Spoilsport."

"You're really weird," she informed him.

"That's what they tell me." He was weirdly cheerful. He was, in fact, the smilingest guy she'd ever known. Maybe he was mildly retarded.

"'They' being . . . ?"

"My Pack."

"Your pack."

"Uppercase *P*."

"Mmm. Of werewolves, right?"

"Yup."

"Who sent you out here to stop me from destroying the world."

"Yup."

"But you're not going to kill me."

"Well . . ." He spread his hands apologetically. "I couldn't, first of all. I mean, really couldn't. I felt bad about it, but I was gonna do it, don't get me wrong. But . . . I didn't. And in case no one's ever told you, an aneurysm hurts like a bastard."

"Thanks for the tip."

"So I figure, we team up, figure out who the *real* bad guys are, and save the world."

"But what if *you're* the real bad guy?"

"Well, I know it's not me. And you were pretty upset about something when you showed up. I'm betting you've met the real bad guys. So, I'll help you get 'em."

"Why?" she asked suspiciously.

"Well. It'll help me both personally and professionally, see, because I've kinda wanted to be on my own, and I figure this is the chance to show what I can do. Just . . . don't blow up the planet in the meantime, okay? I'd never live it down. I mean—how totally embarrassing."

"Team up?" Why was the idea as exciting as it was frightening? "Like that, eh?"

He smiled at her and, oddly, the expression wasn't startling. Maybe because he wasn't showing so many teeth. "Like that. So, what do you say?"

"I say we're both nuts." She pressed the heel of her hand to her forehead. "I can't believe I'm considering this. I can't believe I'm *not* calling the police. I can't believe . . ."

"What?"

"Never mind."

"Oh, that? Don't worry about *that*. I told you, I like you, too."

"Swell," she muttered.

Twelve

"I wish you wouldn't do that."

"Sorry." He pulled back so his head was inside the car. "Can't help it. This place smells *great*."

"Look, it's weird enough that you stick your head out of the car like a big—well, you know. But do you have to do it while you're driving?"

"No," he sulked.

"Take a left at the light."

He did, and Monterey Bay General loomed before them. Sara stared at the brick building. It was completely perfect that they should show up here first. MB General had been her home forever. She'd learned there, worked there, fallen in love there, worked there, got dumped there, slept there, worked there, been forged there, worked there, found out she was an orphan there, grown up there.

Found a father there.

Well, at least Derik hadn't tried to kill her. Again.

"I forgot," she said abruptly. "What's your last name?"

"Gardner."

"Oh." That sounded almost . . . normal. Safe and normal. "Okay. So, I guess you already know my name."

"Yup."

"Of course," she muttered. Stupid! He'd only told her the whole silly story, and more than once. Maybe she couldn't retain the facts because she couldn't swallow them. Frankly, she still wasn't sure if she was buying into this whole "you're doomed to destroy the world" thing, but at the very least, it was more interesting than hanging out in her mechanic's garage.

"You okay?" he asked. "You look like you're about to jump out of the car." He parked. "Which you totally shouldn't do. I mean, you guys are mega-fragile. I don't know how you walk around in those breakable bodies of yours."

"You kind of get in the habit of it, if you're born in one of those bodies."

"Poor thing." He shook his head.

"Never mind."

~ • • • ~

"Okay," she said nervously. "We're gonna go find Dr. Cummings. He's kind of like my mentor. He and my mom were good friends, and he took care of me after she—after she died. He knew a lot of stuff about my family that he would never talk about, and he—he's always been good in a crisis." More like completely unruffled, all the time. And hadn't he recovered awfully quickly from the morning attack? He'd been more annoyed than scared . . . not a typical reaction. Except from him. But it was enough to make her wonder. "Anyway, we'll find him and see what he has to say, and maybe figure out where to go from there. Okay? Is that okay?"

"You're the killer sorceress," he said easily. "I guess we'll go wherever you say."

"Knock that off, or no Milk Bones for you tonight."

He groaned, which caused several female heads to swivel in their direction. Derik was slightly larger than life . . . hell, he was slightly larger than his T-shirt, which bulged and rippled in interesting directions. He was by far the largest man in the hospital lobby. Possibly in the hospital. Or the city. "Don't start with the dog jokes, okay?"

"That depends on you," she said smugly. "Now come on. Dr. Cummings is probably in his office."

"What's he look like?"

"Like an angry Colonel Sanders."

Derik snorted. "Does he have white hair and a white beard? And does he eat tons of Corn Nuts?"

She stared at him and almost didn't get into the elevator. Sheer momentum carried her to his side. "Have you been following me?"

He looked at her curiously. "That's gonna make you mad? That's worse than trying to kill you?"

"People have tried that before. I'm almost used to it. But I fucking *hate* being followed," she snapped. "It's sneaky and dishonest and nasty."

"Take it easy!" He threw his hands in the air. "Seriously, Sara, don't get mad, okay? Just caaalm down. I wasn't following you. I can smell this Dr. Cummings guy on you, that's all."

"That's *all*?" She stabbed the button for the fifth floor. Derik's slight panic was sort of amusing. It was nice to have the upper hand with someone so good-looking. And she knew, she just *knew*, he was one of Those Guys. Every woman in the lobby had been staring at him, and he hadn't even noticed. One of Those Guys never had a clue how great-looking they were. It was annoying. No, it was nice. No, it was annoying.

"He must have hugged you or grabbed you or something. There's a couple of white hairs on your left shoulder. I mean, you got a nose like mine, you don't have to follow anybody. So mellow out, okay?"

"Dr. Cummings knocked me down in the lobby," she admitted. "He was kind of pissed."

Derik frowned. "At you?"

"No, about the killers making us late for grand rounds."

"Seriously?"

"Yes."

"Huh. Yeah, we better go talk to this guy. Shit, maybe we can recruit him."

"I'm sure," she said dryly, walking the Gauntlet—what everyone called the fifth floor physicians' offices—while Derik fell into step beside her, "that he'd be thrilled."

She stopped outside Cummings's office and raised a hand to knock.

"That door says Dr. Michaels," Derik pointed out.

"Mmm. It's one of the many ways Dr. Cummings tries to ensure interns don't bug him."

She rapped twice.

"Go away, or I'll have you fired!"

"That's another one," she explained, and opened the door.

"Oh, wonderful, it's Dr. Nurse Gunn. Or is it Nurse Gunn, Doctor? Don't let the door crush your tiny head on the way out."

"This man here," Sara said, indicating Derik, who was openly fascinated by Dr. Cummings's fuzzy eyebrows, "tells me I'm Morgan Le Fay."

Dr. Cummings grunted and started pawing through the pile of last year's *Lancet*.

"And that he was sent to kill me so I wouldn't destroy the world."

Dr. Cummings found the issue he wanted and settled back in his chair. He grunted again, an invitation for Sara to keep speaking.

"And I was wondering," she continued, feeling foolish, "what you might have to say about that."

"I'm surprised the boy's still alive," Dr. Cummings said, not looking up from the magazine. "And disappointed, I might add. I don't have anything to say beyond that, Your Highness."

She blinked. Thought that over. Started to speak. Changed her mind. Changed her mind again. Said: "Your Highness?"

"Well. You *are* the sister of a king. A centuries-dead king, but there you go."

"Oh, dude," Derik said, and flopped down into the nearest chair. "You're in major trouble, Cummings."

"You keep your hands to yourself, werewolf."

Sara's mouth fell open. Derik nearly fell out of the chair. "Dude! How'd you know? You are so *not* Pack."

"Do I look like I like my steak served *tartare*?" Cummings snapped. "It's all over you. Predators walk, stand, move, and run quite a bit differently from the rest of us. If you want to fool Homo sapiens, I'd advise not walking around sizing everyone up like you're wondering how they'd taste. And as for *you*, Your Highness," he said, swiveling toward Sara, "what are you doing with this—this riffraff? Fooled by his over-the-top handsomeness, I've no doubt. Strongly consider killing him, dear. Werewolves are nothing but trouble, and they do *not* make good husbands."

"That's not true!" Derik said hotly.

"Where's your father, lycanthrope?" Dr. Cummings asked with deceptive courtesy.

"He's . . . um . . . look, let's stay on-topic, shall we? And don't call me that. Cough up what you know, chum. Right now." He turned to Sara, who was desperately trying to follow the conversation. "But let's get back to this for a sec—we do *too* make good husbands. You know—once we find the right girl."

Dr. Cummings made a sound. It was not a sound of encouragement.

"See, most of the guys I know really want a mate—a wife, I mean—and kids. They really do. But there aren't very many of us, and there's tons and tons of *you* guys, so lots of times they don't really think it through before they settle down, and, well, humans are different from Pack, it's nothing to be embarrassed about—"

"Derik." She was exasperated—who *cared*?—and amused at his distress. "Can we stay focused on this whole Your Highness thing? And you!" Dr. Cummings flinched as she shook a finger at him. "Start talking. Start with, 'I moved to Monterey Bay and knew your mother before you were born,' and end with, 'and then you and a werewolf came to my office.' Start *now*."

"Yeah!" Derik added.

"Don't raise your voice to me, pup." Cummings looked at Sara. "I moved to Monterey Bay because by my art I knew Morgan Le Fay was to be born there in seventy-two hours. I found you at this hospital and befriended your mother. I explained to your mother who you were, but she wouldn't believe me, and forbade me to tell you. I kept you safe these many years and looked after you after your mother died. Now Arthur's Chosen is trying to kill you. It has nothing to do with saving the world. They just don't like you. Then you and a werewolf came to my office." He picked up his magazine again.

"Oh, dude." Derik rubbed his forehead. "You are so asking for a heart attack or for your lungs to pop or your eyeballs to explode or something. I mean, I don't even *know* her and that whole story pissed me right off."

"My mother?" Sara coughed and tried again. "My mother knew this?"

"No. You weren't listening, Dr. Gunn, a trait I've discussed with you before."

"Sorry," she muttered.

"Want me to pull his lungs out for you?" Derik asked brightly.

"Try it, lycanthrope."

"I told you not to call me that."

"You guys, cut it *out*!" she snapped. "Finish what you were saying, Doctor."

He sniffed. "Well. As earlier, I said your mother refused to believe the truth. And she did. She willfully would not let herself believe. She went to her grave thinking you were like every other kid. She was, in fact, determined you were like every other kid. No matter what she saw. No matter what you did." Dr. Cummings paused. "A nice woman," he said at last, "but not terribly bright."

"Do *not* talk about Sara's dam like that," Derik growled.

"It's a free country, whelp, and do I look like I'm worried about irritating someone who licks his testicles during a full moon?"

Derik's eyes bulged, and Sara choked back a laugh. She knew at once that the big blond stud was not used to humans in their fifties dishing out shit.

"Okay, okay," she said, holding her hands up. "Let's stay focused."

"I do *not* lick my—"

"So, Dr. Cummings, why you? Why have you been sticking so close?"

"To protect you from the occasional moron who wants to kill you because of who you are." He glanced meaningfully at Derik, whose hands were clenching and relaxing, clenching and relaxing. "Or, rather, who you were."

"And those guys this morning?"

"I told you. Arthur's Chosen."

A long silence and, when it appeared Dr. Cummings had nothing more to say, Sara said, exasperated, "And who are they?"

"Buncha losers, probably," Derik muttered. "Out to get you just because they can."

"And *your* purpose in our fair town was what, exactly?" Dr. Cummings asked sharply. "I'm sure I can guess. Your alpha gave you your marching orders, and off you went, without a question or a murmur. Typical Pack behavior."

"He did not! I mean, I decided to come on my own. Well, um, and what the hell do you know about it, Cummings?"

Dr. Cummings shrugged, and began rooting around for a pack of cigarettes. Smoking was, of course, forbidden in the hospital. Only Dr. Cummings dared to try. "I spent some time—years—in the company of a lady lycanthrope. She'd been banished from your Pack for some trivial reason, and was lonely."

"Where is she now?" Sara asked, interested in spite of herself. She'd never seen Dr. Cummings in the company of anyone but her mother. In fact, there were rumors that he was gay.

"A new Pack leader came to power, forgave her for her unbelievably minor transgression, and off she went, back to the Cape to live happily catching rabbits with her teeth."

"Who was it?" Derik asked. "I probably know her family."

"Never you mind. My point is, I wouldn't start pointing fingers at Arthur's Chosen, because your own reasons for being here aren't exactly beyond reproach."

"Uh-huh! I'm trying to save the world, pal. Grief from puffing human busybodies I so *don't* need."

"Arthur's Chosen," Sara said, again trying to bring them back on track. "What's their story?"

Cummings shrugged and lit a cigarette. "Rabid followers of the King Arthur legend. You know, of course, that Arthur was betrayed by his half sister, Morgan Le Fay, and it's ultimately why he fell in battle. Arthur's Chosen think that if they get rid of *you*, Arthur will finally return."

"So," Derik said, "they're cracked in the head."

"Well, yes. They're fanatics. A tough group to reason with."

"Just a minute," Sara said. "Morgan's supposed 'evil nature' is legend, not fact. In fact, a lot of people believe today that Morgan's wickedness was the invention of misogynist monks."

Both Dr. Cummings and Derik shrugged. Sara resisted the urge to throw up her hands. Men! God forbid they look at history in a woman-friendly fashion. Morgan Le Fay was probably a perfectly nice woman for her time. Strong-willed, sure. But wicked and evil and a dark sorceress? Feh.

"But how do they know Sara's Morgan?"

"The same way I did. The stars, old books, legends, prophecies. How did *you* know?"

"One of my Pack members can see the future," Derik admitted. "She said if I didn't get my butt to Sara's address pronto, the world was gonna blow up, or whatever."

"Hmm. Charming. So, what are your plans?"

Derik looked blank. Sara said, "Plans?"

"To eliminate the threat to your personal safety, to not destroy the world—the prophecies all agree on *that*, I'm sorry to say—you know. Your plans."

"Uh . . ."

"Great," Dr. Cummings grumped. "I swear, Sara, you get dumber every year."

"Watch it," Derik warned.

"And you, I suspect, were never the sharpest knife in the drawer."

"Dude, I am *so* going to make you eat your ears."

Dr. Cumming sighed. "Very well. Arthur's sect has its home base in Salem, Massachusetts. Go there. Smite your enemies. Have a hot fudge sundae. The end."

"Wait, wait, wait. If you knew all this was going to happen, why didn't you warn me? Why didn't you tell me about Arthur's sect ten years ago?"

"Right. I see now that I have failed you. Because you certainly would have believed me and left at once for Salem."

"Might have," she mumbled.

"Don't you see, Sara? I had to wait until forces started moving in on you. It's the only way there would have been a chance of you believing me. The sect would never have harmed you as an infant, because all the prophecies say you don't destroy the world until you're fully grown."

"Wait, wait," Derik protested. "So why not kill her when she was a baby? Save the world that way?"

"Because the sect can't use her if she's dead, stupid mongrel.

And she's not so easy to kill, in case you forgot. Which wouldn't surprise me."

"But how do they use her to destroy the world? These Arthur guys?"

Dr. Cummings shrugged. "No one knows. Only that she is integral to the plot. Kill her as an infant, and who knows what will happen? Wait until she's fully grown—very fully grown, Sara, time to lay off the bagels—and risk the world being destroyed. It's not an easy choice. Most of us decided to watch and wait. Now go away."

"It's not nice to kill old guys," Derik muttered under his breath. "It's not nice to kill old guys. It's not nice to—"

"All I could do was stick close, which I have, and now I'm done, and it's Miller time." Dr. Cummings clapped his hands sharply, making Sara and Derik jump. "Now go! Off to Salem. Good-bye."

Derik and Sara looked at each other, then shrugged in unison. "I'm game if you are," she said. "I don't want to walk into the hospital again and worry about Arthur's Chosen hurting bystanders."

"I'm going where you go."

"How touching," Dr. Cummings said. "I've approved your vacation request as of thirty seconds ago. I suggest you don't delay."

"Why?" Sara asked. "Is there something you're not telling us?"

"No, I'm just bored now. Good-bye."

"What a sweetheart," Derik muttered once they were on the other side of the door.

"Off to Massachusetts," Sara said, "dodging killers along the way, and with a werewolf bodyguard."

"Don't forget about the hot fudge sundaes."

Thirteen

"We can't go back to your place."

"Agreed. Besides, it would take about six hours of cleaning before the house was livable again. Thanks again, by the way."

Derik ignored her sarcasm. "And I sure can't show up at the mansion with *you*."

"Uh-huh. Err . . . why is that, again?"

"Because I was supposed to kill you, duh."

"Don't say duh to me," she ordered. "I get enough of that from Dr. Cummings."

"Yeah, cripes, what a grouch. Guy's not afraid of anything, is he?" Derik said this in a tone of grudging admiration. "But anyway, about you—I can hardly walk through the front door and say, 'hey, guys, here's Morgan Le Fay, didn't feel like killing her, what's for lunch?'"

Sara frowned. "So you're saying you're going to get into trouble for this?"

Derik stretched, wiggling in the driver's seat, then pulled into a convenience store parking lot. "Maybe. Kind of. Okay, yes."

"Derik, you can't—I mean, I appreciate you giving up your sacred holy mission of premeditated murder and all, but don't your kind banish Pack members for, like, teeny tiny reasons? Never mind huge reasons like not fulfilling your mission?"

"We have a group mentality," he explained. "So if you do something that hurts the group, or may possibly hurt the group, it's bye-bye time."

"So you—you can't go back?" Sara tried not to sound as horrified as she felt. She was lonely—well, alone—by circumstance. Her father had died the day she was born; her mother when she was a teenager. But Derik was deliberately giving up his family . . . for her. It was touching. And cracked. "Not ever?"

He yawned, apparently unconcerned. "Well, I figure it's like this: Either you destroy the world, in which case, my alpha can't kick my ass, or you don't, in which case, my alpha will know I was right. Kind of a win/win for me."

"Except for the possible death of billions."

"Well, yeah. There's that."

"But you can never see your friends again?" Sara was having trouble letting this go. "Your family?"

"I was going to leave anyway. It was either that, or—anyway, I had to go."

"Well, thanks," she said doubtfully. "I—thanks. What are we doing here?"

"I'm starved."

"*Again?*"

"Hey, we don't all weigh a hundred pounds and have the metabolism of a fat monkey."

"Oh, very nice!" she snapped. "Well, as long as you're here, let me get my cash card, I'll grab some money."

His hand closed over hers, which was startling, to say the least. He was very warm. His hand dwarfed hers and, in the California sunlight, the hair on the back of his knuckles was reddish blond. She was fascinated to note that his index finger was exactly as long as his middle finger. "Nope."

She stared into his green, green eyes. "What, nope?"

"We're on the way to Salem, right? Chances are, there's gonna be some bad guys on our tail. Right?"

"What, you're asking me? Ten hours ago my biggest problem was finding a pair of panty hose that didn't have a run in them."

"*So*, you can't leave a money trail," he continued patiently. "No cash cards, no credit cards. And if you make a big bank withdrawal, my Pack's gonna know you're alive. They'll assume I'm dead, and then there's gonna be real trouble."

"How would they even know—never mind, don't tell me. We can't go across the country with no money," she pointed out.

"Yeah, yeah. I'm working on that one."

"What a relief," she said, getting out of the car and following him up the sidewalk. "Seriously. You have no idea."

"Aw, stick a sock in it. You—watch it." He grabbed her elbow and pulled her out of the way just as a teenager came barreling through the door of the store. The kid stopped for a minute, utterly panicked, and they all heard the wail of sirens at the same time.

Well, probably not, Sara thought. Probably Derik heard them about a minute earlier. Aggravating man. And what happened when the moon rose? What *then*? Did she really believe he was going to turn into a wolf and run around peeing on fire hydrants?

"Shit!" the teen cried, and started to dart around them. Derik stepped in his way—

"Don't do that," Sara said sharply. "He might have a gun."

"He *does* have a gun," Derik replied, bored.

—and the teen suddenly thrust a paper bag at Sara, who tightened her grip around it purely by reflex.

They both watched the kid race out of the parking lot.

Sara opened the sack, which was bulging with twenties, tens, and fives. "Oh," she said. "Well. Um. I seem to have come into some untraceable cash for our trip."

Derik slapped the heel of his hand to his forehead, then shoved Sara back toward the car. "Let's get out of here before the cops come." He jumped into the convertible, fighting a grin. "You lucky bitch."

~ * * * ~

"So, we need another car."

"Okay," Sara said. They had left the Monterey city limits, and she had just finished counting the money. Eight hundred sixty-two dollars even. No change. "Um, why?"

"Because my Pack rented this one for me. They can track it. We have to leave it and find something on our own."

"Okay."

"So, do it."

"Do *what*?"

"You know. Work your hocus-pocus and wish us up a car."

"It doesn't work like that."

"The hell it doesn't."

"I don't have conscious control over it," she explained, trying—and failing—to smooth her hair out of her face. Convertibles were sexy and cool in the movies, but in real life you couldn't see for all the hair flying around. And she dreaded trying to pull a brush through the mess when they parked. Not that she had a brush. But still. "Heck, until you showed up, I didn't think I could do anything special at all. Except bowl," she added thoughtfully. "I'm great at that."

"Yeah, I bet those pins just happen to fall over for you all the time. Concentrate," he ordered. "We need . . . an untraceable . . . car."

"Stop . . . talking . . . like that."

He slapped the steering wheel with his palm. "Shit. Well, I guess I could steal one . . . except we'd have to do that at least every day or so."

"Why aren't we taking a plane? Isn't it a four- or five-day drive?"

"You want to show airport security your ID? Because I don't think that's, y'know, too cool. Which also lets out renting a car, and taking a train."

"Are there that many werewolves running around the country?"

"No. There's only about three hundred thousand of us, world-wide. But still. I think it's too important to take chances. I'd hate to fuck this up through bad luck, y' know? Not that you exactly have bad luck. But still. I'm not crazy about taking chances. Okay, I am, but not chances of this magnitude. Get it?"

"Hardly. And you can't ask any of your—um, your family—the Pack, or whatever you call it—for a car?"

"Well, I could, but I'd rather not take a chance on anything getting back to Michael—my alpha," he explained. "I'd risk spending a night or two with local Pack members, because my mission is top secret—"

"Excellent, Mr. Bond."

"*Anyway*, most of the Pack doesn't know what I'm up to. Just the East Coasters. So it's no big deal to show up on someone's doorstep and crash for the night. But to do that, and be in a situation where I'd have to borrow a car, and have you in tow . . . that might get back to the wrong set of ears."

"So, what?"

"So, we need a car. We'll drive for a while, then crash."

"I'll tell you right now," Sara declared, "no more convertibles!"

"Aw, how come?" he whined. "How can you not like the wind in your face?"

She pointed to her head, which, thanks to mussed curls, was almost twice as large as usual. "Forget it, Derik. For-get-it."

"Aw, you look cute."

"And you're deranged, but we established that a couple hours earlier. *No* convertibles."

"Well, I'm not driving a zillion miles—"

"Three thousand, five hundred," she said dryly.

"—locked up in a steel box, I can tell you that right now, Sare-Bear!"

"Ew, don't call me that. Sare-Bear? Ugh."

"'Cuz you look like a cute little bear with your hair all over the—"

"Stop talking. What? You're claustrophobic?"

"No. I just don't like being shut up in a steel box for hours and hours a day."

"So, you *are* claustrophobic."

"No, it's just . . . that fake carpet . . . the upholstery . . ." He shuddered. "It reeks, man. It totally reeks."

"You know what we need?"

"For you not to destroy the world?"

"Besides that. We need a truck. A nice big truck with four-wheel drive and a supercab."

"What's a supercab?"

"It's a truck that seats two or three people in the front seat and a couple in the backseat. There's plenty of space to store our stuff, and if you start feeling like the upholstery is closing in on you, you can ride in the back while I drive. Your hair mussed in the breeze, your ears flopping behind you . . . it'll be great."

"Can you destroy the world right now?" he asked. "Because if I gotta put up with one more dog joke . . ."

"And if we don't get a motel room or don't want to stop for long, we can spread some sleeping bags out in the back and sack out there. We'd have to stop and use some of this cash to buy camping equipment, but that'd be easy enough."

He frowned at her. He blinked at her. At last he said, "That's kind of brilliant."

"Well," she said modestly, "I *am* a doctor."

"Okay, so. We try to steal a truck."

"And what are we going to do when we catch up with Arthur's Chosen?"

"Let's get there first," he said grimly, and she had no reply to that.

Fourteen

"This is insane," she commented.

"It is not. Now try to look like we're not stealing a car."

"But we *are* stealing a car."

"Will you cut that out? Look casual. Lean on the door."

"The one you're trying to open?"

Derik resisted the urge to strangle Sara. This was an interesting improvement over resisting the urge to kiss her. You'd think, since he'd saved her life—well, sort of, in that he hadn't tried to kill her again—and because he was helping her hunt down Arthur's Big Fat Losers, that she'd be a little grateful. Or at least nicer. But nooo. It was blah-blah-blah and bitch-bitch-bitch. Like she could do any better than a full-grown werewolf! Okay, well, maybe she could. But that was irrelevant. Wasn't it?

"It's just that this is an extremely insane idea," she was explaining, like he'd gone retarded.

He grabbed the door handle again and tried to smell her hair without her catching on. Roses and cotton—yum! And how cute did she look in the convertible with those red curls flying all over the place? Her nose was sunburned now, and he even liked the shade of pink.

She turned to give him a suspicious look, and he held his breath in mid-sniff. Then, to distract her, he said, "Show me another place that has all the cars lined up, with their keys in the ignition." He spread his arms to indicate the Enterprise Car Rental lot. "Huh? Show me. That's all I ask."

"Show *me* another place that has *less* paperwork on any one of these cars. You don't think they do a head count or whatever—a grille count—before the last guy goes home for the day? They'll know it's gone in a cold minute."

"So we find another car rental place," he said, "and steal from there."

"Help you folks?"

They both spun, Derik swearing under his breath. Sure, the guy had snuck up on him from upwind, and sure, Sara was sort of distracting—she kind of jammed his radar, so to speak—but that was no excuse. No fucking excuse!

"We were just looking," Sara explained, after clearing her throat and trying a smile.

The fella who'd hailed them looked more nervous than they did—and more angry than Derik felt. His gray suit was rumpled, and his tie was flying over his shoulder in the breeze. His brown hair was wisping about, and his watery blue eyes were alternately starey and darting. Derik started to grab Sara's shoulder to pull her behind him when he got a whiff of burning silk—the smell of desperation.

"Uh-oh," he muttered.

"You folks need a car? I'll tell you what. You can have that truck right over there." He pointed to a shiny, brand-new, red pickup truck, complete with supercab and about fourteen antennas.

They looked at the truck, glowing at them almost like a mirage, or the Holy Grail—Derik expected to hear a choir of angels humming—then looked at the sales guy.

"I've had it with this place," he muttered. "Promote *Jim Danielson* over me? The guy comes in an hour late every day and leaves an hour early. And don't get me started on his lunch breaks. They're more like miniature leaves of absence. The guy's fucking the manager's daughter so *he* gets the promotion? *Him?*"

"We, uh, don't want you to get in any trouble," Sara said.

"And we don't want you to get any closer," Derik warned.

"No, look, it's okay, see?" The frustrated Enterprise employee grinned, which looked fairly ghastly. "You guys know how to drive a standard transmission, right?"

"Driving a stick is so *not* the big problem in this scenario," Derik said.

"Shhh!" Sara's elbow jabbed him in the side. "Let him finish."

"It's no problem. I'll just fix it in the computer. Nobody will even know about it. Go on, take it. You can help me stick it to my boss." He stared off at the horizon for a moment, looking haunted. "I just—not today. I put up with it, and I put up with it, but for some reason, today I just—I can't do it. Not one more day. So go on."

~• • •~

"Stop looking so damned smug," Derik told Sara later, as they were leaving California behind.

"Can't help it," she replied.

"So, what are the chances of that happening?"

"About one in a zillion."

"That's what I thought. Nice truck, though."

"*Great* truck."

"You're looking smug again."

"Sorry."

Fifteen

"Okayyy . . . We've got sleeping bags, a cooler, water, backpacks, flashlights, toilet paper, Purell, a first aid kit, dehydrated snacks, a couple of sharp knives, eating utensils, plates, cups, a grill, a frying pan, and a pot. Let's see, what am I forgetting?"

"The fact that I'm a werewolf," Derik muttered, so as not to be overheard.

"Oh, yeah. That. I didn't forget it, I'm just totally discounting it."

"Nice!"

"Quit it, now, you're making me lose track." She squinted at her list, pretending Derik wasn't heaving with indignation less than six inches away. Like Wal-Mart wasn't distracting enough . . . the camping section was bigger than Yosemite.

"Okay, so, we can hit the grocery story for hot dogs, bacon, bread, and—"

"Sara, we don't need all this junk." He fingered the sleeping bag and practically sniffed in disgust. "First off, we have a limited amount of money, so I'll tell you what you don't have to waste the bucks on."

"Oh, would you? That would be swell." She rolled her eyes.

"I can see in the dark, so don't bother with the flashlights. I sure as shit don't need the Band-Aids in the first aid kit. And I'd rather eat my own shit than touch one of those dehydrated beef stews."

"You're so gross," she told him. "And you're forgetting about me. I can neither see in the dark, nor bring my bleating prey down by the neck at a dead run. And I like to be warm at night."

"Why don't you leave that to me?" he leered.

"Why don't you go fuck yourself?"

He deflated. "Aw, c'mon, Sara, it's my job to look out for you. You don't need all this junk."

"Mmmm." She crossed a few more items off the list. "Look, I appreciate that you've aborted the whole 'Kill Sara' plan, I really do. But if I'm going to travel across the country with a homicidal stranger—that's right, I said homicidal, don't puff up like a cobra and glare—then I'm going to take care of myself. Just like I've been doing all along. If you don't mind." *And even if you do, Studboy.*

"That was a good speech," he said admiringly.

"Oh, shut up. And grab that bug spray, will you?"

"Ech! You're not going to actually spray that *on* you, are you?"

"No, I'm going to use it to sweeten my coffee. Just grab it," she said, already exhausted. Long day. Long fucking day, and that was a fact.

~ * * * ~

"You need salt crystals and fresh ground pepper? And vanilla sticks?" Derik cried. "I thought we were roughing it!"

"We are, but there are some things I refuse to give up. I think I've been a pretty good sport up 'til now, don't you? I mean, you turned my whole life upside down, but I'm playing along. Look, think of it as bringing a little taste of home along with us on the road."

"I'm thinking of it as a big goddamned waste of money and space, how about that?"

"A person of limited imagination," she admitted, "and poor cooking skills might think of it like that."

He sniffed the jar that held the vanilla pods and tossed it into her cart. "FYI, sunshine, I am a great damned cook, and these things are a total waste on a camping trip. Not to mention, they're from Mexico, not Madagascar, so on top of everything else, you're getting screwed."

"Say that after you've tried my campfire cocoa."

"Sure I will. How much money do we have left, anyway?"

"Enough to get free range eggs," she said, plucking them out of the dairy section. "Be a good boy and scamper off to get some Asiago cheese, will you?"

"I'm going to pretend you didn't say that," he said, folding his arms across his chest.

"You're just mad because we skipped the Milk Bones aisle."

"Sara, for the love of God . . . if you don't stop with the dog jokes, and I mean, stop with them right now . . ." He followed her, practically wringing his hands, and she hid a smile. It was good to have the upper hand, however momentarily.

Camping across country with a werewolf . . . now *that* was going to be an adventure.

PART TWO

Sorceress and Werewolf

Sixteen

"So you want to stop?"

"I don't mind stopping."

"I didn't ask if you'd *mind*. I asked—"

"Since I'm sitting right next to you," he said, trying not to snap, "I was sorta able to follow the conversation. Look, I can go all night. Drive," he added when she went red. "I can drive all night. If you want to, curl up in the back, go to sleep."

"Well, we bought all this camping equipment."

"You. *You* bought it all."

"Right. And it's"—she looked at her wrist—"eight thirty. We could stop, maybe sleep for a few hours."

"And make some burgers?"

"What?" she cried. "We just dropped twenty bucks at McDonald's!"

"Oh, Big Macs," he scoffed. "They're more like an appetizer than an actual meal."

"Actually," she said frostily, "if memory serves, someone insisted we stop so he could get the toy in the Happy Meal."

"It's for my friend's kid," he tried not to whine. "Anyway, it's not my fault. That stuff doesn't fill you up. Half an hour later—"

"It's been twenty minutes."

"—and you're hungry again."

She smacked herself in the forehead, which looked painful, and left a red mark. He resisted the urge to kiss it. "Okay, okay. So, we'll stop, eat, and sleep. For a little while. We're out of California, anyway. I mean, we're making good time."

"Okay," he said, because really, he didn't know what else *to* say. She was getting nervous, which was making *him* nervous. Which he couldn't stand. It's like she hadn't really thought about the fact that they'd be sleeping right next to each other in the back of a truck until just a couple of minutes ago. Which was extremely weird, because Sara was many things, and stupid wasn't one of them. Shit, it was the first thing that went through *his* mind when they were deciding which nylon bags to buy. "So, we'll stop."

She pointed. "There's a campground."

"Yeah, I see it."

~ • • • ~

Twenty minutes later, they had their one-night camping permit and had selected a teeny campsite that was roughly, given what he'd just paid, ten bucks a square foot.

He decided to kiss her again, break the ice. Well, that, and he wanted to kiss her again. But really, it was, like, a necessity. If she got any edgier, and thus bitchier, he just might try to kill her again, and another brain aneurysm he did *not* need.

So, they'd kiss, and maybe it'd lead to something and maybe not, but she seemed to expect *something*, and he was certainly more than willing to oblige.

Except.

Except, she hopped down from the truck, groped in one of the bags, and was now coating herself head to foot with noxious chemicals. He coughed and gagged and waved the air in front of his face, to no avail. The cloud was suffocating him!

"Enough, enough!"

"Do you *see* all the mosquitoes?" she cried. "We'll get eaten alive."

"Speak for yourself."

"Are you serious?" She walked over to him, and he backed up, terrified—she was a walking biohazard—but she grabbed his arm, forestalling his retreat. He was coughing so hard he missed her question.

"What?"

"It's true! You don't have a mark on you."

"Bugs don't like werewolves."

"Lucky bastard," she muttered.

"Listen, Sara . . ." She was still holding on to him, which he kind of liked. He bent in. "You know, we're going to be spending a lot of . . . um . . . you know, *time* together . . . and . . . and . . . shit."

"What?" She was looking up into his eyes, and oh, she was just so pretty it was a damn crime, that's what it was, and . . .

Shit.

His lungs exploded. Or, at least, that's what it felt like.

"You've got to lay off the bug spray," he gasped after about ten minutes of spasms.

"Well, what do you know about that," she said, and smiled for the first time in half an hour. "It's werewolf repellent."

He laughed in spite of himself. "Deep Woods Off: For those really pesky werewolves."

An hour later, he wasn't laughing. They'd eaten, doused their fire, said their good nights, crawled into their sleeping bags. Well, she did. He couldn't see how she could cocoon herself in a heavy bag when it was eighty degrees outside—humans were *weird*, or maybe it was just females of any species—but whatever. And now he was lying beside her in the back of the truck, slowly going insane.

He'd dated humans before, so it wasn't like he'd never had this problem before. The communication thing. Because he had. But somehow, back then, with other women, it hadn't bothered him so much.

It bothered him now.

If Sara were a werewolf, she'd smell his intent and he'd smell hers, and they'd do it, or she'd say right out: Not interested, pal, take a hike, and they wouldn't do it. Period. The end. But Sara couldn't smell a thing, comparably speaking, and what was worse, she was pretending like she didn't know he was so horny he was ready to have sex with his rolled-up sleeping bag. So it was this big—this big *thing* that they weren't talking about. What was that saying? It was the elephant in the room. A big, green, horny elephant.

He tried to think: What would Michael do? Jeannie had driven the poor guy nuts in the beginning . . . still did, sometimes. And a lot of the early problems were because she had trouble settling into the Pack. And Michael, as alpha, expected her to fall in line. And Jeannie, as a human who carried firearms, thought he should drop dead. So Michael had a lot of experience with the communication thing. He'd been forced to learn, poor bastard. What would *he* do?

He'd talk to Sara, that's what he'd do.

"Sara," Derik whispered.

Nothing.

"Listen, Sara—" I really, really like you, and you smell great, and I think your powers are really cool, if kind of terrifying, and oddly enough this makes you more appealing than any female I've ever known, and I definitely think we should fuck—oh, shit, I mean make love, you know, whatever—and then we can cuddle and I can get SOME FUCKING SLEEP.

"Sara?"

A light snore for an answer.

"Shit."

Saving the world was going to be harder than he thought.

Seventeen

"This werewolf thing," Sara said abruptly. She puffed a hank of hair out of her face and took a break from struggling with her sleeping bag. It was uncanny. You bought the thing in this nice little roll, and after you used it, you couldn't get it back into that nice little roll if someone stuck a gun in your ear. Uncanny! "You know, the full moon's in a couple of days."

"Seventy-eight hours. Yeah, I know."

"So . . . what then?"

"Sara, we could all be dead in seventy-eight hours."

"How many times do I have to tell you?" she snapped. "I'm not going to destroy the world. And what's with you this morning, you big blond grump?"

He mumbled something. It sounded like "I know you are but

what am I?" but even he wouldn't be that immature. And boy, had *he* woken up on the wrong side of the truck this morning!

"I'm just curious about what would happen, is all," she said. "What if you lose control and bite me?"

"What if I do?" he grumped.

"Oh, very nice! Think *I* want to be worried about full moons and biting people and—and getting rabid and eating undercooked food and maybe getting Mad Werewolf Disease?"

He covered his face with his hands and squatted by the smoldering remains of their fire. "It's sooo early . . ."

"Seriously, Derik."

"I am being serious. It's too early for this shit." He took his hands down from his face. "Besides, it's not the flu, Sara. You can't catch it. I could give you a blood transfusion, and you wouldn't catch it. We're two different species."

"Oh. I didn't know that. So all the movies are wrong?"

"Totally, totally wrong." He scrubbed his face with his hands and yawned. "Don't waste your time watching them, unless it's for entertainment value. Also, we don't carry babies off in the moonlight, and I wouldn't eat a person on a bet. Yech."

"Yech?"

He shuddered, and she took offense. "What's wrong with eating a person? You should be so lucky! Not that I want you to."

"You taste terrible, that's what. All of you. The omnivore diet . . . blurgh." He actually gagged!

"Well, nobody's asking you to eat anybody."

"I'd make an exception," he grumbled.

"Very funny. Don't even think about eating me. And if we're two different species, how do you have children with humans? And speaking of blood transfusions, would one of those even take?"

"Yes, and yes. It doesn't happen all the time—cubs with a human—but it does happen. I don't know why, I'm not a goddamned biologist." He groaned again and got up, then loped off toward the truck. "Are we ready? Let's go. Ready?"

"What's the rush? And why are you so scratchy this morning?"

"Couldn't sleep," he replied shortly, stomping on the clutch and starting the truck with a roar. "Went for a walk. All night."

"Well, excuuuse me, Mr. Insomniac—wait!" She ran to throw the last sleeping bag into the back of the truck. "Nobody told me werewolves were such rotten morning people!" She lunged, and just managed to pop the door open as he accelerated.

"Well, now you know," he said, shifting into second as she slammed her door.

"So, what's the plan, Grumpy McGee? Besides a second, possibly third, breakfast by ten o'clock?"

"Drive until we're tired. Stop again. Eat. Sleep. Drive more. Find Arthur's Chosen. Kick their asses. The end."

"A fine plan," she said.

"Except . . ."

"What?"

He yawned again, which was startling—his jaw stretched wider than she thought would be possible, and he showed a lot of teeth. "Well, I have to stay in touch with my people, or they'll start to worry about me. Maybe send someone else out here. So I thought tonight we'd stay at a safe house." This was a rather small lie. He didn't have to stay in the safe house; he could check in from the road. But the thought of having Sara in a warm bed . . . having Sara . . .

"What? I didn't catch that."

"I said okay," she repeated. "I don't mind sleeping with a roof over my head. Don't yawn anymore."

"Huh? Never mind. And a shower. You should shower so you get all the bug spray—"

"Yes, *fine*, all right. So, we stay at a safe house."

"Well, the thing is, I'd have to explain you. Because if any other werewolf ever found out who you were, they'd try to kill you."

"A possibility to be avoided at all costs," she agreed. "So what do you suggest?"

"Pose as my future mate—my fiancée, I mean."

"Oh."

"I have to tell them something," he explained.

"Well. Okay. I guess. I'm against being killed, you know—I'm not totally irrational. We'll just have to hide the fact that we don't know each other very well."

"Um." He cleared his throat. "There's one other small problem."

"Small, huh?" She sighed as he slowed down and took the exit for Burger King. Like he hadn't just eaten a pound and a half of bacon! "I'll bet. Well, bring it on. The week I'm having, I can take it."

"The thing is, they'll know—my people will know—if we're not really, um, intimate."

Her mind processed this, then decided, the week she'd had, she could *not* take it. Probably she had misunderstood. "What?"

"Well, like I said, they'll know if we aren't, you know, sleeping together. So we have to if we're going to pull this off. Sleep together, I mean."

She turned in her seat to glare at him. He kept his eyes steadily on the road, she noticed. Coward. "You're telling me I have to *fuck* you in order to stay at the safe houses?"

"Yeah."

"Well, too damned bad," she snapped, ignoring the surge of heat to her cheeks.

"You'd rather have your neck broken at the safe house?" he snapped back.

"Yes, upon careful consideration, I think that would be preferable!"

"Oh, stop with the drama queen thing. It's just sex, that's all, just sex, sex, that all it is, and frankly, I'm kind of insulted that you'd rather be gutted than see me naked!"

"They're called standards, pal. And I can't help it if I'm one of the few who didn't tumble into bed within five minutes of first meeting you!"

"Standards!"

"Want me to find a dictionary, blondie?"

"I want you to be a realist," he growled.

"In other words, drop your pants and save your life."

"Anything sounds bad if you say it like *that*."

"Forget it."

He pounded the steering wheel, which groaned alarmingly. "Damn it, Sara, you are the most hardheaded, stubborn, infuriating, annoying, stuck-up, curliest, annoying—"

"Curliest?"

"Aw, shut up. Fine, it's your head. We'll sleep out in the woods again, no touchie. And again. And again. Homo sapiens, man, fucking hothouse flowers, I swear to God."

"I am not," she said automatically, inwardly crushed. She'd sort of been looking forward to a shower. And a bed. She'd gone camping quite a bit as a girl, but now that she was in her late twenties, her idea of roughing it was a Super 8 and a hair dryer.

She cleared her throat and then asked timidly, "Can't—can't you just tell them that because I'm not a—a werewolf, you're still working on getting me into bed?"

He hesitated, then shook his head. "Our kind doesn't make a life-commitment without, uh—"

"Sampling the merchandise?"

"Uh, yeah. I mean, it's a totally natural thing to us. We don't have this whole Victorian attitude toward sex that you guys do. And the thing is, I wouldn't bring a casual date to a safe house."

"Oh."

He shrugged. "So, okay. We'll keep camping. I guess I shouldn't have sprung it on you like that, but I thought it'd be worse if I didn't say anything until we were at the house."

She actually shivered at the thought. "No, that's a good point. Well . . . what's a safe house like?"

"It's a house where a werewolf family lives and they take in guests a lot. People on the run, or on a mission, or even making a go-see trip to the Cape to meet Michael and Lara."

"Lara being . . ."

"The next Pack leader."

"Oh. You don't run a patriarchic society?"

"I don't think so," he said doubtfully.

"Who's Lara again?"

"Michael's daughter."

"Ah! Dynastic, then. Never mind. So it wouldn't be . . . weird . . . if we just showed up at this place and asked to spend the night."

"No. It'd be normal."

"But we'd have to share a bed."

"Yup."

"Actually, we'd have to do it before we showed up at the safe house, right? So the other werewolves could tell we'd been intimate? Not that it's any of their damn business," she added in a mutter.

There was a long pause, and then Derik answered, sounding almost like he was strangling. "Yes, we'd have to do it before we showed up."

She drummed her fingers on the seat and watched the scenery go by. "Well. I'm really not that kind of girl."

"Oh, I know," he said earnestly.

"But you're kind of cute."

"Really?" He seemed pleased.

"In an overbearing, totally obnoxious sort of way," she explained, watching him deflate a bit. "And we *are* on a mission to save the world."

He didn't say anything, just pulled into the BK parking lot.

"We could talk about it, I guess. I mean . . . I'd like a shower."

"And I'd like for you to have a shower."

"Bastard," she muttered.

Eighteen

They were still debating the merits of lovemaking—or not—when he pulled up to the Kwik N' Go. "Gotta use the phone," he explained.

"How?"

"Huh?"

"The phone," Sara said. She still reeked strongly of bug spray, but driving around for hours with the windows open had alleviated some of the damage. At least he could think about kissing her without gagging—a crucial step. And the wind had tossed her curls around and around; she looked like an adorable red dandelion. "You can't use your cell phone, for obvious reasons. But how are you paying for a phone call to the Cape from *here*? You can't use your credit card."

"Oh."

"And you can't call from the safe house?"

"They'd hear me anywhere in the house," he admitted.

"Oh. Creepy. I suppose calling collect is out of the question?"

"Only if you don't mind a bunch of werewolves tracking you down."

"Okay, well, let's try this." She hopped out of the truck and walked up to the pay phone on the sidewalk. "This works for me sometimes," she explained over her shoulder. "I used pay phones a lot before I got my cell, and it usually worked out."

She picked up the receiver, listened, then asked, "What's the number?"

He told her.

She tapped in the number, listened, then handed him the phone. "It's ringing."

He took the receiver from her, staring. It *was* ringing. "Won't it ask me for change, or—"

"Wyndham residence."

"Oh, hi, Moira. Listen—"

"Derik! Hey, where the hell are you? How's it going? Are you okay? Michael's been going out of his mind, here! Me, too," she added.

"Tracking her down has been a little harder than I thought," he said with a nervous glance at Sara. Thank God, thank God Moira wasn't anywhere near him. She'd smell a lie, and then kick his ass righteous. He'd deserve it, too. He couldn't remember ever lying before. It was a waste of time in the Pack. It made him feel like a real rat turd now. "But I'm closing in. Just wanted to let everyone know I'm okay. Got that? I'm okay, everything's fine right now. Tell Mike, okay?"

"Okay, honey. Things out here are fine, too. We're basically hanging around, waiting to get the word, you know? So you take care of yourself, okay?"

"Sure. Um, patch me through to Antonia?"

"Sure. She's had a migraine since you left," Moira warned, which made Derik cringe—Antonia was a bear when she was feeling fine—"so I'm not sure she'll be good company, to put it very, *very* mildly, but here she comes, so hold on to your fur." There was a click as he was put on hold.

"I guess this phone's screwed up," he said to Sara. "It's not asking for change or anything."

"Guess so," she replied, looking smug.

"You're scary," he said, and then, "Hello?"

"What are you *doing*? Owww!" Antonia complained. "My head, goddamn it!"

"Well, don't yell if you've got a migraine," he said reasonably. "Listen, Antonia—"

"You chimp, what the *hell* are you doing?"

"Saving the world," he replied shortly. "My own way. And don't call me that."

"But *she's right there!*"

"Duh. Listen, don't tell Mike, okay?"

"Aw, man, Derik, you're killing me," she complained. "You are *fucking* killing me!"

For a moment he actually thanked God that Antonia had a

persecution complex. She was one of the few Pack members who would actually consider helping him deceive Michael. Moira, for example, would never, ever do it. She'd feel bad, she'd apologize the whole time she was kicking his ass and then dragging him by the scruff of the neck to take his medicine, but friendship was one thing, and Pack was Pack.

"Look, Antonia, I wouldn't let you twist in the wind on this. We've got a plan. I'm pretty sure it will work."

"*Pretty sure?* Owww!"

"Look, I must be on the right track, or you would have ratted me out to Mike by now, right? I mean, your visions must be showing you that something's going right. Right?"

Sullen silence.

"Right," he repeated, on slightly surer ground. "So, listen, I'm okay, she's okay, and we're gonna get the bad guys and save the world. See, I think the bad guys will accidentally trick her into destroying the world, so if we take care of them, we take care of anybody else."

"And how the blue hell do you know that?"

"Well, I don't. Know it, exactly. You know, like you know two plus two makes four. But I feel it. I mean, I know Sara would never do something that bad on purpose. So the bad guys must do it, or trick her into doing it, or something."

"You're talking out your ass. And besides, you're not an alpha, Derik," Antonia pointed out through gritted teeth. "It's not your call. I mean . . . you could run a Pack, but Michael's the boss of this Pack, and he told you what to do. And *you're not doing it.*"

"Just . . . don't say anything yet, okay?"

"Derik . . ." This was more a howl than a groan.

"Antonia."

"You're fucking crazy, you *know* you're crazy, right?"

"Just do this one thing for me."

"Sure," she snapped. "The first favor he ever asks me in twenty-two years, and *this* is it!"

For a moment he was startled . . . Antonia was so annoying, so bitchy, so harassed because of her visions, it was easy to forget she was still just a baby. She was barely voting age, and look what he was asking of her!

"Thanks," he said, because that was her way of saying yes. "I owe you one."

"You owe me *twenty*, you big, stupid, lumbering, asshole moronic—" He hung up on her. The conversation had gone as well as he could have hoped; no need to drag it out.

"Okay," he said, letting out a deep breath. "I bought us some time, anyway."

Sara smiled at him. It was the first smile of the day—they'd spent the afternoon screeching at each other in between bouts of fast food—and it knocked him out all over again, how gorgeous she was, how funny, how cute, how—"Yeah, sounds like you did. Thanks. What do you say we go find this safe house of yours?"

"Great," he said. "Showers all around."

"Enough rubbing in how bad I smell," she muttered, trailing him to the truck.

"I just meant that I could use a shower, too."

"Sure you did."

Nineteen

They had eaten (twice, in Derik's case), drunk cocoa, and roasted marshmallow after marshmallow. Sara knew if she gobbled one more soft white squishy candy she would explode. But she couldn't stop herself from eating them.

Quit stalling, she ordered herself.

Ugh, she answered herself.

"Okay," she said thickly, noticing Derik was watching her with amazement. "Let's do it before I lose my nerve."

"How romantic," he commented. He was crouched over the fire, balanced on the balls of his feet. "Are you all right? You look a little . . . bloated."

"Do me," she commanded, and stripped off her shirt. Her belly, bulging with marshmallows, pooched out over the waistband of her jeans. "You know you want to."

"Uh . . . right this minute? I wouldn't bet the farm. Maybe you should lie down."

"No, no, no. We're gonna do it. We *have* to do it, to save the world." She groaned and massaged her belly. "And to sleep in a warm bed tomorrow night. And to have a shower! Think of it, all that warm water . . . and soap, think of the soap!"

"I can't do this," he announced. "It's too much like taking advantage."

"You're right about that, but I'll be the one—hurp!—taking advantage. Now get over here." She painfully wiggled out of her jeans, then lay, gasping like a landed trout, beside the fire.

Derik was trying not to laugh, and as a result his face had gone an alarming shade of apple-red. "I don't think you're up to this tonight," he gasped.

"Aw, shaddup, when I want you to think, I'll yank your leash."

"Now you're just being mean."

"Whatever works, pal. Now strip."

"Oh, it's like that? Strip?"

She reached out and cupped the warm bulge in his jeans. "Like you're not dying to."

"Well, that's true," he said, and quit arguing, and in a minute he was naked, and helping her out of her bra and panties—

"What's burning?"

"Your bra . . . sorry."

—and then they were rolling in the grass beside the truck, kissing and groping and moaning and for a minute Sara forgot about her grotesquely distended belly, and the mosquitoes munching on her legs.

And then he was easing inside her and that was fine—it was a little uncomfortable, because he was large and she wasn't ready, but it was all right, because she just wanted this over with, but oh, oh, she hadn't expected it to feel good, she hadn't expected . . . expected this.

He rocked against her, obligingly smacking the mosquitoes he saw on her, and then his rocking speeded up, and she wriggled in the grass to give him better access, and then he stiffened all over, the cords on his neck standing out like steel.

"Ooofta," she said when he collapsed over her.

"I swear," he mumbled into her neck. "I swear I'm usually much better at this."

"No, no, it's all right. Speed impresses me!"

"Sara, you're killing me."

She laughed, and stroked the back of his neck.

Twenty

"Hi, I'm—Jon?"

Sara poked him in the side. "Your name's Derik," she whispered.

He ignored her—and embraced the red-haired man in the doorway so hard, the poor guy left his feet. "Jon, you son of a bitch! I thought that was your scent!"

"Never mind my mother," the other man replied, laughing. "Or my scent. And put me down. Derik, what the hell are you doing here?"

"It's a long story," he said, jerking a thumb over his shoulder at Sara. "This is my fiancée. We need a place to crash for the night. Okay?"

His old friend's face lit up like a moonrise. "Shit, yes, okay! Can you stay longer?"

Derik shook his head and trailed the shorter man into the house. Sara, after a doubtful look around, followed. "Got to get to the coast. Long story, which I won't bore you with. What are you doing in Kansas?"

"Hi," Jon said, extending a hand for Sara to shake. "I'm Jon; Derik and I grew up together, and he's still got no manners at all. Welcome to my home."

"Thank you," she said, jerking her head to get her hair out of her eyes. She thought about trying to straighten the mess and immediately dismissed it as a lost cause.

Jon was a redhead, too, except his hair was a rich, deep auburn, cut brutally short, and his eyes were the green of old Coke bottles. He was a couple of inches shorter than Derik; in fact, exactly her height. It was disconcerting to say the least, being able to look him straight in the eyes. His pupils, she noted clinically, were enormous. She had to swallow against the sudden blockage in her throat. Were all werewolves so . . . unsettling and charismatic? And green-eyed? "I'm Sara," she managed at last. "It's nice to be here. Nice to meet you, I mean." She noticed Jon trying not to wrinkle his nose, and sighed. "I'll let you two catch up. Meantime, can I use your shower?"

~• • •~

"So, what the hell?" Derik had polished off the last of his steak tartare, and was now rooting through Jon's fridge for a beer. "Last I heard, you got mated, Shannon was pregnant, and you were off to see the world. Now you're here? And where's the rest of the family?"

"Visiting Shannon's mother." Jon shuddered. "I decided to pass. I don't like talking to grumpy old women who are hairy when the moon *isn't* full. I'm sorry you couldn't see my cub, though."

"Heard you had a girl? Katie?"

"Mm-hmm. She's got my eyes and Shannon's brains, so that worked out nicely."

"Very nicely," he agreed, still rooting. "Listen, how come you left in the first place?" *Ah! Hello, beer, my old friend, I've come to glug you once again.* He twisted the bottle cap off—werewolves disdained bottle openers—and took a deep drink. "Oh, yeah, that's the stuff. Oooh, baby. Anyway, how come you left? We all wondered."

"Well, you know how it is." Jon had been tipped back in his kitchen chair, now he brought it forward until all four legs were on the floor. "I mean, you're not there now," he pointed out. "You can love the Pack but not necessarily want to be with them every second. I needed a little space. The mansion, big as it was, felt crowded after I mated."

"I can relate. Mike and me almost got into a huge fight before I left."

"Over what?"

"Over nothing."

"Come on, cough up."

"It was stupid."

"Did it have anything to do with you being an alpha now?" Jon asked quietly.

"What, did Moira put it in the newsletter?"

"No. You're different. You walk different, stand different . . .

even smell a little different. I bet Michael knew before you did and just waited for you to figure it out."

"Well, we almost tore each other's heads off. I had to get the hell out of there before I did something really stupid. Even for me."

Jon pondered that one in silence, while Derik finished the beer. Finally, he said, "It's a dangerous business, I guess. Sometimes. You're lucky you didn't really fight. The last thing you need is to be running the Pack. Also," he added matter-of-factly, "Jeannie would have shot you in the face."

Derik shrugged.

"And now you're with that cute, curly haired redhead."

"Yeah."

"Human, huh? Well, congratulations."

"Thanks."

"You don't seem like a happy mate-to-be, you'll excuse me for pointing it out."

"We've been fighting a lot." Finally, an unvarnished truth! "She might be having second thoughts."

Jon shook his head. "She hasn't even had first thoughts. How long have you guys known each other?"

"Never mind."

"So, less than a week."

"Never *mind*, you nosy S.O.B."

"Swept her off her feet, huh?"

"Something like that," Derik said lamely.

"Uh-huh."

"Well, it was." He'd thought it would be bad, trying to fool a regular Pack member, but this was Jon. Practically his littermate! Of all the safe houses in all the world, why'd he have to walk into Jon's? "It's been kind of a stressful week."

"Mmm. You know what your mom always said."

"If you chew on my hardwood floors one more time, I'll break your neck?"

"The other thing."

"Yeah," he said sourly. "Stick to your own kind."

Jon spread his hands, but didn't say anything.

Twenty-one

"So!" Sara said brightly, bouncing into the living room, which was floor-to-ceiling windows on the entire west side. She'd thought Kansas was supposed to be flat and boring, but it had a kind of wild beauty about it—like a prairie rose. And the windows in this place! Werewolves must not like being unable to see out. Well, of course she already knew that from Mr. "Can't we please get a convertible?" "What should we do?"

Derik, the big dope, nearly fell out of his chair. "What? Now? What are you talking about?"

"It's only nine o'clock, calm down," she said. "Do you guys want to watch a movie? Play a game?"

"A game?" Jon asked. He was a yummy one, all right, with that build and that hair and those green, green eyes. No Derik, of course, but who was? He was a watcher, though, while Derik was a doer. She could tell . . . Jon didn't say much, but his eyes were always calculating, judging, weighing. She pitied the house burglar who tried to crack *this* place. "What kind of game?"

"I don't know . . . this is *your* house. Whatcha got?"

"The only games we have are Candyland and Chutes and Ladders," Jon admitted.

"Oh, you have a little girl, that's right—I saw the pictures in the hall. She's adorable." Adorable, with about six hundred too many teeth. A truly frightening smile for a four-year-old. "Really darling."

"Thank you. Shouldn't you guys—um—aren't you tired? Don't you want to go to bed?"

"No," Sara said, at the exact moment Derik said, "Yes."

"Uh-huh," Jon said, narrowing his eyes at Sara. "Tell me again why you guys are—"

"Deck of cards?" she said hurriedly. "You've got to have one of those lying around."

"Right!" Derik said heartily. "I could really go for a—a game of—um—"

"Cards!" Sara said brightly.

Jon sighed and got up. "I think I can find one around here somewhere. Be right back."

Once he left, Derik muttered, "Very smooth."

"Shh! I thought you said he could hear everything."

"He can. When are we going to bed?"

"When you stop being an asshole." She glanced at her watch. "Shouldn't take more than a few years."

"Very f—"

"Here we are," Jon said with fake heartiness.

"This isn't such a great idea," Derik said.

"Horny bastard," Sara muttered.

"Well, yeah, but besides that."

"Don't be such a spoilsport." Jon sat down on the end of the couch and pulled the coffee table closer to them. Though the tension was thick enough to swim through, he ignored it and, ever the polite host, handed the cards to Sara. "One or two games, big deal."

Sara was blinking in confusion. "What are you guys talking about?"

"Sare-Bear, we've sort of—"

"Got to stop calling me that."

"—got the advantage. I mean, you can't bluff us. We'll know it. Your body language gives it away, even your smell changes."

"Gross," she commented.

"We'll always know when you have a good hand or a bad hand. It's not really fair. Now checkers . . . we could play checkers . . ."

"That's okay," she said. "Cards will pass the time. Consider me warned."

"Seriously," Jon said, shifting uncomfortably on his end of the couch. "It's like playing cards when we can see your cards, but you can't see ours. Not very sporting."

"Oh, hush up and deal. It'll be fun. What are we playing for? Got any quarters?"

~ ◆ ◆ ◆ ~

"Oh, boy," Derik said half an hour later.

Sara, stacking her quarters, didn't look up.

"Let me get this straight, no pun intended," Jon said. "In ten hands, you've been dealt a full house, queens over jacks, a straight, a straight flush, four aces, another straight flush, another full house, aces over kings, and another four of a kind. Aces again."

"What can I say? Lady luck likes me."

"Uh-huh."

"Told you it'd be fun."

"Uh-huh. Derik, can I talk to you a minute?"

"No," Derik said.

"*Now.*"

"That's what I said, now. You just misheard. Back in a minute, Sara."

"You, uh, want me to come with?" she said, nervously watching Jon grab Derik by the shoulder and haul him away.

"No! Don't go near him. I mean, I'll be fine. I mean—"

Then they were in the hall, and then they were in the office with the door closed.

"Okay," Jon said.

"Now, Jon—"

"What the hell are you up to?"

"Shh! Sara will hear."

"She couldn't hear if I left the door open, and you know it. What's going on?"

"You wouldn't believe me if I told you."

Jon glared, and Derik didn't drop his gaze. Finally, Jon dropped his and said to the floor, "For the record, you're both full of shit. You're not engaged, you barely know each other. You're hiding something huge, and there's something weird about your lady friend. *Really* weird. I can't put my finger on it . . . can't even get my nose around it . . . but it's making me really nervous." He rubbed the back of his neck, frowning.

"Like I said. You wouldn't believe it." Derik could feel his heart rate—which had been trip hammering at about one-eighty—slow down once Jon quit challenging him. Maybe this wouldn't be ugly. Maybe—

Jon dragged his gaze up. "Derik, you're my friend, we grew up together. So I'm giving you the benefit of the doubt, here. And I don't want to fight, and I don't want to call Michael."

"Well, shit, Jon, I don't want to fight either."

"Uh-huh. But you better get your thumb out and do whatever the fuck it is you're supposed to do. I have a family."

Derik nodded. "I know, Jon. Mike has one, too, and it's like my own family. *You're* like my own family. You think I'd screw around if it meant hurting you, or someone important to you? I'd never do that. I'd kill myself before I'd do that."

"Finally," Jon commented, "a truth."

"Look, I'm not sure what's going to happen myself yet, but I've got it covered." *I think.*

"Maybe I can help. Can you tell me about it?"

"Not really. It's hard to explain, but Sara and me—we make a good team. She can—you wouldn't believe it. But we're gonna do the right thing. She'll see to it, and I'll see to it. I swear it on my life, man. Not your family's, or Mike's, or Lara's life . . . *my own life.*"

There was a long, tense moment, and then Jon relaxed. "All right, Der. We've known each other too long not to trust each other when it gets down to the wire. Do you need help? I can come with you if—"

"No!" Christ, no. He didn't want Jon anywhere *near* Arthur's Chosen when it went down. Bad enough he and Sara were going to be there. "No, you stay here. Take care of your family. I'll come back and tell you all about it, when we're done."

"Swear."

"Swear."

Jon nibbled his lower lip, cut his eyes away for a moment, then finally said, "All right, then."

~◦ ◦ ◦ ◦~

Derik staggered down the hallway. He'd gotten away with it! Jon knew—it had been stupid to even try to fool him—but the sensible bastard was letting it ride. It wasn't the first time Derik had thanked God for Jon's basic levelheadedness. Werewolves really did have it better . . . Jon knew Derik was good for his word, and thus the unpleasantness of a fight to the death was avoided. Good deal!

Even better, he and Sara didn't have to have sex, which sucked for him but was nice for her, so that was—

He tapped on the door and walked into the guest room, just in time to see Sara drop her robe and slip between the covers. He got a tantalizing flash of cream-colored skin and streaming red curls, and then she was snuggled beneath the quilt.

"There you are," she whispered. "Close the door."

He did.

"Come over here."

He did.

"Well, come on."

"Uh?"

"Let's get this over with." Then she blushed to her hairline. "Sorry, I didn't mean it to sound like that. But let's do this before your friend gets any more suspicious. I was really worried about you when he whisked you away."

He was trying not to rock back on the heels; he couldn't get the smell of roses out of his nose. Not that he wanted to. Except he better. Yeah. Because if he didn't—"Uh . . . we . . . uh . . ."

She threw the quilt back, and he could see her bare leg, bent at the knee, the pale joint inviting kisses, inviting—

"Come *on*," she said impatiently. "Before I lose my nerve, or your friend gets any nutty ideas."

"Okay," he said, and was out of his clothes in about six seconds. He ignored the twinges—okay, the big giant pokes—of conscience. It wasn't as hard as he thought it would be.

Her knee . . . that's what did it. It was as erotic to him as if she'd dropped the sheet and shown him her tits. And her smell. Her wonderful sweet smell. She was like—like dessert.

You'll pay for this one later, his inner voice, the one that sounded annoyingly like Michael, informed him. *Oh, boy, will you pay.*

He didn't doubt it. And he couldn't help it. He was about to dance with possibly the most dangerous woman in the world . . .

. . . and he couldn't wait.

Twenty-two

I'm about to do it with a werewolf. A werewolf. Again! Sara kept saying it in her head, and it kept not working. This was weirder than the time she did it with the UPS guy. That had been like a bad porn movie come to life: "Got a package for you, ma'am." "Ooooooh, a package! Bring it over here, stud." And then, natch, she never heard from him again. It was like he'd changed routes or something. Probably he had. But anyway, this had that beat by a country mile. A werewolf. A *werewolf*!

Telling herself this was all part of saving the world didn't work, either. Truth was, Derik was magically delicious, and she meant to have another piece of him. The fact that they *had* to do it was icing on the cake. A big, blond, yummy cake. A big, muscle-y, preternaturally strong, sexy, fabulous cake. A—

Whoa.

He'd stripped in about half a second, and she barely had a glimpse of his ridiculously perfect body—washboard abs, long, long legs, flat stomach, bulging biceps, and a fairly fabulous dick, which jutted up like some sort of orgasm-seeking divining rod—before he was on her.

"Oh my God," he said, and then his mouth was on hers, he was tearing the quilt away, his tongue was in her mouth, and then he was nibbling her throat and breathing deeply, as if he couldn't get enough of the way she smelled. "Oh, Jesus."

"Are you going to talk through this whole thing? Because I'm trying to think of England, here."

"Sara, for the love of God, *please* shut up."

"Make me."

Then he was trailing kisses down her throat, her collarbone, her breasts. He played with her nipples until they were stiff and hard, and now she was doing a few "oh my Gods" herself. She squirmed beneath him, trying to give him better access, and gripped his shoulders, which were rigid with strain.

Now he was kissing her stomach, and now her mons, kissing and taking big gulps of air, and, weirdly, he was shuddering like he had a fever. Then he was coming up to her again, grabbing her thighs and slinging her legs over his shoulders. "Sorry," he panted, and then she could feel his cock between her legs, urgent and heartless, and then he was shoving himself inside her.

She shrieked in surprise, then yelled again when he nipped the side of her neck. "Sorry," he groaned again.

And here was the weird part. The weird, sick part. It hurt, sure.

It was tight as hell. It had been a while for her—last night barely counted, that was for damn sure. And she was certainly accustomed to more than forty seconds of foreplay.

But she loved it, too. She loved that he was taking her, that he was so overcome by her they weren't playing nice. He needed to fuck her, and so he was.

And she needed to be fucked, and so she was.

He buried his face in her hair and gripped her thighs harder. The bed rocked and squeaked. She felt the change in him as his orgasm approached; his muscles, already rigid with strain, seemed to get even harder for a second, and then he was shaking over her, and then he was done, and couldn't look at her.

"Well," she said, after waiting twenty seconds.

"I swear," he said, still not looking at her. "I swear I don't usually suck so much in bed. I'm aware you've heard that before."

She laughed; she couldn't help it. "It's all right. You seemed, um, like you needed to do it."

"Oh, I needed to do it. And in about ten minutes, I'm gonna need to do it again."

"Gee," she said dryly, ignoring the bolt of excitement that it brought to her belly, "I can hardly wait."

"Nice try," he said, slipping out of her and kissing her deeply, deeply. He sucked on her tongue for a long minute, then added, "But I can tell you like the idea."

"Insufferable bastard," she muttered into his mouth.

"God, you smell *so* good. Anybody ever tell you? I mean, seriously good." He stretched, and the bed creaked. "They should bottle you."

"I can safely say no one has ever suggested bottling me. So, uh, do you think Jon heard?"

He hesitated. "Well, yeah."

"Okay. I mean, creepy, and I'll be freaking out about this tomorrow, but at least you won't get in trouble."

Another odd hesitation. "Right."

"Breakfast should be fun," she muttered. "But at least that's done, right? So, good."

He didn't answer, just rolled over and kissed her again, then licked her nipples for what seemed like a delightful eternity. He cupped her left breast and brushed his thumb over her nipple again and again, while licking and kissing the other one, and then he would switch, until she was groaning and writhing beneath him.

He went lower, nuzzling between her legs, then separating her folds with his tongue, darting and licking, and then his tongue was inside her and she nearly hit the ceiling.

He settled between her thighs and over her clit and licked steadily for what seemed like an hour, until she was clawing at the bedsheets and whimpering like a maddened animal. Her orgasm hit her like a freight train, and he backed off, then was immediately on her again, spreading her apart with his hands and stroking her with his tongue and even, very, very gently, biting her.

When he came up to her again she was more than ready; she wrapped her legs against his waist and was thrusting up at him before he was even seated all the way within her.

"Oh, Christ," he managed, and propped himself up on his hands, and they went at each other for another eternity. She could come again if she tightened her thighs around him as he thrust, and did, and he groaned like he could feel it, feel her coming around him, and after a while she was begging him, begging him to come, and he was nibbling the sweet spot behind her ear and ignoring her, and they were so slick with sweat they were sliding against each other, and finally she bit him on the ear, hard, and that was it, that was what he needed, and then they were done, and it took her about ten minutes to get her breath back.

When she did, she said, "This doesn't mean we're married or anything, right?"

"Unfortunately, no."

"What?"

"I said, no."

"Oh. Okay. That was—" *The best in my life. Probably the best in anybody's life. Good work, old chap!* "That was really great."

"I knew it'd be really great," he said softly, and picked up her hand, and kissed her palm.

"Mmm. Conceited much?"

"Sara. Can I ask you something?"

"Mmm."

"What happened to your mom?"

She squinted at him, trying to see his face in the dark. "Why would you ask me that?"

"I don't know . . . something Dr. Cummings said. Actually, the way you reacted to something he said. It got me wondering."

"Well, she was killed in a stupid accident. And it was her own fault—she wasn't watching where she was going. Plus she was jaywalking."

"Oh. I'm sorry."

"It's against the law for a reason, you know."

"Yeah, okay. Well, I'm sorry," he said again.

"Thanks. What about your folks?"

"They died helping Michael's dad take over the Pack."

"Oh. Well, um, my mom got run over by a garbage truck." Pause. "It's not funny, Derik."

"I'm not laughing."

"You big liar."

"I'm really sorry," he said, sounding truly sincere. "It was just . . . unexpected."

"The really weird thing was, the city paid. I mean, I didn't sue or anything, they just gave me a big check. Just in time," she added glumly, "for me to pay for the first couple years of college."

"Oh."

"Yeah, it was like living in 'The Monkey's Paw.' Gee, I wish I could afford to go to college . . . whoops, my mom's dead, and the city's paying for school."

There was a long pause. "That's creepy."

"Tell me about it," she said, and sighed.

~ ♦ ♦ ~

Later, Sara dozed off, her small hand nestled on his chest. Derik was wide awake, ignoring the clamoring of his conscience.

Oh my God, that was so so good.

Oh my God, I'm such an asshole.

But it was so good!

And you'll pay for it, ass face. What the hell are you going to tell her? And when? Jerk.

So, so good. Like, once-in-a-lifetime good. And her poor mom! I'm glad she told me. Imagine living with—

Stay focused. Jerk.

And oh Jesus, her smell, and the feel of her, the way she held on and whimpered and squirmed, the way—

The way you were a jerk. The way you didn't tell her she didn't have to. The way you didn't want another sleepless night.

Well, look at it this way, he thought. Maybe she'll destroy the world, and I'll never have to tell her tonight was completely unnecessary.

Nice, his inner voice—Michael's voice—said snidely. *Maybe billions will die so you don't have to face the music. You're sick, dude.*

Twenty-three

Derik rolled over and saw Sara sitting on the edge of the bed. "Didja blow up the world yet?" he mumbled, scrubbing his face with his palm.

"Stop asking me that. And the answer is no." She took a sip of her coffee and grinned at him. "So you have to get up."

"Aw, man . . ."

"It's ten o'clock in the morning! I'm pretty sure the good guys don't laze away in bed, giving the bad guys plenty of time to plan."

"Ummm . . . can I have a sip of your coffee?"

"Touch my cup and die. Jon's got a whole pot out in the kitchen. Besides, I put a ton of sugar in mine, and you don't like that."

He yawned. "How'd you know that?"

"I pay attention, numb nuts. Rise and shine."

"Ummm . . . c'mere."

She scooted out of his reach. "None of that, now. It's time to go." She smiled at him again. He supposed that in the movies the sun would be shining on her and she'd seem all godlike and bright to him, but this was real life, and so she only looked really, really good. She was wearing a scoop-necked T-shirt that tantalized him with her cleavage, and when she smiled, her eyes lit up and looked like the deep end of a pool on a hot day. "Play your cards right, though, and maybe we'll stop early for the day."

"It's a date," he said, and bounded out of bed.

She nearly spilled her coffee. "Jesus! A little warning before you do that."

"Wait until I've had my coffee. Then you'll see something." He yawned again and scratched his ass, then remembered someone he wanted to impress was in the room, and stopped. "Sleep good?"

"After you wore me out last night? I'm sort of surprised I didn't slip into a coma around two A.M."

"Awww," he said, and twined one of her red curls around his finger. "That's so sweet." He let go, and it bounced into her eye.

"Ow!"

"Oh, shit! Sorry."

"As a tender moment," she informed him, "that left a lot to be desired. Go take a shower."

"Come with me," he wheedled.

"Forget it," she said. "Better hurry, or all the coffee will be gone."

~• • •~

They were finishing breakfast when Jon snapped his fingers, said, "Forgot," got up, left, came back. "Picked this up for you when I went out," he said, and slid a glossy magazine across the table.

"Oh, dude! Thanks! I've been waiting for this one." To her complete and total amazement, Derik started thumbing through the current issue of *Fine Cooking*. "I don't even know why I subscribe to this thing, it's really hard to wait for it to show up in the mail. I always end up buying it on the stands, too. Oh, well, I can always sell the extra ones on eBay."

"What just happened?" she asked.

"If you're going to be with Derik," Jon said, "you must also be obsessed with cooking."

"What? Seriously?" She looked at the big, strapping blond across from her. "Big homemaking fan, are you?"

"No," Jon said as Derik became absorbed in an article on cilantro, "but he's a big cooking fan."

"I only get it for the articles," Derik said defensively.

"Didn't you notice the shirt?" Jon added, referring to Derik's black shirt with white lettering: FREE MARTHA.

"I could hardly miss it," she said, "but I thought it was some werewolf thing."

Jon snorted. "To our everlasting relief, it's not."

"Okay, *this* is the weirdest thing to happen to me this week," Sara said.

Derik slapped the magazine closed. "I can't concentrate with you two jabbering like apes."

"Hey, hey!" Jon protested. "Watch the language."

"Sorry. Sara, are you ready to hit it?"

She blinked. "Sure, I guess. Are *you*?"

"I'll cook for you sometime. Then you won't give me shit."

"You've been letting me slave over a hot campfire all this time?"

"I need my kitchen tools to do a really good job," he explained.

"Great. Hey, I love to cook, too. At last, something in common! Not that, as an engaged couple, we don't have tons in common," she added hastily, realizing her slip. "Because we totally, totally do. Have tons in common, I mean. *Tons*."

"That's quite a hole you're digging with your mouth," Derik observed.

"It's true," Jon supplied, rescuing her. "Derik's an amazing cook. His tomato-less pizza will make you cry like a tiny girl. Don't get me started on his butterscotch cookies."

Sara said nothing. For the life of her, she couldn't think of a thing. Not that she was some sort of reverse chauvinist, all "men shouldn't be in the kitchen because they're too big and strong," but it was hard to picture Derik in a KISS THE COOK apron.

The three of them stood around the table, Derik cradling his magazine, and there was a long, awkward moment, followed by Jon clearing his throat.

"Well, good luck, you guys."

"Thanks for letting us stay over," Sara said, giving him a hug. "And for the, um, reading material."

"Sure, Sara, anytime." Jon was looking at Derik. "Sure you don't want an extra pair of hands?"

"We've got it covered," Derik replied. "And by 'got it covered' I of course mean, we're pulling it out of our asses as we go along."

"But don't worry," Sara added.

"Right. Don't do that."

"At least stay through the full moon," Jon coaxed. "Rest up, figure out the rest of your plan."

"We gotta hit it, Jon. It'll be fine. We'll be in a state park somewhere when She comes up."

"Don't forget your promise," Jon said.

"We'll be back," Derik said.

"We're like terminators that way," Sara added brightly.

Twenty-four

They were in another campsite, supper was done, even the dishes were done. Now they were snuggling beside the campfire, and when Sara looked up into his face, she noticed his eyes glowed back yellow-green. It was startling, yet comforting.

"You know, the thing about Jon," she began.

"Oh, good, I was hoping you were going to talk about another guy."

She ignored that. "He seemed like a regular person, you know? I mean, to look at him, you wouldn't think, 'Thar's a werewolf, git the gun, Paw.'"

"Christ, I hope not. And I guess it makes sense. There's not very many of us. And there's tons of you. So I guess we blend in pretty good."

"I mean, I see you all the time, and I forget about it a lot, unless you do something to remind me. Like this morning. I blinked, and you were on the other side of the room. It freaked me out."

"I can't help it"—he sighed—"if I've evolved as a genetically superior being."

"Oh, shut the hell up. Listen, what's the real reason you're avoiding your family? The Pack?"

"Huh?"

"Well, you just seem awfully concerned that they'll catch up with us, but not just because they'll try to ice me. So what's up with that?"

"It's . . . kind of complicated."

"Derik . . ."

"Well . . . you know what an alpha is, right? Like the boss of a group? And our Pack has an alpha. It's Michael. Which is totally fine. But sometimes . . . sometimes alphas aren't born, they're made. And I don't know how it happened, but in the last couple of weeks I've wanted . . . wanted things I don't deserve. At least I think I don't deserve them. And I left before things could get . . . well, you know."

"Oh."

"I can't go home again. So," he added, forcing cheer, "it's just as well that this whole save-the-world thing came up, you know?"

"Well, what I don't get is—"

"Can we change the subject?"

"Uh . . . sure. So, what's the plan for tomorrow night?"

"Before or after we have hot, wild monkey sex?"

"Can we have a serious talk, here? Like for thirty seconds? Is that too much for you?"

"I can't help it if I'd rather picture you naked than talk about our feelings, or whatever."

"I'm not even talking about our feelings, you half-wit!" She saw that he was delighted he'd teased her into yelling. "Very funny. Are you gonna answer the question?"

"Well. We'll have to make sure we're pulled over by the time the sun goes down, that's all. I'll Change, you'll sleep, I'll probably bring down a couple of rabbits and then curl up next to the fire, blah-blah."

"Blah *blah*? This is the most surreal conversation I've ever had," she announced, "and it's been quite a week for me, in case you hadn't noticed. You'll curl up next to the fire? Like a good boy? Should we pull over and get you some Milk Bones?"

"You know," he grumped, "*some* people would be a little nervous about spending the night in the woods with a werewolf."

"Some people cheat on their taxes. It's a weird world." She slipped her hand under his shirt. His pro-Martha Stewart shirt. Best not to go that route, if she wanted to maintain her horniness. "So, uh, you got any plans for the rest of the evening?"

"Well, I was thinking about jumping your bones and then taking a nap."

"Excellent! Oh, wait a minute, I'm not that easy." Heck, two nights ago she'd been fervently . . . well, a little bit . . . opposed to making love with a perfect stranger. Although Derik was far from perfect. "What the hell." She sighed as he bent and nibbled on her throat. "Yes, I am. By the way, I'm on the Pill. And I assume you're disease-free, being a genetically superior irritating being and all."

"The Pill?" He paused in mid-nibble. "Oh. Okay. That's good."

It didn't sound like he thought it was good. In fact, it sounded like he thought it was the opposite of good. "What, you wanted me to get pregnant?" she joked.

"No, no."

Weird. Because he sounded . . . disappointed? Maybe it was a cultural thing. She'd figure it out later.

She slapped a mosquito and kissed him back, delighting in the feel of his hard stomach beneath her fingers, the way his taut muscles rippled under—

"Ouch, damn it!"

"What? What?"

"I'm getting eaten alive, here."

"Yeah, I know," he murmured into her ear. "And if you give me another minute, I'll—"

"I meant by bugs, idiot."

"Oh."

"Where's the Off?"

"Poison in a can? No. No, Sara. Please," he begged as she got up in search of relief. "Don't put that stuff all over you. Please!"

"Derik," she said, exasperated. "I'm going to be one big mosquito bite tomorrow. I'm sorry you don't like the smell, but—"

"Let's go in the truck," he suggested.

She paused and slapped another flying vampire. "Good idea."

In another minute, they were groping and moaning on the front seat.

"Oh, God . . ."

"Um . . ."

"Oh, that's nice . . . here . . . move over here."

"Ah . . . oooh."

"Yeah, like that . . . oh, God."

"Ooooh, baby."

"That's—ow!"

"What?"

"The gearshift is sticking into my neck . . . there. Um. Okay, that's better. Move your hand an inch to the . . . yeah. Oooh."

"Mmm."

"Ow!"

"*What?*"

"Your foot is caught in my shirt."

"Sorry . . ."

"That's better . . . yeah . . . um . . . here, raise up . . . a little more."

"Oh, Christ."

"Yeah."

"Do not stop."

"Well, I don't—ow!"

He sighed. "What?"

"*What*, what? My head is on the floor mat, and you're confused?" She puffed hair out of her eyes, but due to her upside-down position, it just flopped back. "It's a mystery why I'm protesting?"

"Sorry. How's that?"

"Derik, this isn't working."

"What are you talking about?" He was panting, disheveled, bottomless. She would have laughed if she hadn't been so uncomfortable. "It's fine."

"What are you, high? You are, aren't you? And you aren't even sharing the good drugs."

"You're the one with a prescription pad. Besides, you're just not giving it a chance."

"Your *foot* was in my *shirt*. And now I have Raisinettes in my hair."

He burst out laughing. "Okay, okay. You win. Go put the fucking poison on."

"Forget it. Let's just bag it for tonight."

"Aw, man . . ." He indicated his dick, which was happy to see her. "I'm kind of in an awkward situation, here."

"So? Your erection will go away." She grinned. "You know, eventually."

"Aw, Sara . . . you're killing me. I mean, sincerely killing me. I think your luck is going to make my balls blow up."

"Yeah, yeah, cry me a river." She paused. He really did look pathetic. "Maybe I could help you out."

"Please?" he begged.

She wriggled and squirmed around and finally found herself in a position that didn't make her want to scream with pain. She gripped him by the root, pumped up and down, then bent and licked the pearly drop off his tip.

"Oh my God," Derik gasped, his hips thrusting toward her. "Oh, Christ, do *not* stop."

She licked and pumped and licked some more, and then his hand was on the back of her neck and she had a sense of his crushing power, power held in fierce check, heard him moan, "Don't stop . . . don't . . . don't . . ." Then he was pulsing into her mouth.

"Yech!" she said a minute later, while he lay gasping and limp as a noodle—all over. "What have you been eating?"

He rolled his eyes until he was looking at her. "Can't you just let me bask in the moment, here?" he sighed.

"Go jump in the lake," she replied. "Literally."

Twenty-five

Sara kept looking at him out of the corner of her eye, but she did it once too often, because finally Derik said, exasperated, "What?"

"Sorry."

"I can tell you that when I Change, you'll definitely notice. How 'bout that? So stop sneaking looks at me; it's creeping me right the hell out."

"Give me a break," she said, slightly defensively. "It's been a weird week. I can't help being a little nervous."

"Well, don't be. I'd never hurt you."

"No, just kill me."

"Yeah, but it wouldn't have hurt," he said easily.

She could actually feel her eyes bulge in her head as her blood pressure zoomed. "Oh my God, you're serious!"

He just looked at her.

"Okay, well, you can go run off in the woods now," she said. "I'm pissed again."

"In a few minutes." The sky was a gorgeous blaze of pinks and reds—a truly staggering sunset. And she was too annoyed and freaked out to appreciate it. "You okay?"

"Sure. Sure I am." She sneaked a glance at her wristwatch. It had been a long day—she'd spent it staring out the window, at the moon. Last night—heck, the night at Jon's—seemed a thousand years ago.

"Look, you're all set here, right? Just stay with the truck. I'll probably stick close, anyway. Stop looking at your watch, it's making me nuts."

"Sorry," she said, and like a bad dream, her gaze snuck to her watch again. "So, is it, like, *Farmer's Almanac* sunset that you change? Or actual full dark? Because it's a full moon right now, you know."

"I know," he said, and did his voice sound . . . thick? She snuck another glance at him and noted he was staring dreamily at the sky. "Sunset to sunrise. That's when we run with Her."

"Oookay. I'll be cringing in my sleeping bag if you need me." She started toward the truck, and quick as thought, he had her by the arm, gently restraining her. His nails, she noticed with a detachment that was almost like being drugged, were quite long, and curving under.

Sure, it was like being drugged. She was scared, and her brain was trying to help her deal with that fear by going into analyze overload.

Oh, for God's sake, Sara! This was Derik, and bad first impressions aside, he'd chew off his left hand before hurting her.

That was true, and she felt better, even if the sight of those nails—claws, really—was a bit upsetting. "What? What is it?"

"Stay with the truck," he said again, and it *wasn't* her imagination; he *was* speaking with difficulty.

"Okay," she said. "You told me that already, but okay."

Then he was kissing her, almost devouring her, his tongue was in her mouth, and he'd picked her up off her feet, his arms were tight around her back. And he seemed—bigger? Was that possible? Or maybe he just seemed more there, because he was so close to his change.

His mouth moved to her throat . . . and then he abruptly pulled back.

"Well," she said, almost panted. "That was . . . um, interesting. Could you let go of my arm now?"

He did, and was rapidly shedding his clothes, in fact, the only time she saw him undress quicker was when they were about to have sex that first time. Was it only the day before yesterday?

"Easy," she said as the button fly on his Levis went flying. She could hear something—was he grinding his teeth?

No; he was Changing. If she had blinked she would have missed it. He fell to his hands and knees, and his blond hair grew out, and his fingernails were digging into the dirt of the campsite, and then an enormous wolf was looking up at her, a wolf with fur the exact color of Derik's hair, a wolf with green eyes like lamps in the dark.

The wolf leaned forward, and she bent to it—to him—and he nuzzled her, a quick snuffly kiss, and then she heard the growl ripping out of him and turned so quickly she nearly lost her balance.

There was a smaller wolf at the edge of their camp, hesitating as if sensing the borders of their territory. This one was coal black, with the yellow-gold eyes of a calico cat. And quite small, really very small; Derik quit growling and loped over, and it was shocking how much bigger he was than the other one.

They sniffed each other, and she noticed Derik was at ease with his enormous size, and was trying to put the other one at ease, too. The other one was almost timid, backing off but not running away.

Then she realized: The other one was female. And they were . . . they were going off together! Without so much as a backward look, that fuzzy slut went and nabbed her would-be assassin/boyfriend/fake fiancé.

"Well, shit," she said, and kicked one of the truck's tires.

~ ◦ ◦ ◦ ~

Derik bounded up to their campsite the next morning, lured by the smell of frying bacon. He was so relaxed, and in such a good mood, it took him a while to realize something was wrong.

He supposed he should have expected it. She *was* human, even if she was an extraordinary one. And he did turn into a wolf in front of her. That was probably pretty weird for her. He'd thought about going off into the woods a good half hour before the sun set to spare her the admittedly odd sight, and in the end he'd shitcanned the idea. Because this was who he was, and if she didn't like it, tough.

But it was more than that: He wanted her to see. See all of him, and not be afraid.

"What's wrong?" he finally asked, deciding to grab the bull by the horns.

"Nothing."

"Oh. Are you, uh, mad about something?"

"No," she lied.

"Oh." Honest to God, he had no idea what to do now. She was lying, and he knew she was lying, and she probably knew he knew she was lying. So what the fuck? "So, uh, everything go okay last night?"

"Fine."

"That's good." Tell her she was lying? Ignore the fact that she was lying? Tell her but at the same time forgive her for lying? Tell a lie himself? What? "Are you mad because I didn't bring back a rabbit? I thought about it, but to be honest, skinning and cleaning one would be a pretty messy job, and I didn't think you—"

"I really don't care, Derik."

"Oh."

"So," she grumped, poking the fire.

"So, what?" He stretched, feeling pleasantly pooped. "Is there any bacon left?"

"You know damned well there is," she snapped. "Where's what's-her-fur?"

"Huh?" He sat up, puzzled. She wasn't kidding around. Not at all. She was *pissed*. She smelled exactly like the campfire. "What? Did you wake up with a spider on you? *What is it?*"

"That hair-covered-whore you took off with last night, as if you don't remember. That's *what*."

"Hair-covered . . . oh, you mean Mandy?"

"Mandy," she sneered.

"She's not a hair-covered-whore," he said defensively. "She owns her own accounting firm. And she's not here. She went home."

She shook the spatula at him, and he dodged drops of hot grease. "Look, all I want is the truth. Just tell me the truth, okay? I promise I won't get mad."

"But you're already mad," he said, wondering if he could crawl underneath the fire. The truth was, he was sort of morbidly curious . . . what would her powers do to him if she was just mad, but not defending her life? Maybe just give him dandruff, or a sprained ankle. "Really, really mad."

"Oh, shut up. Did you guys do it out there in the woods?"

"Do—oh. Oh!" He laughed out of relief, then dodged as she jabbed the spatula at him. "Sara, for crying out loud. Mandy's *got* a mate. We just paired up to hunt. Remember: Way more of you guys than us. It's really rare to just run into one of us in the woods. So we teamed up. She was on her own, because it was his turn to stay home with the cubs."

"Hmm." She was staring at him with narrowed eyes, but he could tell she felt better.

"I can't believe this! You've been stewing about this all morning?" He was trying to stop laughing; it wasn't likely to make her less mad. "The most powerful sorceress in the world is jealous of an accountant?"

"M'not jealous," she muttered. "Just wanted to know, is all."

"Well, now you do. And thanks for the vote of confidence, by the way. Yes, we werewolves are so slutty we do it with anything on four legs."

"I didn't mean it quite like that," she mumbled.

"Yeah, sure you didn't."

"Well, I'm sorry," she grumped.

"Besides, I'd never go off with another female now. I'd—" He'd shut his mouth with a snap.

"You'd what?"

"I'd get some of that bacon, like, pronto. I'm starving!"

"And the Universe," Sara said dryly, "realigns itself."

"Seriously," he said after a long moment. "That was really dumb."

"Oh, shut up," she said, but he knew she wasn't mad anymore. Even if she hadn't smelled like roses again, she fixed a whole 'nother pound of bacon, just for him.

Twenty-six

They were in St. Louis, and to tell the truth, Sara was getting pretty damned sick of the truck. And sick of sleeping outside. And sick of the smell of campfire, how it clung to her hair and clothes and skin.

And really, really sick of bacon. Derik, it appeared, could eat it with every meal. She could not.

But none of that mattered, none of it was important, because, as sick as she was of the whole thing, she didn't want it to end. She wanted to stay like this with Derik—in this adventure limbo—forever.

Because the world would end, or it wouldn't, and either way Derik would be out of her life.

Unacceptable.

That's nice, she told herself. *Put off saving the world so you can get boned a few more times. Very nice.*

"Over halfway there," Derik said.

"Uh-huh."

Right. Because werewolf lovers come along all the time. Why shouldn't I want to hang on to some happiness?

She coughed. "Listen, is there a plan for when we get there? How do we find these guys, anyway? And then what do we do, once we find them?"

"I figured your luck would help us out with finding them. Shit, you'll probably trip and fall on the leader and accidentally give him a fatal concussion. As for the rest of it . . . I can take care of the rest of it."

"You have no idea what the plan is, do you?"

"Never mind," he said primly, which made her laugh.

"It's okay," she said. "We've got some time to work on it, thank God."

"Mmm. Listen, this Morgan Le Fay business . . . maybe if Arthur's Idiots find out you're a good enough gal, they'll stop trying to kill you. I mean, we've only got Dr. Cummings's word for it that they're the bad guys."

"That and what I saw with my own eyes at the hospital," she pointed out.

"Oh, right. Well, like I said, maybe once they find out you're not bad, they'll forget about the whole thing."

"And maybe," she added brightly, "I'll get caught up on my laundry this week. But probably not."

"Seriously. Morgan's whole deal was that she was wicked, bad, blah-blah, but you're not like that."

"Morgan's whole deal, as you so annoyingly put it, is that Merlin set her up, screwed over her family, *splintered* her family, and then took off after he did all that damage."

"Oh." He paused. "Really?"

"Listen, without his interference, she could have been Arthur's greatest champion. She really could have. But she's been totally screwed over, not just by real life but by history, too. Men write the history books," she added neutrally. "So naturally their take on it was that Morgan was this wicked terrible evil witch who destroyed Arthur because she could. But that's not true at all. She was *set up* to destroy him. And then she did. But if things had been different . . ."

"Oh."

"If she'd had a normal family life . . . a normal upbringing . . . who knows?"

"Huh."

"This is the part where you say, 'I never thought about it like that.'"

"Well, I never did."

"Exactly. Men. I mean, I'm not mad about it or anything, because you can't help thinking with your dicks all the time—"

"As long as you're not mad."

"Stop the truck!" she shouted suddenly, and Derik stood on the brakes. Sara was half strangled by her seat belt, but finally fought free of it and opened her door. She reached back, grabbed the large duffel bag they were using as a communal suitcase, and said, "Come on."

"Come on, what?"

"Trust me."

She ran toward the . . . Amtrak station, Derik belatedly noticed. He ran after her. "A train?" he called. "You want to take a train? Why didn't you say so when we first started seeing trains?"

"I dunno. I'm sick of that truck," she explained, entering the busy station. "And I'll bet you a million dollars we can find a train that goes to Boston. We can ride instead of driving."

"One of us *has* been riding instead of driving."

"That's because you're a wheel hog. You wouldn't let me drive after that one time."

"You can't drive a stick."

"I can, too!"

"So we were stalling all the time, why again? And what are we doing looking for a train?"

"I don't know," she said, "but I think it's going to be all right."

"When we don't have a ticket? What am I saying. The ticket guy won't notice us, or will pretend like we have tickets, because his wife left him this morning, or Amtrak's entire computer system will crash, and they'll be too distracted to worry about two strangers on a train."

"Exactly."

"So, this is like instinct?"

"Exactly."

He was following her past the ticket windows. "Okay."

She turned to look at him over her shoulder. "Really okay?"

"Sure. I'm a huge believer in instinct. Besides"—he smiled at her—"you haven't steered us wrong yet."

Twenty-seven

"You know, I could get used to this," Derik said, climbing into the sleeping berth beside Sara, who was propped up on one elbow, looking out the window. "No ticket, no money? No problem!"

"I was wondering if it would work," she said, not looking around. "I'm sick of my power—my whatever-it-is—being passive, you know? I wanted to see if I could make it work."

"And you did."

"I *think* I did . . ."

"And say, hon, can you see anything out there?"

"*I* can't," she said, looking over her shoulder and smiling at him. It was ridiculous what a gorgeous smile she had. "Come here and narrate."

He curled up behind her and peeked over the top of her head, out the window. "Well . . . that's a farm . . . and that's another farm . . . oh, there's a herd of cows, sound asleep . . . mmm . . . cows . . ."

"Don't start, you just ate."

"What, 'just'? Half an hour ago. Oh, now look here, the land's thinning out, probably because . . . yep, there's a river . . . you can see those lights, right? Probably a town right on the river. Where the hell are we?"

"Somewhere in the Midwest."

"Well," he said, nuzzling the back of her neck, "that narrows it down."

"Off my case, hose head, I'm not a walking atlas. You know, this time tomorrow, we could be getting stomped by Arthur's Chosen."

"What a cheerful thought. Thanks for the subject change."

"It could all be over in just another day or two," she said, sounding weirdly neutral. "Just think."

"Yeah. All done. And either the world ends, or we go back to our lives."

"Yeah," she said.

"Um . . . Sara . . . this is going to sound dumb . . . and slightly retarded . . ."

"Thanks for letting me brace myself."

". . . but I'm actually having a great time with you. I—I sort of don't want it to end."

"You asshole," she said, and he was startled to see she was crying.

"What? Jeez, don't do that. I freak out when you do that.

Actually, it's the first time I've seen you do that, and I'm definitely freaking out."

"Shut up," she sobbed. "You talk too much."

"Sara, what's wrong? Besides, um, everything."

"That about sums it up," she said, wiping her eyes. "Everything. I don't want it to end, either. I'd rather stay on this train forever than fight and mess up and maybe die, or maybe the world dies, or maybe you die."

"It'll be all right," he said with a total lack of conviction.

"You're a terrible liar. Really. The worst I've ever seen."

"What can I say, we're not bred for it. Not like you guys. You guys are total experts," he said, trying to cheer her up. "Homo sapiens is the most deceitful, rapacious species the planet has ever—"

"Shut up. And have you—have you thought about—I mean, what if you're wrong?"

He snuggled closer to her in the berth. "I have no fucking idea what you're talking about, darling girl."

"Maybe you should kill me tonight," she said quietly, and he nearly fell off the bunk. "Save the world."

"Bullshit!"

"Don't yell, I'm right here."

"You're not evil, Sara. Not even a little bit evil. So how can you destroy the world?"

"What if it's not a conscious act?"

"What if it is?"

"Quit that," she snapped. "We'll get nowhere like this."

"Exactly. So drop it, all right? I didn't go through all this crap to kill you now. Besides," he pointed out, "I probably couldn't, remember? I mean, really couldn't. In addition to feeling just awful about it and not being able to make myself try again."

"Oh. That's true," she said, cheering up. "Your heart would probably explode if you tried."

"Yeah, so quit crying, okay?"

"Shut the hell up and kiss me. Dumb ass."

He did, and she kissed him back, fiercely, almost desperately, and he smelled her fear and anxiety, and soothed her as best he could with his mouth and hands. And after a while, her anxiety gave way to lust, which kindled his own.

They shed their clothes and slid against each other, whispering, nibbling, teasing, sighing, and toward the end, he closed his eyes and breathed her perfume, and they rocked together as the train rolled through the Midwest.

~ ♦ ♦ ~

"If I tell you something," he said just as she was drifting off, "you have to promise not to get mad."

"Could you sound more like a big girl? What? What is it?"

"You have to promise not to get mad."

"Whenever somebody says that, it's code for, 'you're gonna get mad as hell, so watch out'."

"Yeah, well, you have to promise you *won't* get mad."

"No."

"*No?*"

"That's right."

"Shit. Sara, I've got to tell you this. I mean, it's been, like, haunting me."

"So tell me."

"But I don't want you to get mad," he whined.

"Tough."

"Cripes." He took a deep breath; the berth was so tiny she could feel his chest heave. "Okay. We didn't have to have sex at Jon's. Or the night before, in the woods."

"We didn't have to what what at where?"

"We didn't have to have sex. He knew you weren't really my fiancée."

"And you kept this little tidbit to yourself, because . . . ?"

"Well, because I wanted to get laid," he said reasonably. Then, "Owww!"

"What? I didn't lay a finger on you."

"Oww, damn it, Sara!"

"You jerk! You creep! You ass! Oh, *fuck*!" When she thought of the way she threw herself at him . . . dropping the robe and pulling the quilt back like a big old slut . . . telling herself they were Doing It for a good cause . . . she was furious with embarrassment.

And what did it say about him, that he just boned her and never told her the truth? Other than the fact that he was a lying, sneaking, opportunistic—

"Owwwwww!"

—bastard.

"What are you whining about?" she snapped. "I haven't even gotten started. You son of a bitch! You piece of shit! You—"

"Ow, my fucking sac!" He was cradling his groin and rocking back and forth, as much as their crowded berth would allow. "Sara, will you stop it?"

"Stop what?"

"Calm down," he begged. "For the sake of our unborn children."

"I told you, I'm not doing anything." But was she? She was certainly angry enough to picture a groin-related disaster. Possibly more than one. Though his yelps of pain were doing wonders for her temper. "Quit complaining."

"Ow, ugh, ow! Oh, man." He moaned piteously. "I think my testicles just imploded."

"Serves you right," she snapped.

"I'm serious, Sara. This is the worst pain I've ever known."

"Good."

"Look, I'm sorry, okay? Really, really, really, really sorry. I was sorry before you blew up my balls."

"I did *not*—"

"It's just, I couldn't have this hanging over us anymore. Especially not after what you said, about how tomorrow might be the big day, you know?"

"So?" she sulked.

"So, I wanted to tell you."

"So, you did."

"Yeah, but you promised not to get mad."

"I did not."

"Okay, well, you got your revenge, right?" He gingerly felt himself. "Oh, boy. I think I'm out of the Sexual Olympics for a while, Sare-Bear."

"Serves you right," she said again, and flopped over on her side, as far away from him as she could get, which wasn't very far. "Asshole."

"Aw, c'mon," he coaxed. "I said I was sorry. It's not my fault I wanted to fuck you so bad I was willing to—"

"You're not helping your case," she said grumpily, but when he snuggled contritely behind her, she let him.

Twenty-eight

"Ah, Boston, the sweet smell of—Sara, what the *hell*!"

She had tripped, and he was too close on her heels, and went sprawling down the steps and over her. She hit the platform with a thump that made him wince and bit her tongue, hard.

"Oww!" she cried unnecessarily. "I mit my mongue!"

Derik rolled over, quick as a cat. "You what your what?"

"My mongue! I mit it!" She rolled it out, crossing her eyes in an attempt to look at it. "Ith it mleeding?"

"No," he said, pulling her to her feet and ignoring the curious stares of their fellow passengers.

"You nint even look!"

"Sara, if you were bleeding, I'd know it. Now what's the problem?"

"The *mroblem* ith that I nipped over my own two eet an—ow!"

She'd said "ow" because he had grabbed her by the scruff of the neck and hauled her back up onto the train, brutally shoving passengers out of his way and ducking behind the window.

"What? What's wrong? Is it Arthur's Chosen? They're waiting for us, aren't they?" She clawed frantically in her pocket, came up with a Kleenex, dabbed her tongue, checked for blood, then re-addressed the situation at hand. "It's them, isn't it? Funny how imminent death totally took my mind off my sore tongue. Which still hurts like hell, FYI. It's the Chosen, isn't it?"

"Worse," he said grimly, peeking out the window. "It's my Pack leader and his wife."

"Really? More werewolves? Oh, that's so cool. And terrifying. Where?"

"Get *down*, idiot."

"Idiot? How'd you like another broken testicle?"

He was ignoring her, peeking out the window. "They're down-wind . . . thank God. But how in the hell did they know we'd be here at this particular train station at this particular . . . Antonia."

"I don't think so," Sara said, looking up at him from the floor. "From what you told me, it sounded like she was keeping your secret."

"How else can you explain it?"

"Well. There's me. I mean, my power."

"Maybe." He peeked out the window again. "Is it possible? Would your luck have brought them here? But how come? If Mike sees you, he'll try to kill you, and Jeannie will back him up. I mean,

Mike's a toughie, but Jeannie's *insane*, especially when she's knocked up. So why would your luck put you in that position?"

"Are you actually having a conversation with me?" she asked. "Or thinking out loud?"

"It just doesn't make sense," he continued. "The whole point is that we're trying to avoid my Pack. So what would bring them here now, right before we're about to go after the bad guys? Why are they here?"

"Why don't you ask them?" Sara replied. Then she waved, looking past him. "Hi there."

"Don't kill her!" he screeched before he even turned all the way around.

"It's nice to see you, too, Derik," Michael said, yellow eyes glinting in amusement. And . . . something else. Surprise? No. Shock. They were both shocked, and covering.

"Uh . . ."

"This is the part where he says, 'I can explain'," Sara said helpfully.

"I sure as shit hope so," Jeannie said. She was looking bodaciously gorgeous as usual, with that shoulder-length mess of sun-colored curls, freckled nose, and flinty gaze. Terrifying *and* beautiful, the perfect mate for his alpha. Right now she was nervously chewing on her lower lip. "Start talking, or I start shooting."

Sara was slowly getting to her feet. "Did you guys hear all that? You know, what he was babbling while you were walking up to us?

Because I'm kind of curious, too. Not that it's not nice to meet you. Because it is, I'm sure. But what brings you here?"

Jeannie and Michael looked at each other, then looked at Sara. "We had to drop off a friend. She doesn't fly. Then I saw you, so we came over."

"That makes perfect sense," Sara said. Derik was amazed; she wasn't scared at all. Meanwhile, his adrenal gland had dumped what felt like about six gallons of fight-or-flight into his system. "I can't imagine werewolves like to fly. Stuck in an iron tube hurtling through space. I mean, it freaks me out to think of it, and I'm not claustrophobic. I don't think."

"Just . . . everybody stay calm," Derik said.

"We *are* calm," Michael pointed out.

"Everybody relax, and I can explain everything."

"Derik, we're fine," Sara said.

"Just, nobody panic."

"What's the matter with you?" Jeannie asked. "You're all twitchy and sweaty. You're usually much more laid back."

"Well. You're armed, which makes me kind of nervous. And, uh, I didn't—we didn't—expect to see you here. Today, I mean. At the train station."

"We didn't expect to see you, either," Jeannie said. "And with a friend." Blond eyebrows wiggled suggestively.

Michael stepped close and sniffed Sara. "A *good* friend," he said.

"Quit that," Sara said, throwing up an elbow. "It creeps me right the hell out."

Jeannie cleared her throat. "Please note how I restrained myself from smelling your butt."

"For which I will be forever grateful," Sara giggled. "Seriously, cut it out." She shoved Michael back, gently enough. "If you want to know something, just ask me."

"Are you Morgan Le Fay?"

"Well, um, yes."

"But she's not evil," Derik said quickly.

"She doesn't smell evil," Michael agreed. He added, "Evil usually smells a little more clove-like. But what I really want to know—"

"*I* want to know why I haven't gotten a hug," Jeannie said, spreading her arms wide. Relieved, Derik stepped close for the embrace, and then Jeannie's face shot over to the left and the entire side of his face was numb.

"Ow!"

"That's for putting my kids and husband in danger while you concentrated on getting laid," she snapped, tapping the butt of her Glock.

"Yeah," Michael said, a familiar look on his face—amusement and disconcertedness. Jeannie had, literally, beaten him to the punch. "What she said."

"Hey, working on saving the world here, okay?" he snapped back, rubbing his sore cheek.

"That's why I didn't shoot you."

"And what 'kids'? There's just Lara, because you're, like, five minutes pregnant."

"Seven weeks."

"Congratulations," Sara said. "Don't touch him again."

Jeannie didn't even glance at her. At least she had taken her hand off her gun and buttoned her jacket back up, which was always a good sign. "But Derik, I swear to God, if you put my family in jeopardy ever again because you've got a personal agenda . . ."

"Ow!"

"Yeah," Michael added, pointing to Derik's face. "Um, there'll be plenty more where that came from."

"Don't *touch* him *again*."

"Or what, Red?" Jeannie asked, supremely unimpressed.

"Or I'll make you eat that Ann Taylor knockoff."

Jeannie gasped. "It's *not* a knockoff!"

"Regardless. Stop smacking him around. If anybody gets to hit him, I do."

"Knock it off. This doesn't have anything to do with you, Red, so pipe down and shut the hell up."

"How about instead I kick your ass up and down the railroad car?"

"I don't know about you," Michael said to Derik, "but I'm experiencing a fantastic degree of sexual arousal."

"I'm too nervous to get hard," Derik muttered back. "Besides, I had kind of a bad night." Then, louder: "Now, ladies, ladies . . ."

"I mean, talk about nerve," Sara was saying. "Sneaking up on us—"

"We walked up to you at five o'clock in the afternoon in broad daylight—"

"And being all annoying and threatening, and all we're doing is trying to save your ass, and everyone else's ass, and we get attitude for it—"

"He's chasing his dick instead of getting down to business! My kids are supposed to come before his sex life. And—and—"

"You never mind about his sex life."

"I will when it's putting my family in danger."

"Well then," Sara snapped back, "you'd better shoot me."

Jeannie blinked.

Derik said, "Don't shoot her."

"I'm waaaiting," Sara sang, folding her arms across her chest.

"Don't shoot her," Michael ordered.

"Aw, can't I? She's so mouthy, it'd be a pure pleasure."

"Look who's talking," Michael muttered, giving his wife a squeeze.

"It won't work, anyway," Derik said. "Don't you think I tried to ice her? It's sort of all tied up in this mess we're in."

"I'm sure I could pull it off," Jeannie announced.

"Try it, you dyed blond, homicidal, gun-toting weirdo."

"I do *not* dye my hair!"

"Please stop," Derik begged.

"Stop," Michael said, not begging, and Jeannie and Sara both closed their mouths.

"Thank you," Derik said, relieved.

Michael was frowning. "Derik, you think we're here for a reason? For real? Because we thought we were here dropping a friend off because—because of something else."

"Getting to shoot someone," Jeannie added, "would just be icing on the cake."

Sara crossed her eyes at her and stuck out her tongue. Jeannie started tapping the butt of her gun again.

"Why don't we go get a drink, get off this train?" Derik suggested, jabbing Sara in the ribs at the same moment Michael jabbed Jeannie. "Talk about it?"

"Oh, going off and having a drink is your solution for everything," Jeannie snapped.

"It makes a pleasant change from me killing you, and my wife shooting your friend," Michael said.

"We could do that later," Sara suggested. "If you get, you know, bored."

Jeannie's forehead smoothed out, and she laughed, taken by surprise. Michael just shook his head, smiling.

Twenty-nine

"So you've got money . . ."

"Yeah."

"Okay, and you can take our car, we'll grab a rental for the trip back."

"Thanks."

"All right then. Good luck."

"Mike, what's bugging you? It's not me blowing you off."

"No?"

Derik looked over at Jeannie and Sara, who were standing in the doorway of the restaurant, pretending to be polite to each other. Well, it wasn't surprising. In his experience, strong-willed women usually didn't get along. And hardly anybody got along with Jeannie. It was the alpha thing—somebody needed to be in charge. It made her perfect for the Pack, but low on girlfriends. "No. I guess it's pretty bad. I guess you'd better tell me."

Michael hesitated, then plunged. "We were really shocked to see you. Because Antonia . . . Antonia is very upset."

"Upset like screaming foul names upset? Upset like—"

Mike didn't crack a smile. "She said it was too late. She was lying down all morning and then she came to us and said it was too late. That it couldn't be fixed."

"Oh. Well . . . oh."

"Yeah."

"But . . . oh."

"Yeah. So we were all hanging around the mansion waiting for the world to end—"

"I bet that was fun."

"—and Rosie finally said she couldn't take it anymore, that if the world was going to end, she might as well head home for it, so we ran her up here to the train station. It was actually a relief to have something to do."

Derik didn't know what to say. It couldn't be *over*. They hadn't even tried to get the bad guys yet. How could it be over? But Antonia was never wrong.

And now here was his friend, talking about the end of the world like it was a normal everyday thing.

"So," Michael continued, "I'm glad we didn't spend what might be our last day fighting."

"Me, too."

"Good luck," he added with a total lack of conviction.

"Mike," Derik said, then fell silent for a moment. Then, "It'll be all right."

"Yeah?"

"Yeah."

His friend shrugged. Derik still couldn't get over the weirdness of it all. They should be fighting. That's what an alpha did when a Pack member didn't do what he was told—kicked some ass. They should be fighting, and Jeannie should be doing what she did best, which was overreact when her family was in danger, and there should be a brawl right here on Milk Street.

Hell, when you got right down to it, Derik should have listened to his leader in the first place.

And he didn't really believe it was done, did he? That it was too late? It couldn't be fixed?

"Look," Mike was saying—uh oh, he'd better start paying attention—"you're doing fine so far with all the, uh, ignoring my orders and hooking up with the most dangerous woman on earth—"

"Thanks."

"—but I've just got one piece of advice for you."

"I'm waiting breathlessly, oh, wonderful Pack leader whose lightest utterance gives my life meaning."

"For Christ's sake," Michael muttered. "How does she put up with you? Anyway. The advice is this: Stay focused."

"Stay focused."

"Yeah."

"Okay."

"I'm serious. Keep your eye on the ball."

"It's good that you used a cliché," Derik replied, "or I might not have understood your meaning."

"Just keep it in mind," his friend said, super-mysteriously, which was annoying, but hey, at least they weren't fighting to the death, so that was all right.

~ ♦ ♦ ~

"They seemed nice," Sara commented. "For a couple of killer were-wolf psychos."

"Hey, hey."

"He *did* sic you on me, Derik."

"Yeah, but he didn't know you then."

"What a relief," she said mockingly. "Now I feel so much better. But at least now we know why they were here."

Derik looked at her, which was unnerving, because his pupils were unusually large; the rings of his irises were just thin hoops of green. In fact, ever since Michael and Jeannie had left, he'd been twitchy as hell. Which was making her twitchy as hell. "I know why they were here," he said. "I didn't know you knew."

"It's obvious. Now we have money, and a car, and you're not worried about the Pack sniffing up our backtrail. We can focus on the matter at hand, right?"

"Right," Derik said. "Focus. That's good advice. Actually, the reason they were here was— Oh my God!"

"What?" She jerked back and looked around wildly. "What's wrong? It's the bad guys for real this time, isn't it? Get 'em!"

"It's Rachael Ray! Look!"

Sara looked. They had been walking past the New England Aquarium and Legal Sea Foods, and she saw the cameras, the techs, the vans, the wires, and the lights; all evidence of a television show being taped. And in the distance, just disappearing into Legal's, a perfect brunette bob . . .

"Oh my God!" Derik was rhapsodizing. "I can't believe it! Look! They must be doing a show on Boston, or seafood. Or seafood restaurants in Boston." He gripped her arms and shook her like a maraca. *"Do you realize Rachael Ray is in that building less than a hundred feet away?"*

"This is so completely the opposite of staying focused," she informed him.

Incredibly, he was straightening his hair, which was so short it really never got mussed . . . not even after sex! Which was quite a trick. "Do I look okay?"

"You look very pretty, Mabel."

"God, I wish I had my cookbooks with me! I'd have her sign *Thirty-Minute Meals Two*." He looked around wildly, as if expecting the book to pop out of nowhere. "Shit! Oh, wait . . . I know! She can sign my shirt." He tugged his T-shirt out of his jeans and smoothed it.

"If you take off the shirt, she can sign your nipple."

He shot her a withering look. "This is serious business, Sara."

It was getting downright impossible not to burst out laughing. "It is?"

"Look . . ." He was holding her fingers, completely unaware that his grip was crushing. Annoying enhanced werewolf strength . . .

arrgghh! "I have to do this. I mean, I *have* to. I've been watching her show ever since she started on the Food Network. Both her shows . . . *Thirty-Minute Meals* and *Forty Dollars a Day*. She's just the greatest. And I have to find out. This is my chance!"

Sara was having a little trouble following the conversation, which she didn't beat herself up for, because it was pretty bizarre. "Your chance for what?"

"To find out if she's Pack. I mean, she must be. No ordinary human could be cute *and* charming *and* a great cook *and* do two shows for one network."

"It's a persuasive argument," she admitted.

"But I don't know for *sure*. If I get close enough to smell her, I'll know."

"How can you not know?"

"What, there's a humongous list of werewolves, and I memorized it?"

"I guess not," she said. "But doesn't Michael know?"

"He won't tell me. I've been after him for years, trying to figure it out, and he won't tell me! Bastard. How do I look?"

"I already told you."

"Okay, well, I'm gonna go do this now." He took a few deep, steadying breaths. "I have to do this."

"I understand." She gestured toward the bright lights. "Go to her."

"Great!" He bent, kissed her, loped off.

Sara watched him go, beyond amused. He was like a kid with a crush. A big, scary kid. She hoped Rachael would be nice to him.

Minutes later, he returned, looking so disappointed she knew at once he hadn't had a chance to meet his idol. "There were too many people around," he said glumly. "I mean, I could have gotten past them without too much—but I didn't want to scare her or make her think I was a stalker or something."

"Maybe next time. Did you find out if she's a werewolf?"

"No. I could smell a Pack member, but I couldn't get close enough to sort it out from the rest . . . it could be a techie, could be her assistant, could be the guy who owns Legal's, for all I know." His eyes narrowed thoughtfully. "But it's gotta be her. It *must* be her."

"Well, you tried."

"Yeah." He looked at her, a serious look. Uh-oh. "Sara, I just wanted to say I really appreciate your support."

"If by 'support' you mean 'mocking you behind your back,' then yes, I am chock-full of support."

"No, really, Sara. And I just wanted to say—I mean, to tell you, that maybe when this is all done, we can, you know, hit the road again, maybe try to run into Rachael again."

What an unbelievably weird idea. "Okay. I mean, that'd be nice. I'd like to do that." As she said the words out loud, she realized it was true. "When this is all done."

He took her hands again, more gently this time, she was relieved to note. "I'm just saying, there's nobody I'd rather follow the *Thirty-Minute Meals* show with than you."

"That's . . . so sweet." She bit her lip so she wouldn't laugh. Then, to her total shock—and his, too, she'd bet—she burst into tears.

"Oh, good," he said, hugging her. "Because this is exactly the reaction I was hoping for."

"I'm sorry," she sobbed. "It's just that I want this to be over—over in a good way—so we can do dumb stuff like stalk Rachael Ray. Together."

"Dumb?" Then, "I love you, Sara."

"I love you, too."

He cradled her in his arms. His big, strong arms. She resisted the urge to melt.

"Oh, Derik. How the hell did we get ourselves into this?"

"Who cares? I love you, and we'll fix it. I loved you," he added nostalgically, "from the moment I tried to kill you."

"It took a little longer for me," she confessed.

Thirty

Sara had suggested, in a ploy to divert them from their mission and cheer Derik up, that they stop by Wordsworth and pick up a new cookbook. Derik agreed at once.

"Is it totally lame that we're putting off going to Salem?"

"No."

"Well, good." She paused, then walked into the bookstore as he held the door for her. "Why isn't it lame, again?"

"We don't even know where we're supposed to go once we get to Salem," he pointed out reasonably. "Maybe if we keep hanging out, your power will kick in, or the bad guys will make a move, or something."

"Uh-huh. Is it just me, or has quite a bit of this world-saving trip entailed waiting around for something to happen?"

"It's just you," he said, and trotted toward the cooking section.

"Like hell," she muttered. She had no desire to add to her cookbook collection, but maybe she could check the New Fiction section and see if Feehan had a . . .

Oh. Oh!

After a couple of minutes, she was sitting on the floor in the History section, looking up King Arthur. Which was really kind of silly, after all, she had done lots of papers in school on King Arthur and Morgan Le Fay, so it was unlikely there would be a book here with information she didn't have on—

Arthur's Chosen. Also referred to as Arthur's Sect, Arthur's Guild, and Morgan's Bane. A mysterious sect founded in the year of King Arthur's death, Arthur's Chosen believes Arthur will return one day, but only with the help of his half sister, Morgan Le Fay . . .

Well. That was lucky. She'd just sit here and find out all about the bad guys, thank you very much.

Sara became absorbed.

One Hour Later . . .

Idiot. Fucking Idiot!

"You know better," he said out loud, startling the clerk standing a few feet away. He shot her an apologetic grin and followed Sara's scent out the door.

Well, isn't this what you were waiting for? Something to happen?

"Shut up," he said—damn it, he was talking out loud again!

Bad move, bad guys. He could find Sara's backtrail in a snow-storm; he could certainly track her to Salem. And if they harmed *one* hair . . . one *half* of one hair . . . if they touched her . . . *breathed* on her . . . *thought* about her . . .

He noticed people jumping out of his way and supposed he should calm down—he was scaring perfect strangers and really shouldn't growl in public—but he was too fucking annoyed.

~ * * *~

They weren't in Salem. They hadn't even left town. Tracking them—Sara—down had been totally super easy. He supposed he should have been suspicious, but he was too relieved.

He stomped over to the building—an abandoned warehouse near Logan Airport, of course, naturally, it was the sort of thing that all bad guys hung out in, and clearly these bad guys had been watching all the right movies—and was just about to rip the door off its hinges when his cell phone rang.

This was startling, as it hadn't rung since he left the Cape. In fact, most of the time he'd forgotten it was on his hip. He let it charge overnight and clipped it to his belt in the morning and never gave it a thought, just like he never gave pulling on Jockeys a thought. Everybody knew what he was supposedly working on, and no one wanted to bother him. Not to mention, werewolves weren't big on calling each other up and asking about the weather.

So who was calling him? And why now, when he was about to go all Search and Rescue?

He sneezed—the stench of hydrocarbons in the area was really vomit-inducing—and flipped the phone open. Before he could even say hello, Antonia was screeching in his ear.

"Don't do it! Derik, don't go in that building!"

"When this is over," he told her, more than a little rattled, "we have to sit down and talk about how scary you are. You and Sara would get along great, by the way."

"Turn around. Walk away. Leave now. Now!"

"I can't. Sara's in there. I have to go—"

"Shut the fuck up! Derik, if you go in that building, you'll die. I saw it. You'll—" Antonia's voice broke, and he nearly dropped the phone. Antonia? Worked up into tears over *his* ugly ass? "You'll die. Don't go in, Derik. Don't."

"I appreciate the warning," he said. "But I have to. If I don't see you again—"

"Don't!"

"—thanks for all your help."

"You numb fuck! Men! I told Michael it couldn't be taken back, and what does *he* do? Goes to Boston for a day trip! You guys would think I was, like, wrong occasionally."

"We know you're not wrong," he explained. "But that doesn't mean we're going to lie down and wait for the world to end."

An inarticulate screech was her only answer.

"And thanks for trying to save me. I don't suppose you saw what'll happen to Sara?"

"Ape! Chimp! Gorilla!"

"Now you're just being mean," he said, and closed the phone.

Nuts, he thought. *I forgot to ask her how I die. Well, I suppose I'll find out in a few minutes.*

He was weirdly sanguine about it, and after a moment's thought he knew why. He could face dying, if Sara was all right. He could even face the end of the world, if Sara was all right. But he couldn't stay out in this smelly parking lot and play it safe while the redhead was in trouble.

So, he would go in. And die, because Antonia was never wrong. But maybe Sara would come out of it okay. And maybe not.

It was worth trying, anyway.

He kicked the door off its hinges, belatedly realizing it hadn't been locked. "D'oh!" he said, then picked the door up and sheepishly set it against the wall. "Hello-o?" he called. "You guys better come get me! Quit whatever you're doing to what's-her-name and come on over here. Let's dance."

"Let's dance?" a thrillingly familiar voice said. "That's really bad, Derik."

"Sara!" He avoided three of Arthur's Losers—the cranberry-colored robes were a dead giveaway, *why* did they do that?—and ran to her. "Oh, man, thank God you're all right!" He hugged her, lifting her off her feet. Then he shook her. "And what the hell did you think you were doing, going off with the bad guys?" Then he hugged her again. "I don't know what I would have done if something had happened to you, oh, baby, baby." Then he shook her. "Kicked some ass, that's what I would have done! And what is your *problem*? I tell you to stay put, and you leave? Have you never watched a horror movie in your life?" Then he hugged her again. "Oh, Sara, Sara . . . you sweet, sweet dumb ass."

"Will you stop?" She extricated herself with difficulty and puffed a curl out of her face. "I'm gonna throw up if you don't quit that. And I had to go with them."

"What, had to?"

"They said—they said they had snipers. Trained on your head. And I didn't know if it was the truth or a lie. It seemed a little far-fetched. But I know they use guns, because of that time in the hospital—God, was it only earlier this week? I wonder if my car's fixed yet."

"Could you stay focused, please?"

"I *am*. Anyway, I couldn't take a chance. I didn't think you—even you—could survive a head shot. They said if I went with them they wouldn't kill you. So, I went."

"Dumb ass."

"In retrospect, yeah." She lowered her voice, which was stupid, because the Chosen were right there, hearing every word. "They needed my blood." She showed him the inside of her elbow, which had a drop of dried blood on it. "And they didn't even disinfect the needle site. Bastards."

"Your blood? They needed your blood?" That didn't sound good. That didn't sound remotely good. "Like, for to do magic? Like a spell?"

"I've missed their last few meetings," Sara said dryly, "so I don't know exactly what they need it for."

He put his arm around her, protectively, then turned and glared at the Robed Weirdos. "What's up, fellas? What'd you need her blood for?"

The shortest Arthur's Chosen blinked. "Who are you?"

Derik was almost crushed. These guys clearly had access to powerful magicks, at least one of them could see the future, and they had *no* fucking idea who he was! How totally embarrassing.

"I'm this one's mate, so there," he snapped, squeezing so protectively that Sara yelped. "Oh. Sorry, babe."

"Mate, huh?" Sara muttered back. "Aw. I didn't know you cared."

Weirdly, the robed fellas were bowing. He could smell quite a few more and looked up . . . there were at least a dozen on the catwalk, and even more in the back where he couldn't see. They were *all* bowing.

"Why are you doing that?" Sara asked, and he was so puffed up with pride—she didn't sound afraid at all, though he knew perfectly well she was—that he almost squeezed her again. "I don't think you should do that. Do you think they should do that, Derik?"

"Definitely not."

"You are our sworn enemy," they all said in unison. Then the one who had spoken first added, "But you are also the daughter of a king, and the sister of a king."

"Um . . . I'm the daughter of an ad exec, and the sister of nobody," Sara said. "But, thanks anyway."

"In *this* incarnation," one robed fella said.

"And I'm not going to destroy the world," she added, "and you can't make me!"

"Darned right you're not," another of the Chosen said. "Why do you think *we're* here?"

"To, um, kill me?"

"To try," Derik added silkily, in his turn.

"We knew you were coming. Did you think we weren't ready? We've had years to arm ourselves with formidable magicks."

"Whoa, whoa." Sara made the time-out sign with her hands. "The only reason I'm here is because your Chosen Ones showed up at my hospital! My mentor told me all about you and sent us to Massachusetts. If you hadn't tried to kill me, I'd still be in California."

"I'm such a loser," Derik muttered in her ear. "Because that actually depressed the shit out of me. We'd never have met!"

"Stop thinking with your dick," she hissed back.

"Your mentor is a traitor to our cause and will be killed on sight . . . as soon as we attend to this other business."

Sara gaped. "Dr. Cummings was one of you?"

"Used to be one of us. Then we discovered he was a foul traitor."

"He was only using us to get information for one of his doctorates," another one explained. "He didn't care about our cause."

"Yeah, that sounds about right," Sara agreed. "He's really aggravating that way."

"Nice of him to warn us, though," Derik said.

"Extremely nice." Then Sara added, "Besides, I can't do magic. I don't know any spells, or anything. I'm a nurse, for God's sake!"

"Then, as a nurse," one of them said from the catwalk, "you

know that sometimes it's necessary to hurt a patient to heal an-other one."

"Uh . . . we're talking theoretically here, right?"

"Your blood will bring back His Majesty, King Arthur. Without your interference, *woman*"—he spat that word out like someone else would have said "child molester"—"he will be the greatest of all of us. He will raise Britain to heights only dreamed of. He will . . . *not! Be! Dead!*"

"Oh, boy," Derik muttered. "Someone forgot their meds today."

"Probably more than one day," Sara said. Then, louder: "You mean you're not going to make me destroy the world? You're going to use my blood to—I dunno—clone or resurrect a new Arthur?"

"Well, sure," another robed one said, one not quite so frothy at the mouth. "What'd you think we were going to do?"

"But Sara doesn't do magic," Derik said. "In case you guys weren't listening the first time."

"That's a relief," the mellower one said. "It makes this all so much easier."

A few of the robed fellows in the corner, who had been bustling busily about during their conversation, now revealed the small lab table where they'd been working. Evil-smelling smoke was pouring from various beakers. Its color exactly matched the cranberry of their robes!

"They don't know about your luck," Derik whispered. "How can they not know?"

"Shit, Derik, *I* didn't know until a few days ago. But how are they going to make Arthur just appear? Even if they cloned him, somehow, he'd have to grow. He wouldn't just appear—"

"We can hear you, you know," one of them said. "I mean, you're only standing ten feet away."

"Aw, shut up," Derik said.

"Arthur—the dead king Arthur—can't just appear," Sara was reasoning out loud. "It doesn't make sense. Unless—"

"*Doseda nosefta kerienba!*"

"—unless they know some sort of magic spell," she finished, and sighed. "Magic. Cripes! I'm from California, and I still don't believe it. Oh, yuck! Look. They're splashing my blood all over the table. Gross! And I don't see a single biohazard sign, thank you very much."

"Uh, if you don't need any more of her blood—"

"Yes, yes, you're free to go," one of them said, without looking up.

Derik and Sara looked at each other.

"Seriously?" Sara finally asked.

"Yes, yes. Go."

"Go as in *leave*? Or go as in wait quietly in the corner for you to come over and kill us with an axe?"

"This makes *no* sense," Derik said. "You tried to blow her brains out at the hospital, but now she can leave?"

"We just needed some blood to complete the spell," Surprisingly Reasonable Robed Guy explained. "It was the last thing. We've spent years collecting the other ingredients. And she *is* a foul sorceress. We didn't want to take any chances."

"Which, since she accidentally killed all the bad guys, wasn't the worst plan, I suppose," Derik said grudgingly.

Surprisingly Reasonable Robed Guy shrugged. "That was mostly Bob's plan."

"So we're *leaving*?" Sara blurted. "We can just go?"

No answer. The robed ones all took turns muttering chants and moving things around on the lab table. Sara pointed to the pentagram outlined in what looked like green chalk, which she had just noticed.

"I have to admit," Derik admitted, "I didn't really see this coming."

"What do we do?" Sara asked, gripping his hand. "Do we leave? We can't just leave. Can we?"

"I . . . guess not."

"We didn't travel all the way across the country so they could snatch a few cc's of my blood and then kick us out. *We're* the good guys. *We're* supposed to save the world from *them*!"

"Hey, Sara, I'm with you, okay? What do you suggest?"

"We stop them from the spell they're working on!"

"I don't know if messing with them when they're in the middle of performing black magic is the best idea . . ."

"True, but I don't think anything good can come from trying to raise the dead. It's, like, a philosophy of mine."

"Even if it is King Arthur who, you gotta admit, would be kind of cool to talk to. Okay. You stay here. On second thought, you come with me. Maybe if they try to stab me, you can give them a brain-bleed or something." He gripped her hand, then loosened his grip when she yelped again, and started forward. "Hey! You guys! In the robes! Stop what you're doing!"

Thirty-one

"Modesa noeka birienza doseda nosefta kerienba modesa noeka—"

"That's totally the opposite of stop what you're doing," Derik said, and Sara almost laughed. What a day. What a week! Nothing was turning out the way she had expected. Was that a good thing, or a bad thing?

A bubble, poison green and clear as glass, rose from the table, enveloping the chanters as it grew. With every spoken word, it got bigger. There was no pain when it enveloped her and Derik, and no smell. Suddenly, the world was green, and the bubble was still growing.

Derik rushed forward, tossing robed fellows like red checker pieces, and as she hurried to help him, the lab table fell over. The screams of the Chosen Ones almost drowned out the glass breaking.

The world was still clear green—it was like being trapped inside a mucous bubble—but now an ominous humming had started. Sara clapped her hands over her ears—the sound was so low it made her teeth hurt—but the sound went on, and she realized it was going on inside her head.

"We did not finish! We did not finish!"

"Let me guess," she said, taking her hands down—what was the point? "That's bad."

"The moGhurn! The moGhurn!"

Derik was standing, brushing glass and blood off his T-shirt. "What the hell is a moGhurn? And where are all of you guys going?"

There was something in the bubble with them. It was so sudden . . . one minute there was breaking glass and pandemonium and yelling, and the next she felt so heavy she had trouble breathing. The air had gotten heavier, or—it sounded dumb, but—her spirit had gotten heavier. Something had appeared, had been conjured up out of blood and despair and desperate hope, something the sect was trying to run from, but they were all trapped in the green bubble together.

The moGhurn looked like a devil crossed with an elm tree. It had a face, of sorts, and eyes and arms, and was terrible, all terrible—she could think of nothing good to describe it. It swept up members of the sect in its—arms?—branches?—and dashed them to the ground, or pulled their limbs off like her mother used to pull the leg off a chicken, and for a funny thing, it made much the same sound, the sound of gristle tearing and parting from meat, and then she bent, and stared at the green floor, and worked hard on not throwing up.

In the panic she had been separated from Derik, but now the dead gaze of the moGhurn fell on her, and it moved toward her with the rapid, inhuman speed of a snake. She backed up as far as the bubble would let her and she saw . . .

. . . she saw . . .

She saw the sect killed, all of them, heaps of robes everywhere. She saw Derik, dead. She saw the moGhurn reach for her, and then the bubble burst in a feat of amazing and unlikely luck—and the moGhurn, delighted to be free, forgot about her and moved out into the world.

The moGhurn killed everyone in the Boston area, from the oldest man in the Chelsea nursing home, to the infant girl who was born forty minutes ago. This took the demon about two and a half hours. In a day, it had finished with Massachusetts; in a week, the Eastern seaboard. The more it destroyed, the stronger it grew—no magical green bubble to keep it in check any longer— and in a month, North America was gone.

Except for her. Lucky, lucky Sara, spared by the moGhurn, who was distracted at exactly the right moment.

And in another thirty days, she was alone. She was alone in the world. She had not meant to, but everyone was dead all the same, and the moGhurn was still hungry . . . this time, Morgan Le Fay had triumphed, and her reward was a dead world.

Sara blinked, and the bubble was back. There were still bad guys running around in robes—though quite a few of them were dead. Derik was punching the bubble, trying to get out. Everything was green.

She groped, saw what she wanted, leaped for it. An empty hypo amid the broken glass and blood. She pressed the plunger, then pulled it back. Right in the heart. Instant embolism. No more luck. MoGhurn stays put. *Good-bye, cruel world. Oh, Derik, and you'll never know how brave I was.*

Do embolisms hurt?

No time like the present to find out. She slammed the needle forward, gritting her teeth, and then—

"Ow!"

Derik's hand, protectively across her chest. Goddamn it! That spooky werewolf speed could be a real pain in the ass sometimes.

"Derik, you idiot!" she shouted. "I have to!"

He jerked the needle out of the back of his hand, then tossed it. "Like hell!" he shouted back. "Bad, bad, bad, *bad* plan. Bad Sara! No suicides today, please. If this fucking weird green circle thing ever breaks, you run like hell, Sara." He kissed her hard, then thrust her back. "Run!"

She wanted to scream after him but didn't have the breath—it had been knocked out of her by what she was seeing. Derik was running right for the moGhurn, knocking Chosen Ones out of the way like bowling pins.

"We're supposed to be scared of a mutated oak tree?" he shouted, then leaped for the demon, who caught him and shook him like a doll.

Shook him like a *doll*?

Her Derik?

Her Derik?

"Get your tree limbs off him!" she roared, stomping toward the demon. "You piece of shit! You overgrown nightmare from a Tim Burton movie! You leafy motherfucker! *Let him go or I will kill you, I swear it, I swear it!*"

She stomped through broken beakers, barely feeling the glass slice through her sneaker, her sock, her foot. "Right now! Not tomorrow now, not an hour from now, *now*, now!"

It towered over her, and Derik was dangling, limp, from its awful grip. She was afraid, but on top of the fear was anger—true, dark anger, that anyone, anything should treat her love like that. The moGhurn tossed Derik aside like an empty milk carton, and she saw red. Literally, saw red. It was reaching for her and she knew she was no match for it, knew it would kill her—*but that was okay because it looked like Derik was dead, too, so who cared?*—and she did the only thing she could as it bent toward her: She kicked it.

It screamed—horrid, awful, terrible noise—and staggered away from her. This was gratifying, if startling. It screamed, and screamed and shook, and knocked over Robed Ones, and ran around like an evil leafy tornado, and fell over, and twitched like it was being chopped down by a chain saw, and then it shrank down into itself and disappeared.

Then the bubble popped, and she realized her foot hurt like hell, was, in fact, bleeding pretty good.

"Who cares?" she muttered, racing over to Derik, who was

lying in the corner all crumpled and banged up. She skidded to her knees beside him, hesitated,

I could . . . I could . . . I could hurt him more by moving him

and then turned him over. He came into her arms with a loose, boneless feel that scared her worse than the tree demon had.

"Derik," she said softly, and cried at his dear, battered face, the way his head was tipped too far back in her arms—broken neck at the axis for sure, maybe the atlas as well—and the blood, all the blood. His eyes were open, but he wasn't seeing her. She groped for a pulse, found nothing. Nothing. "Oh, Derik, you big dumb ass . . . you weren't supposed to die. Me, okay, and the rest of the world—a faint possibility. But not you. Never you."

He's only clinically dead, you dumb ass! What, you've got no training? Get to work!

But his neck . . . his neck was . . .

Get to work!

Right. She set him down on the cement floor and started a closed chest massage. One and two and three and four. One and two and three and four. *Oh, don't be dead. Don't.* One and two and three and four. *Oh, don't you dare leave me. Don't you dare. Like I could settle for an ordinary guy after this. Don't.* And one and two and three—

"Sara . . ."

"Now I'm alone," she panted. And two and three and four. "Alone with a zillion people in the world, and where the hell am I going to find someone else like you?"

"Sara . . ."

"What?" she wept. She stopped pumping and pulled him back onto her lap. "What, idiot?"

"Where's the bad guy?" The whites of his eyes were blood red, and blood was even leaking from his left eye like dark tears.

"I kicked him and he died," she sobbed.

"Way to make . . . make a guy feel . . . useful," he gasped, and coughed, and now there was more blood, oh, God, like there wasn't enough before.

"Does it hurt?" she cried. Probably not, she realized clinically; shock would keep much of the pain at bay.

"It's pretty fucking excruciating," he admitted.

"It is? Oh my God, Derik, I'm so sorry, let me go pull some robes off these dead idiots, you must be freezing."

"I just want a drink," he groaned. "Possibly ten. Help me up."

She almost burst into fresh tears—he had no idea how badly he was hurt. How he had minutes, at the most, to live. How he had already died, and she'd only brought him back through luck and some brute skill. The damage she could see was bad enough—she couldn't imagine what had happened internally. Crushed liver. Collapsed lungs—it was a wonder he had the breath to talk at all. *Oh, Derik.* "Just—just lie still and the ambulance will come."

"Sara, it stinks in here, I've had a bad day, and I'd really like to get off this disgusting floor," he snapped. "Help me up."

"Just lie still, Derik," she soothed.

He rotated his neck on his shoulders, irritably, like a man trying to work out a kink. She heard the crackling sound of air popping free of bones, and then he coughed again, wiped the blood off his chin with a grimace, and sat up in her arms. His left eye was still bloodshot. The right was entirely clear.

"What a dump," he said in disgust, looking around the chaos of dead bodies, scorched robes, broken glass, upended tables. "What a day! Let's get the hell out of here. Stop it, that tickles."

She was feeling him all over. "Oh my God. Oh my God! So quick, it was so quick!"

"Yeah, well, superior life form, baby. I told you this already." He rubbed the eye that was still bloody, and when he quit she saw that it was now clear. "Doesn't hurt that the full moon's not that far behind me. And I think you had something to do with it, too."

"Me?" she gasped, feeling him.

"Yeah, I wouldn't be able to heal this fast normally. I think your power—your sorcery—I dunno, wrapped me up in a magical envelope, or whatever."

"Really? Let's consider this caref—"

"Later. Cripes, I'm sore. What a day."

"Shut the hell up." She put her thumbs on his lower lids and pulled them down. The sclera of both eyes were a perfectly healthy pink. "I can't believe it, I can't believe it! It was so fast!"

"Like I said. I think I've got you to thank for that. I mean, I'm a fast healer, but that was extra special. Maybe your power sort of wrapped me up, like a lucky hug. Or something." He grinned. "*I'd* hug you, but first I need a new shirt. And possibly new underpants—that tree demon thingy was scary."

"What about Arthur's Chosen?" she asked, almost whispered.

She'd never been in a room full of dead bodies before—not since nursing school.

"What about 'em? They're all dead. *Luckily*, the demon killed them all, and then you fucked him up before he could do anything else."

"You're right," she said after a minute. "I *am* scary."

"Scarier than taxes, babe."

He took her hand and led her from the warehouse she'd honestly thought was to become her tomb.

PART THREE

Mates

Thirty-two

"I guess the question, 'will they be surprised to see us?' has been answered," Sara commented as they pulled up to Wyndham Manor. A huge banner reading GOOD WORK SAVING THE WORLD was strung across the front entryway.

They got out of the car, just as a dizzying parade of people poured out of the doors of the house—mansion, really. Sara found herself picked up and hugged by Michael and several other ridiculously good-looking men she'd never met before. Jeannie was kissing and hugging Derik, and a petite, stunning blonde was climbing all over him like a monkey, laughing and saying over and over again, "You did it! I can't believe you did it!"

Then intros: Michael and Jeannie (whom she already knew), and their daughter, Lara, who had her father's odd yellow brown eyes and her mother's aggressiveness, and the petite blonde was

Moira, and oh, several others that she lost track of, but she didn't mind, because even though they were all strangers, it was exactly like coming home.

~ • • • ~

"So you told them we were coming, huh?" Derik asked.

Antonia, who was just as ridiculously breathtaking as the rest of them, shrugged. "Don't get pissy. It's what I do."

"Thanks for all your help," Sara said.

Antonia grunted. Sara had never known that someone who looked like a swimsuit model could be so sullen.

"So, what's next for you two?" Jeannie asked, picking up the pitcher of lemonade, pouring herself a glass, then promptly draining it off. They were sitting in a gorgeous sunroom, the remains of a glorious lunch laid out before them. "And why did I do that?" she griped aloud. "Like I don't have to pee often enough. Pregnancy," she finished in a mutter.

"You're glowing," Michael said automatically.

"That's because of all the puking," she retorted.

"So?" Michael prompted. "You guys? What's next?"

"Um . . ." Sara said, because she didn't have a clue.

"Well, we're getting married in a couple of days, and Mike's going to give us an RV for a wedding present, and then we're going to drive around the country looking for Rachel Ray."

"That's the lamest marriage proposal ever," Sara commented, while Antonia actually cracked a smile.

"Yeah, but you're gonna go along with it." When she didn't say anything, he dropped the cocky pose. "Right, Sara? Sara? Right? You're gonna be my mate, right? Sara?"

"Oh, Christ, tell him yes," Antonia said, rolling her great dark eyes. "Before I pick up this fork and jam it into my ear, just so I don't have to listen to any more of that."

"Actually, it's a refreshing change," Michael commented, biting the chicken leg in half and sucking out the marrow in one slurp. Sara managed to conceal her shudder. "Keep him on the hook, Sara."

"Never mind," she told them, and then said to Derik, "It would have been nice to have been asked, jerk. But it sounds like a fine plan."

"Congratulations," Antonia said, bored. Then she leaned forward and speared Derik with her gaze. "And before I forget, numb nuts, who told you to go to her house and kill her?"

"Huh? I mean, you did."

"No, I told you to *take care of her*. As in, look out for her, so she could destroy the moGhurn when it manifested."

"*What?* Wait just a goddamned minute! You *never* told me to look out for her. You told me—"

"Well, I knew you wouldn't be able to ice her, but I wanted you to stay close anyway," Antonia explained. "The world was saved because you were fated to love her, not because you were fated to kill her. Not to mention, you were fated to die . . . but not for too long. Dumb ass."

"Now *wait one minute*." Derik was as furious as Sara had ever seen him. She clutched at his sleeve, trying to get him to sit down, but he towered over Antonia and ignored Sara's tugging. "You sent me there to—"

"Take care of her—do I have to get out the hand puppets? Look, Derik, I couldn't tell you the whole thing. We probably wouldn't be sitting here right now if you'd known what I'd known. Not that you could ever be bright enough to know what I know—"

"God*damn* it, Antonia!"

"Oh, take a chill pill. Everything that happened this week, you guys had to do. It *all* led to the big showdown. High noon in Boston, so to speak."

"I still don't get it," Sara confessed. "The bad guys—Arthur's Chosen—made the demon-thingy on purpose? No?"

"No, it was an accident. You screwed up the spell. They were trying to bring Arthur back, remember? With your blood. But the spell screwed up—which anybody who watches *Charmed* will tell you—and then they were in over their heads. I mean, that's the trouble with screwing around with black magic. You make one slip, and suddenly there's a world-devouring demon in your warehouse."

"Which Sara got rid of," Derik said, calming down. "You guys shoulda seen it."

Sara laughed, which calmed Derik down even further. "I was so scared, I didn't know what to do. I think I kicked it—the whole thing's kind of a blur. I guess my blood did away with it? Because my blood conjured it up?"

"Do I look like I'm wearing a pointy Merlin hat?" Derik griped.

"Track down your mentor, Dr. Cummings. Ask him. He can probably explain the whole thing."

"And this whole 'everything is for a reason' bushwah . . . you mean my car conking out was part of the big plan, too?"

"The universe is a mysterious place," Antonia said, popping the last cherry tomato into her mouth.

Derik sat down. "Fucking miracle it all turned out all right," he muttered. *"Miracle."*

"Oh," Sara said, leaning forward and kissing him on the cheek. "My specialty."

"At least the alpha thing is taken care of," Moira said. "Thank God."

"What alpha thing?" Sara asked.

"It doesn't matter now," Derik said, visibly uncomfortable.

"What?" Michael said. "It's fine, Derik. Shit, I'm not one to argue fate." He glanced fondly at his wife. "Not anymore."

"What are you guys talking about?" Sara asked.

"Derik's an alpha, too, which usually means trouble for us," Moira explained, "because our Pack already has an alpha."

"I don't suppose he can, like, try to win the next alpha election, or whatever . . ."

"It doesn't exactly work like that," Antonia said dryly.

"But part of the problem of *being* alpha is the overwhelming urge to *prove* it . . . men," Moira added, shaking her head.

Sara decided she would like the tiny blonde, if the woman wasn't so damned cute. Thank God she was married!

"Anyway, not only does Derik not have to prove anything," Moira went on, "he's aligned himself with a mate who is quite possibly the most powerful being on the planet."

"Oh, now, well," Sara said self-deprecatingly.

"Know anybody else who can get rid of a demon by kicking it?" Antonia asked rudely.

"Kicking it," Jeannie said, shaking her head. Then, "Excuse me. I gotta pee."

"Anyway," Moira continued, frowning at Antonia, who sneered back, "it sounds like you guys aren't even going to be around that much. So the problem has, essentially, been solved. Both internally—feeling alpha and feeling the need to prove it—and externally, because you'll be traveling."

"Oh," Sara said. It all sounded like a lot of werewolf bullshit to her. She'd have Derik go over it with her later. Probably. "Well, that's good."

"Real good," Michael said, "because I would have broken out all his teeth, and then I really would have gone to work on him. And I would have hated to do that."

"Dude, what have you been sniffing? You were so *toast* if I decided to bring the smackdown. I would have spanked you!"

"And then I would have snapped your spine."

"You're high! You are on *serious* uppers, dude! You gotta know I would have totally . . ."

"God, I'm bored," Antonia mumbled. "At least when we thought the world was gonna end, it was interesting around here."

"Maybe you can go off and have an adventure of your own," Sara suggested.

"Yeah, yeah . . ."

"So," Sara said to Jeannie, who had just returned and was working on her third glass of lemonade, "how are you feeling?"

"Oh, fine. I haven't started craving raw meat yet—thank heavens."

"Are you thinking about names?"

Jeannie set down her glass and shook her blonde hair out of her face. "Well, you know, Sara," she said seriously, "we really haven't been lately. Because of—because we weren't sure what was going to happen."

"Oh. Sure, I get it."

"But I guess now we have to get back to it. And I think, just for the record, that Sara is a lovely name."

"Oh, vomit," Antonia said, which was just as well, because Sara was too choked up to say anything.

Epilogue

"Hi, and welcome to *Forty Dollars a Day*. I'm Rachael Ray, and I'm here today at the annual San Antonio rattlesnake festival with Derik Gardner, who has taken first prize with his *wonderful* dish, Rattlesnake *en croûte*. I know, I know, it sounds kind of yerrrgggh, but you *gotta* try it. Derik has come out of *nowhere* and unseated last year's champion with his awesome dish. Derik, congratulations!"

"Thanks, Rachael."

"Your dish is *delicious*. I mean, yum! Who would have thought something made out of snake could look so delicious? I mean, look at that, so crispy and golden and just . . . gorgeous! And it's very tender. It really doesn't taste like chicken at all. So, Derik, do you catch the rattlesnakes yourself?"

"Yes, I do, Rachael."

"That's *amazing* . . . do you use a net, or a trap?"

"Something like that, Rachael."

"And this is your wife? Sara?"

"Yeah, hi."

"Do you help Derik catch the rattlesnakes?"

"God, no. The whole thing just creeps me out. I stay in the RV, while he does that."

"Well, it looks like you get to partake in the fruits of his labor, then . . ."

"Yes, lucky me."

". . . and is it true you two travel around the country going to cooking shows and the like?"

"Yes, that's true, Rachael."

"Well, that's certainly working out well for you so far, at least from where I'm standing."

"Thank you, Rachael."

"You're right about that one, Rachael."

"Oh, whoa now! I guess you would call that the newlywed effect . . . and congratulations, by the way."

"Thanks, Rachael."

"Yeah," Derik said, beaming. "Thanks."

MONSTER LOVE

Prologue

From the private papers of Richard Will, Ten Beacon Hill, Boston, Massachusetts

"Becoming a vampire was the best thing that ever happened to me. The very, very best. Which is why I don't understand all the literature, how the vampires are usually these moody fellows who rue the day they ever got bitten, who pray for some illiterate European to plant a stake through their ribs. Rue the day? If the mob hadn't torched my killer the next night, I'd have kissed his feet. I'd even have kissed his behind!

"After all, what else was there for me? Take over the farm when my father died? *No, thank you.* Farming is back-breaking work for very little reward and even less respect. And I could hardly endure being in the same room with my father, much less work for him the rest of my life. (Punch first and punch second, that was my dear departed papa's motto.)

"Lie about my age to join the army and get my head blown off? (All so sixty years later we can ignore the Holocaust and pretend the Germans are good guys?) But back then, if you didn't fight you were a coward. Of course, two wars later, the young men were *encouraged* to go to Canada, to avoid responsibilities to their country. If they fought, and lived, their reward was to be spit upon at the airport. It just goes to prove, nothing changes faster than the mind of an American.

"No, life wasn't exactly a bowl of fresh peaches. I was in a box, and each side of the box was equally insurmountable. I wasn't the only one, but I was the only one who noticed the shape and size of the prison. I was always different from my chums. At least, I think I was . . . it was a long time ago, and don't we always think we're different?

"So when Darak—that was his name, or at least the name he gave me—bought me a drink, then two, then ten, I didn't turn him down. What did I care if a stranger wanted to help me forget about the box? I was big—twenty-three years working on a farm made for a big boy—and if he wanted to get inappropriate, I was sure I could handle it.

"Yes, there was homosexuality in the forties. People like to pretend it's a modern invention, which always makes me laugh. Anyway, I figured Darak wanted to see what I had inside my drawers, but I had no intention of showing him—what men did with other men was none of my concern. Of course, my drawers weren't what held his interest at all.

"I'd been supremely confident I could toss Darak through a window if I needed to, which just goes to show I was something of a naive moron when I was a boy. Darak took what he needed from me, and never mind pretty words or even asking permission. He stopped my heart and left me on a filthy floor to breathe my last. The last thing I remember was a rat scampering across my face, how the tail felt, dragging across my mouth.

"I woke up two nights later. It was dark and close, but in a stroke of luck, I hadn't been buried yet. I didn't know it then, but the town's only mill had blown up and there were forty bodies to be interred. Plus they'd cornered Darak and set him on fire. Yes, things had been positively hopping in the small town of Millidgeville, pop. 232 (actually 191 now). They were in no rush to get me in the ground. They had more important things to worry about.

"I was thirstier than I had ever been in my life. And strong . . . I meant only to pop open the door to the coffin and ended up ripping it off the hinges. I lurched out of the coffin and realized instantly where I was. And I knew what Darak was . . . I'd read Bram Stoker as a teenager. But even through the mad haze of my unnatural—or so it seemed to me then—thirst and the disbelief of my death, the main thing I remember is the relief. I was dead. I was free. I silently blessed Darak and went to find someone to eat.

"Being a vampire is *wonderful*. The strength, the speed, the liquid diet . . . all solidly in the plus column. The minuses—no sunbathing (so?), sensitivity to light (sunglasses fixed that nicely), no real relationships other than those of a transitory nature (call girls!)—are bearable.

"I miss women, though. That's probably the worst of it. No more sunsets? Phaugh. I saw plenty of them on the farm. But I haven't had a girlfriend since . . . er . . . what year is it? Never mind.

"I can't be with a mortal woman, for obvious reasons. She'd never understand what I was, what I needed. I'd constantly fear hurting her—I can lift a car over my head, so being with a mortal woman is not unlike being with a china doll. And being dead hasn't affected my sex drive one bit. I was a young man of lusty appetite, and while I still look young, my appetite has increased exponentially with my age.

"I've only met six other vampires in my life. Of the six, four were women, and let me tell you, they were complete and unrepentant monsters. They ate children. *Children!* I killed two, but the other two got away. I could have gone after them, but I had to get the child to a hospital and—well, I wouldn't have wished their company on my fiercest enemy, much less welcomed them to the marriage bed.

"Yes, I'm lonely. Another price to pay for the eternal life and the liquid diet. But I'm young for a vampire—not even close to a hundred yet. Things are bound to look up. And even if they don't, my patience—like my thirst—is infinite."

One

A monkey. *A fucking monkey!*

Janet Lupo practically threw her invitation at the goon guarding the doors to the reception hall. Bad enough that one of the most eligible werewolves in the pack—the world!—was now off the market, but he'd taken a pure human to mate. Not that there was anything wrong with that. Humans were okay. If you liked sloths.

She stomped toward her table, noticing with bitter satisfaction the way people jumped out of her path. Pack members walked clear when she was in a *good* mood. Which, at the moment, she was not.

Bad enough to be outnumbered a thousand to one by the humans, but to marry one? And fuck one and get it pregnant and join the PTA and . . .

The mind reeled.

Janet had nothing against humans as a species. In fact, she

greatly admired their rapaciousness. *Homo sapiens* never passed up prey, not even if they were stuffed—not even if they didn't eat meat! They'd kill each other over *shoes*, for God's sake. They had fought wars over shiny metals and rocks. Janet had never understood why a diamond was worth killing over but a pink topaz was hardly worth sweating about. Humans had fought wars over the possession of gold, but iron ferrite, which looked *exactly the same*, was worthless.

And when humans started killing, watch out. Whether it was "Free the Holy Land from the Infidels!" or "Cotton and Slave's Rights!" or "Down with Capitalism!" or whatever was worth mass genocide, when humans went to war, your only chance was to get out of the way and keep your head down.

But marry one? Marry someone slower and weaker? Much, much weaker? Someone with no pack instincts, someone who only lived for themselves? It'd be—it'd be like a human marrying a bear. A small, sleepy bear who hardly ever moved. Fucking creepy, is what it was.

And there was Alec, sitting at the head table and smirking like he'd won the lottery! And his mate—uh, wife—sitting next to him. She was cute enough if you liked chubby, which the boys in the pack did. A bony wife wasn't such a great mother when food was scarce. Not that food *was* scarce these days, but thousands of years of genetic conditioning died hard. Besides, who wanted to squash their body down onto a bundle of sticks?

Okay, there wasn't anything wrong with her looks. Her looks were fine. So was her smell—like peaches packed in fresh snow.

And the bimbo knew what she was getting into—her old lady had worked for Old Man Wyndham, way back in the day—so the whole family had experience keeping secrets. But to call a sloth a sloth, the new Mrs. Kilcurt was not pack. She wasn't family. And she would never be, no matter how many cubs Alec got on her.

Jesus! First the pack leader—Michael—knocked up a human, and now Alec Kilcurt. Didn't any of her fellow werewolves marry *werewolves* anymore?

"Dance, Jane?"

"I'd rather eat my own eyeballs," she said moodily, not even looking to see who asked. Why was she going to her table, anyway? The reception wasn't mandatory. Neither was the wedding. She'd just gone to be polite. And the time for that was done.

She turned on her heel and marched out. The goon at the door obligingly held it open. Which was just as well, 'cuz otherwise she'd have kicked it down.

~ ◦ ◦ ◦ ~

Janet vastly preferred Boston in the spring, and as cities went, Boston was not awful. Parts of it—the harbor, the aquarium—were actually kind of cool.

Thinking of the New England Aquarium—all those fish, lobsters, squid, and sharks—made her stomach growl. She'd been too annoyed to eat lunch, and when she had walked out of the reception, she had also walked out on her supper.

She turned onto a side street, taking a shortcut to Legal Sea Foods, a restaurant that did not suck. She'd have a big bowl of clam chowder, some raw oysters, a steak, and a lobster. And maybe something for dessert. And a drink. Maybe three.

A scent caught her attention, forcing a split-second decision. She turned onto another street, one much less crowded, curious to see if the men were going to keep following her.

They were. She hadn't seen their faces, just caught their scents as they swung around to follow her on Park Street. They smelled like desperation and stale coffee grounds. She was well dressed and probably looked prosperous to them. Prime pickings.

She turned again, this time down a deserted alley. If the two would-be robbers thought they were keeping her from supper, they were out of their teeny, tiny minds. She could easily outrun them, but that would mean kicking off her high heels. The stupid pinchy shoes cost almost thirty bucks! She wasn't leaving them in a Boston alley. If push came to shove, she'd bounce her stalkers off the bricks. Possibly more than once, the mood she was in.

"Halt, gentlemen."

Janet jumped. A man was standing at the end of the alley, and she hadn't known he was there until he spoke up. She hadn't smelled him, even though he was upwind. When was the last time *that* had happened?

He was tall—over six feet—and well built for someone who wasn't pack. His shoulders were broad, and he definitely had the look of a man used to working with his hands. He had blond hair the color of wheat, and his eyes—even from fifteen feet away she could see their vivid color—were Mediterranean blue. He was wearing all black—dress slacks, a shirt open at the throat, and a duster that went almost all the way to his heels. And—what's this now? He was squinting in the poor light of the alley and slipping on a pair of sunglasses. *Sunglasses*—how weird was *that*, at ten thirty at night?

"I have business with the young lady," Weirdo continued, walking toward them. His hands were open, relaxed. She knew he wasn't carrying a weapon. He moved with the grace of a dancer; if she hadn't been so fucking hungry, she might have liked to watch him prance around. "Much kinder business, I think, than you two. So be on your way, all right?" Then, in a lower voice, "Don't be afraid, miss. I won't hurt you. Hardly at all."

"Stand aside, four eyes," she snapped, and with barely a glance, she stiff-armed him into the side of the building and hurried past. She had no time for would-be muggers and less for Mr. Sunglasses-at-Night. Let the three of them fight it out. She had a date with a dead lobster.

Behind her, Sunglasses yelped in surprise. There was a flat smack as he hit the wall and then slid down. She'd tossed him a little harder than she meant—*oopsie*—and then the other two jumped him, and she was out of the alley.

She could see the restaurant up ahead. Just a few more steps, and she could order. Just a few more . . .

She stopped.

Don't you dare!

Turned.

C'mon, enough already! They're human . . . it's none of your business.

She started back toward the alley. Sunglasses was a weirdo, but he was vulnerable to attack because of what she had done. Yeah, they were human, but it was one thing to mind your own business and another to turn your back on a mess you helped make.

You moron! Who knows when you'll get to eat now?

"Fuck off, inner voice," she said aloud. People thought the outer Janet was a bitch; God forbid they should ever meet the inner Janet.

She stepped into the alley to help and was just in time to see the second mugger crumple to the filthy street. The first was half in and half out of the Dumpster. And Sunglasses was hurrying, hurrying toward her, licking the blood off his knuckles. "As I was saying before you tossed me against the wall, I have business with you, miss. And where on earth do you work out?"

She was so surprised she let him put his hands on her shoulders, let him draw her close. He smiled at her, and even in the poorly lit alley, she could see the light gleaming on his teeth. His very long canines. His fangs, to be perfectly blunt. He had fangs, and it wasn't even close to the full moon.

"What the hell are *you*?" She put a hand to his chest to keep him from pulling her closer. His heart beat once. Then nothing.

He blinked at her. "What? Usually the lady in question is halfway to fainting by now. To answer your question, I'm the son of a farmer. That's all."

"My ass," she said rudely. "I came back to give you a hand—"

"How sweet."

"—but you're fine, and I'm hungry."

"What a coincidence," he murmured. He tapped a sharp canine

with his tongue. Beneath her palm, his heart beat again. "My, you're exceedingly beautiful. I suppose your beaux tell you that all the time."

"Beaux? Who the hell talks like that? And you're full of shit," she informed him. Beautiful? Shyeah. She wasn't petite, and she wasn't tall—just somewhere in the middle. Average height, average weight, average hair color—not quite blond and not quite brown—average nose, mouth, and chin. She could see her average eyes reflected in his sunglasses. "And you'd better let go before I hit you so hard, you'll spend the rest of the night throwing up your teeth."

He blinked again and then smiled. "Forgive the obvious question, but aren't you a little nervous? It's dark . . . and you're quite alone with me. Why, I might do anything to you." He licked his lower lip thoughtfully. "Anything at all."

"This is really, really boring, fuck-o," she informed him. "Leggo."

"I decline."

She brought her foot down on his and felt his toes squish through the dress shoe. Then she knocked him away from her with a right cross. This time, when he went down, he stayed down.

Twenty minutes later, she was happily slurping the first of a dozen oysters on ice.

Two

He knew he was lurking like a villain in a bad melodrama, but he couldn't help it. He had to catch her when she came out of the restaurant. So he was reduced to watching her through the restaurant window from across the street.

Richard rubbed his jaw thoughtfully. It didn't hurt anymore, but if he'd been mortal, it likely would have shattered from the force of the woman's punch. She hit like a Teamster. And swore like one, too.

She was stunning, really very stunning, with those cider-colored eyes and that unique hair. Her crowning glory was shoulder length, wavy, and made up of several colors: gold, auburn, chestnut . . . even a few strands of silver. The silky strands gleamed beneath the streetlight and made him itch to touch them, to see if they were as soft as they looked.

She had been fearless in the near dark of the alley, and he'd become utterly besotted. He had to see her again, take her in his arms again, hear her say "fuck" again.

Ah! After a five-course meal, here she came. And look! She had spotted him instantly and was now stomping across the street toward him. Her small hands were balled into fists, and her lush mouth was curled in a snarl.

"Fuck-o, you don't learn too quick, do you?"

"You're marvelous," he said, smiling at her. Few people were on the street at this hour, but the ones who were around caught the tension in the air and did a quick fade. Most mortals had zero protective coloring, but something about the proximity of a vampire put their wind up, even if they weren't consciously aware of it. "Just charming, really."

She snorted delicately. "I see you're heavily medicated, on top of everything else. Get lost, before I belt you in the chops again."

"You came all the way over here to tell me to go away?"

A frown wrinkle appeared on her perfect, creamy forehead. "Yeah, I did. Don't read anything into it. So blow, okay?"

"Richard Will."

"What?"

"My name is Richard Will." He held out his hand, hoping she wouldn't be startled by his long fingers. Most people—women— were.

"Yeah? Well, Dick, I don't trust people with two first names."

She stared at his outstretched hand and then crossed her arms over her chest.

He let his hand drop. "And you are . . . ?"

"Tired of this conversation."

"Is that your first name or your last?"

Her lips curled into an unwitting smile. "Very funny. You never answered my question."

"Which one?"

"What are you? Your heart . . ." She started to reach for him but then stopped. "Let's just say you should get your ass to a doctor, pronto."

"You know what I am." He bent toward her and was thrilled when she didn't back off. "In your heart, you know."

"Dick, as my family will tell you, I don't *have* a heart."

He rested his palm against her chest, feeling the rapid beat. "Such a lie, dearest."

She knocked his hand away and sounded gratifyingly breathless when she said, "Don't call me that."

"I have no choice, dearest, as you never told me your name."

"It's Janet."

"Janet . . . ?"

"Smith," she said rudely, and he chuckled. Then he laughed, a full-blown guffaw that sent more stragglers hurrying away. "What the hell's so funny?"

"Don't you see? We simply must get married. Richard and Janet . . . Dick and Jane!"

She gaped at him for a long moment and then, reluctantly, joined him in laughter.

~ ♦ ♦ ♦ ~

"So you don't like the new wife?"

Janet moodily stirred her coffee. It was after midnight, and they were the only couple in the coffee shop. "It's not that I have a personal problem with her. She's just . . . not our kind, is all."

"She's Polish?"

She snorted a laugh through her nose. "Nothing like that . . . I'm not *that* big a bitch. It's hard to explain. And you wouldn't believe me anyway."

He grinned, flashing his fangs. "Try me."

"No way, José. I want to hear about *you*. I didn't know there were such things as vampires. Assuming you're not some pathetic schmuck who filed his teeth to get the girls."

He considered lifting her, in her chair, over his head, but decided against it. Among other things, it was unnecessary. She knew what he was, oh yes. She had felt his heart. And he had felt hers. "I didn't know there were such things either, until I woke up dead."

She leaned forward, which gave him an excellent view of creamy cleavage in her wine-colored dress. "How old are you?"

"Not so old, for a vampire. Not even a hundred yet. And as it's not polite to ask a lady her age—"

"Thirty-six."

Perfect. Giggling girlhood was left behind, she was closing in on her sexual peak, and the best was still ahead. He tried very hard not to drool.

"I'm the old maid of the family," she was saying. "Most of my friends have teenagers already."

"You have plenty of time."

She brightened. "See, that's what I always say! Just because we're trapped in this damned youth-obsessed society doesn't mean we have to do *everything* in our twenties. What's the fucking rush?"

"Exactly. That's what I—"

"Except my family thinks totally differently," she said, her shoulders slumping. "They're very *in-the-now*, if you know what I mean. Sometimes there's . . . there's fights and stuff, and you never know if today's your last day on Earth. There's lots of pressure to make every single day count, to cram *everything* you can, as often as you can. Nobody really stops and smells the fuckin' roses where I come from, you know?"

"That's fairly typical of . . . of people." He'd almost said "of mortals," but no need to push things. As it was, he had a hard time believing this conversation was taking place. She'd insulted him, pounded him, knew what he was, and was now having coffee with him. Amazing! "If your life span is so brief—what? seventy years or so?—well, of course you want to make every minute count."

"My family's life span is even shorter," she said moodily.

"Ah. Dangerous neighborhood?"

"To put it mildly. Although it's better since . . . well, it's better now, and I just hope it lasts."

"Which is why you can take care of yourself so well."

She cracked her knuckles, which made the lone counterman cringe. "Bet your ass."

"Indeed I would not." He stirred his coffee. He could drink it, though all it would do was make him thirstier. Instead, he played with it; he enjoyed the ritual of cream and sugar. "How long are you in town?"

She shrugged. "Long as I want. The wedding's over, so we'll probably hang out for a couple days, then head back to our homes."

"And home for you is . . . ?"

"None of your fucking business. Don't get me wrong, Dick, you seem pleasant enough for a bloodsucking fiend of the undead—"

"Thank you."

"—but I'm not opening up to you with all my vitals, no matter how good-looking and charming you are."

"So my powers of attraction aren't completely lost on you," he teased.

She ignored the interruption. "And if you don't like it, you can stop dicking around with your coffee and get the hell gone."

"I cannot decide," he said after a long pause, during which he guiltily put down his spoon, "if you're the most refreshing person I've ever met, or the most irritating."

"Go with irritating," she suggested. "That's what my family does." She glanced at her watch, a cheap thing that probably told time about as well as a carrot. "I gotta go. It's really late, even for me." She laughed at that for some reason.

He leaned forward and picked up her warm little hand. Her

palm was chubby, with a strong life line. Her nails were brutally short and unpolished. "I must see you again. Actually, I would prefer to spirit you away to my—"

"Creaky, musty, damp castle?"

"—condo on Beacon Hill, but you're quite a strong young lady and I seriously doubt I could do so without attracting attention. So I must persuade you."

"Damned right, chum." She jerked her hand out of his grasp. "Try anything, and—"

"I'll vomit my teeth, or be split down the middle, or my head will be twisted around so far I'll be able to see my own backside." She giggled. "Yes, yes, I quite understand. Have dinner with me tomorrow night."

"Don't you mean 'let me watch you eat while I play with my drink'?"

"Something like that, yes."

"Why?" she asked suspiciously.

"Because," he said simply, "I've decided. You're refreshing because you're irritating. Do you know how long it's been since I've had a nice conversation with a lady?"

She stared at him. "You think this has been a nice conversation?"

"Nicer than 'Help, eeeeeek, stay away you horrible thing, no, no, noooooooooo, oh, God, please don't kill me!' I can't tell you how many times I've had *that* conversation."

"Serves you right for being a walking wood tick," she said. "Dinner, huh? On you?"

"Of course." *Possibly on you*, he thought, suddenly dizzy with a vision of licking red wine off her stomach.

"Mmmm. All right. I'll admit, it's nice to be myself with a guy and not have him be such a fucking Nancy boy whenever I say something the least bit—"

"Fucking obscene?"

She giggled again. "But you gotta tell me all about waking up dead and what it's like to be on a liquid diet. And how come my family didn't know about you and your kind?"

"Why would your family know about my kind?"

"We're pretty far-flung. There's not much going on on the planet we *don't* know about. So you'll feed me, and we'll talk. Deal, Dick?"

"Deal . . . Jane."

"I find out you've got a dog named Spot, and dinner's off," she warned.

Three

The phone rang, that shrill "pay attention to me!" sound she hated. She groaned, rolled over, groped for the phone, and knocked it off the hook. She relaxed into the blessed silence, which was broken by a tinny sound.

"Hello? Jane?"

She burrowed under the covers.

"Jane? Are you there? Janet. Hello??"

She cursed her werewolf hearing. Tinny and faint the voice might be, but it was also unmistakable. "What?"

"Pick up the phone," the voice coming through the telephone squawked. "I want to be sure you're getting all this."

"Can't. Too tired."

"It's six o'clock at night, for God's sake. Pick up the phone!"

She muttered something foul and obeyed the caller. "Whoever the hell this is, you'd better be on fire."

"It's Moira, and I practically am . . . the high today was eighty-two. In May!"

"Moira."

"You should see what the humidity did to my hair."

"Moira."

"I look like a blond cotton swab."

"Moira! This is fascinating, but you sure as shit better not be calling me to babble about your for-Christ's-sake *hair*. What do you want?"

"It's not what I want," Moira went on in her irritatingly cheerful voice. "It's Michael. The big boss wants to see you on the Cape, pronto."

Finally, the silly bitch had Jane's attention. Her eyes opened wide, and she sat straight up in bed. "Michael Wyndham? Wants to see me? How come?" And on the heels of that, a panicked thought: *What'd I do?* And resentment: *Come, girl, good dog, here's a treat for the good doggie.*

"Mine is not to reason why, girly . . . and neither is yours. I suggest you get your ass out here yesterday."

Jane groaned. "Aw, fuck a duck!"

"I'll pass."

"I've got a date. Today." She squinted at her watch. "Tonight, I mean."

"You *do?*" Moira sounded—rightfully so—completely astonished.

She modified her tone, too late. "I mean, of course you do. Sure. It's only natural, a . . . a lively and . . . er . . . opinionated young lady like yourself. With a date on a Saturday night. Yep."

"Cut the shit. You're embarrassing both of us." *Young lady.* Right. Moira was at least ten years younger, half Jane's size (and weight), and twice the brains. Calling Moira a silly bitch was only half right. "Fuck! I don't need this now. You don't have *any* idea what it's about?"

"Um . . ."

"Come on, Moira, you and the boss are practically littermates. Spill."

"Let's just say that in his newfound happiness with mate and cub, our fearless leader thinks it's high time you settled down—"

"No, no, *no!*"

"—and he's met *just* the right fella for you," she continued brightly. "He's sure you'll hit it off."

"Doesn't the head of the pack have anything better to do than fix me up on yet another stupid blind date?" She could hear plastic cracking and forced her fingers to loosen around the receiver.

"Apparently not. Now tell the truth; the last one wasn't so bad."

"He cried like a third-grade girl when I beat him to the kill."

"Well, you *did* hog all the rabbits yourself. *Tsk, tsk.*"

"Figures," Jane grumbled, swinging her legs over and resting her feet on the floor. "The first halfway decent guy I meet in forever, and the boss wants me to blow him off to meet some new dildo."

"Sorry," Moira said, sounding anything but. "I'll leave the dildo part out when I tell Michael you're on the way. And now, having imparted my message, I'd say something like 'have a nice day,' except I know you—"

"Hate that shit. Bye." She hung up and resisted the urge to throw the phone against the wall. Fuck. Fuck fuck!

She'd been so excited about dinner with Dick, she'd had a hard time getting to sleep. She'd finally dozed off near dawn . . . and slept the entire day away. Now she had to beat feet for the Cape of all places . . . fuck!

She did throw the phone. But it didn't make her feel any better, not even when it shattered spectacularly against the wall.

~ ◦ ◦ •~

She was tapping her foot on the curb, waiting for the slothlike doorman to hail her a cab. She could hail her own damned cab, thanks very much, but when in Rome, do what the sheep do. Or something like that.

She'd packed like a madwoman, and it showed—she could see the corner of her dress sticking out of the suitcase. *Aarrggh!* Fifty-nine ninety-nine at Sears, and she'd probably never get to wear it again. Like clothes shopping wasn't an unending horror anyway—now she'd have to go *again*.

And Dick. She felt really bad about up and leaving town. He'd think she stood him up. Like *that* would happen. He was ridiculously good-looking but, even more important, she could talk to him. Not be herself—not completely—but close.

Shit, she couldn't even be herself with the pack; they'd written her off as an old maid a decade ago. Pack members mated young, dropped kids young, and died young. And she didn't want kids, which, among her people, made her *El Freako Supremo*.

Getting knocked up—assuming your mate could get you pregnant without getting his bad self hurt—was one thing, but then you were a slumlord to a fetus for ten endless months. At least the humans only had to suffer for nine. Even worse, you puffed up like a blowfish and ate everything in sight, then squeezed out a kid during hours of blood and pain . . . *blurgh*.

And afterward! Just the thought of having to tote around a nose-miner who cried and screamed and puked and shit—and that was just the first week!—was enough to curl her hair. She hadn't liked kids even when she was one. The feeling had been mutually—and heartily—returned. She'd felt that way at eighteen, twenty-three, thirty, thirty-four. Sure, kids were necessary—for other people. Janet preferred to sleep late, wear clothes that hadn't been puked on, and not watch her language.

"Where to, ma'am?" the doorman asked, breaking her anti-infant reverie. He was ineffectually flapping a hand at the occasional cab. She could have hailed four on her own by now. Shit, she could have *jogged* to the airport by now.

"Logan," she practically snapped. It wasn't Door Boy's fault she'd been ordered to leave town, but the big boss wasn't here for her to take her anger out on him. "Quick as you can."

She thought about leaving a note for Dick and reluctantly decided against it. Better find out what Boss Man Michael wanted first. And if it wasn't life and death, she'd let him have it. Who gave a rat's ass if he was the pack leader? She had a life. Well, before yesterday she really hadn't, but *he* didn't know that. It was his privilege to snap his fingers and have any one of them come at a dead run, but it was hers not to like it.

She observed the doorman shivering and realized the sun had nearly set, and the temperature had dropped a good ten degrees. Still, it wasn't *that* cold. And why did the kid look like he was ready to drop a steaming load into his trousers? She was irritated, but not at him . . . surely he knew that.

God, the reek the kid was giving off! Like mothballs dipped in gasoline. His fear—his terror—burned her nose. It put her wind up, and she cupped her elbows, shivering. From grumpy to edgy in less than five seconds . . . a new record!

The ball dropped, and she understood a half second too late. She was spun around and had time to take in burning blue eyes before there was a walloping pain in her jaw and Dick turned off the lights. And everything else.

Four

He didn't care. He really didn't. She was fine, and if she wasn't, who cared? He hadn't hurt her. Not really.

He checked on her for the eleventh time in sixty minutes and was relieved to see the bruise on the underside of her jaw had faded to a mere shadow. Guilt rolled off his shoulders like a boulder.

To save time and steps—if he left he'd just be in here five minutes later—he sat down in the chair beside the bed. He cupped his chin in his hand, leaned forward, and watched her sleep.

Jane scowled, even in the throes of unconsciousness. It would have made him smile if he hadn't felt so angry and betrayed.

Betrayed? All right, tell the truth and shame the devil . . . yes. *Betrayed!* And angry and sick at heart and *furious* with the little twit tied to his bed. Most of his anger was directed at himself, it was true, but he had a nice helping saved for Miss Jane.

She'd fooled him; that was all. A simple thing, but unforgivable. She made him believe she accepted the monster, when in fact she most assuredly had not. The duplicitous wretch agreed to join him for dinner to placate him and then made arrangements to slink out of town like a thief. If he hadn't shown up early to escort her to dinner, she would have disappeared and he might never have known what had become of her. He would have wasted years of his life worrying about her fate.

Instead, he'd taken in the situation at a glance and acted accordingly. Well, all right, that was a rather large lie. He had panicked— all he could think of was to get her home, stop her from leaving him. Leaving *town*, rather. And in his panic, he'd smacked her when he only meant to tap her. The one bit of luck was that it had happened too quickly for the lone witness—the doorman—to see much more than a swirl of cloth. Dusk and speed were his friends, even if Jane was not.

And that was the rub of it. He'd allowed himself to forget, for one evening, that he was the monster in the fairy tales. He had forgotten there could be no relationship with a woman other than the most carnal type. He wouldn't have vampire women, and mortal women wouldn't have him. Well, that was fine. That was just fine.

He was a monster, and he was done pretending otherwise.

But Jane would pay for making him forget. She'd pay for making him think, however briefly, that he was a man first and a beast second.

Five

Jane groaned and tried to roll over. The phone was ringing. It would be Moira, telling her to get her ass to the Cape. She couldn't see Dick tonight. She had to answer the phone and tell Moira to go fuck herself, and then—

Wait.

That had already happened. So why was she still in bed?

She opened her eyes and tried to sit up. Three alarming facts registered immediately on her brain: 1) she couldn't sit up, and 2) she was tied to a bed. She was, in fact, 3) tied down in the same room with an annoyed vampire. And not a prayer of room service.

"Ohhhhhh, you *idiot*!" she howled. If she could have slapped her hand over her eyes, she would have. If she could have slapped *him*, she would have. As it was, her ankles and arms were spread wide and tied to each poster of the bed. "Do you have any idea of the trouble you've landed me in, numb nuts?"

Dick, sitting in the chair next to the bed, blinked at her. He did that a lot . . . a long, slow, thoughtful blink when he was taken by surprise. It was like a stall for time or something. She thought it was kind of cute yesterday. "I shouldn't have expected maidenly protestations," he said after a long pause.

"You *should* expect a fractured skull, you undead idiot! What the *fuck* am I doing tied to your bed? *Is* it your bed? It damn well better be your bed! If I'm in some strange dead guy's bed, your ass is grass!"

He brought a hand up to his chin . . . and then got up and abruptly left. She used the chance to yank at her bonds—no good. They were soft, like cloth, but amazingly strong. Were her bonds lined with bubble gum or what?

She strained to hear and, very faintly, could hear muffled laughter coming from about thirty feet away. Dick had trotted out to the hall to have a giggle at her expense—fucking great.

The door was thrown open a moment later, and when Dick returned, he was stone-faced. "Sorry about that. I thought I left something on the stove. Now where were we?"

She kicked out at him. The bonds let her leg leave the bed, but not by much. "We were talking about how you're going to die a painful and horrible death—again! What the hell have you trussed me up with?"

The left side of his mouth twitched. "It's elastic lined with titanium wire. It won't hurt you if you pull on it, but it's impossible to break. Even I have trouble breaking it, and I'm quite a bit stronger than you are."

Wanna bet, Dead Man Walking? "Do you have any idea—*aarrgh!* I'm supposed to be meeting my boss right this minute! What time is it?"

"About two A.M."

"*Aaaarrrgggghhh!* Jerk! I'm five hours late!"

"Another date?" he asked silkily.

"No, Deaf and Undead, I *told* you. My boss called—well, *he* didn't call, one of his lackeys did—and told me to get to the office, pronto. And when he says jump, we *leap*, dude. I didn't have time to leave you a note, but I would have come back!"

"Sure you would have."

Jane was so annoyed, she felt like biting herself. Instead, she yanked impotently on her bonds again. "Yes I would have, dill-hole!"

"Your boss calls you on a weekend, and you must drop everything and race to his side? Really, Janet. I was expecting a better story than that."

She snarled at him. If he made her much madder, she'd start barking at the goddamned ceiling. "Jesus, to think I was actually looking forward to seeing you! And this is how you take rejection . . . pervert!"

Something flashed in his eyes then. Way down deep. She was suddenly reminded of the lake back home she used to do laps in. The blue water was pretty and inviting, but the lake was spring-fed and freezing cold, even in July. You didn't know how cold it was until you committed yourself and jumped. Then you were stuck, and you got moving or you froze.

"So you admit you rejected me?"

"No, doorknob! I told you the truth. You can believe it, or you can go fuck yourself."

"Is there a third choice?"

"Yes . . . untie me so I can make a phone call!"

"I decline."

"You can't just keep me here like a . . . a . . ." She practically spat the word. "Like a *pet* or something."

"Can't I?"

Suddenly he was standing over her, casually unbuttoning his shirt and sliding it off his shoulders. Her eyes widened until they felt like they were practically bulging. "What the hell are you doing?"

"You're a bright girl. You'll figure it out in a minute."

"Don't you *dare*!"

"I dare much, now that my heart—" He cut himself off abruptly, and she heard the click of his teeth coming together. What the hell was going *on* with this guy?

Off came the trousers, the socks, the underwear. Nude, Dick was exceedingly yummy . . . long legs, broad shoulders, and a tasty flat stomach that made her think about hot fudge sauce and whipped cream. His chest was lightly furred with blond hair two shades darker than the hair on his head. His muscle definition was excellent, and she had a sudden, maddening urge to touch him to see if his skin was as smooth as it looked. It would be, she thought, like velvet encased in steel. Or marble . . . he was quite pale.

He reached out and flipped off the light . . . *click*. She consciously dilated her pupils and could see him again, a pale blur in the dark. A blur with glittering blue eyes.

She felt his cool hand on her thigh and then his fingers were nimbly unbuttoning her dress. She kicked out again, to no avail. He popped open the clasp on her bra—stupid front clasps!—and with odd care, gently tore her panties down the middle. She hissed at him. Twelve bucks at Victoria's Secret! The bitch's secret was that she marked up her underwear by six hundred percent!

"You are an asshole," she said clearly.

"True enough." He pulled her panties free, spread her dress wide, and then pushed her bra out of the way. "Umm. Very nice."

"Go fuck yourself, perv."

"I'd rather not . . . besides, *you're* here, so why should I have to? We have hours until sunrise." He chuckled. It sounded like cold water flowing over black rocks. "And Jane . . . I'm sooooo hungry. I've been waiting and waiting for you to wake up."

"I hope I poison you. I hope you choke until your lungs explode. I hope my blood burns your windpipe. I hope—"

"I get the gist. *I* hope the next time you agree to spend the evening with me, you keep your word." Then he was on her so suddenly she didn't have time to pull in air for a gasp. She braced herself as best she could for his brutal entry, for teeth and blood and pain. *Oh, when I get out of here I'm going to use your vertebrae for dice. See if I don't. And I won't cry, either. So there.*

His mouth skimmed her jaw, and she felt him lick her jugular and nibble gently at the tender flesh. His cool hand closed over her breast, pressed against her warm flesh, and she felt her nipple harden against his palm. Then he was kissing her throat, the middle of her chest, and her stomach. She felt his thumbs on her cunt, spreading her wide, and she felt his tongue snake inside her. The shock of it nearly bent her up off the bed. His mouth was cool but quickly warmed, and she flinched back, thinking of his sharp canines.

But there was nothing to fear—or there was, but she quickly forgot it as waves of heat started from her crotch and radiated upward. His tongue was flicking in and out of her little tunnel, stabbing her clit, and then he pulled back and licked . . . excruciatingly slow licks that made her shake. She gritted her teeth as hard as she could and locked away the sounds she wanted to make. So he wasn't being a hard guy—fine. This still wasn't her idea. It still wasn't any different from smacking her around or shoving her up against a dirty alley wall or—or—

He stopped. He pulled back. She started to relax but then felt the sharp sting as his teeth broke the skin over her femoral artery. She gasped—she couldn't help it—and tried to jerk away, but his hands held her fast.

His fingers smoothed the soft pelt between her thighs and then he was parting her lips again and stroking her throbbing clit. One of his fingers dipped inside her while his thumb pressed gentle circles around her increasingly slick flesh. Meanwhile, his mouth was busy on her inner thigh, and she could hear soft sucking.

This went on and on . . . she quickly lost track of time. She was screaming inside. Whenever she started to get close, he somehow knew and his fingers would still or pull away entirely. His mouth *never* stopped. Then he'd resume again, careful not to push her over the edge. After a while she still wasn't making any sounds, but the bed shook with her trembling.

At last he was sated. He pulled back and then bent to her and gave her a long, leisurely lick. "Ummm. You're so wet. I love that. And you taste *soooo* good. Everywhere, it seems. Your blood is really rich. What on earth have you been eating?"

She ground her teeth at him for answer. She felt his pelvis settle over hers, heard him chuckle. "Your rage could set the room on fire—better than being cold, I think?"

She didn't dignify that with an answer. Besides, if she opened her mouth—what might she say? She was horribly afraid she might ask—beg—to be fucked. Hard. For a long, long time. Her cunt throbbed. Her thigh throbbed. It wasn't pain; it was sheer yearning. She had never needed to come so badly.

When she felt him start to enter her, it took every ounce, every drop of her willpower not to strain to meet him. She resisted by listing his many odious offenses inside her head.

That part of him was warm. And hard, and huge. His cock was parting her slowly and gently, and she had a quick thought: *He has to be gentle . . . he wasn't a few times before, and he hurt his partner. That's how he knows to tongue fuck first.* But that thought spiraled away into confusion as he shoved, and she felt him slam into her. She made a sound, some small sound, and his mouth was instantly on hers. She could taste her lust, and her blood, and then he was whispering into her mouth, "I couldn't help that, I'm sorry—am I hurting you?" His hands were fisting in her hair, he was groaning and thrusting, and her breath was coming in harsh gasps.

"Please," she groaned. "Please—" *Don't stop. Don't ever stop. Harder. More. Faster. Please. Please. Please.*

He groaned, too. "I wanted to hurt you but not like . . . I'll make it up to you, my own—" She heard him grind his teeth . . . and then he stopped so suddenly he was rigid with the strain of it. She was afraid to move, to breathe, but it didn't matter. He did the unthinkable anyway—slowly pulled out of her. She closed her eyes and whimpered as he went, hating herself for it even as she knew she could have done nothing to quell the sound.

"Jane. Tell the truth, love. Am I hurting you?" She felt his hand caress her cheek and opened her eyes. His teeth were set so hard his jaw trembled. Here was a perfect opportunity for revenge. And she couldn't do it.

"Twice," she whispered.

He bent closer and dropped a kiss to her shoulder. "What?"

"Twice. This is my second time. Ever. In my life."

"You—*what*?" She could have laughed at his horrified expression if she hadn't been ready to claw his eyes out for not letting her come. "Oh, Christ! I had no—I thought you—you seemed so tough I was sure—"

Tough? Sure. Real tough. She'd grown a shell around her soul the night she lost her virginity. The night she, in her ardor, broke her lover's back. It had happened on the last day of her freshmen year in college, and her then-boyfriend, as far as she knew, was still in a wheelchair. It was the first and last time she'd chosen someone who wasn't pack. It was, in fact, the last time she'd chosen anyone, until tonight. And she hadn't exactly chosen this, had she?

"You can't say *Christ*," she whispered. "You're a vampire."

"One of the many myths," he whispered back. He stroked her hair. She could feel his cock on her leg, throbbing impatiently. *It* didn't give a fuck if she was hurt or not. It had business to get back to. And so did she. "Jane, why did you try to run away from me?"

"I didn't, dimwad. I told you the truth."

"Hmm."

"Now will you *please* finish and untie me?"

"Pick one."

She nearly screamed. "What?"

"Pick one." He tapped her clit with a teasing finger. "And I'll do it." He kissed her again. He ducked down and licked her nipple and then sucked, hard. In their bonds, her hands curled into fists. "Whichever one. I'll do it. Thoroughly."

"I hate you," she nearly sobbed.

"I know."

"Finish."

"Oh, thank God." In an instant he was pushing his way inside her again, and for a half second, she understood why he had been concerned—the friction was delightful, *so* delightful, it was just this side of pain. Then he was pumping his hips against hers, and it became more than delightful; it was exquisite.

"Kiss me back," he said into her mouth. "Give me your tongue."

Half blind from the swamping pleasure, she did so. He sucked on it in time with his thrusts, and she could hear someone making high, whimpering noises and realized with amazement it was *her* making those silly bitch sounds. The bed thumped in time with their fucking and then he tore his mouth from hers. "Now," he hissed in her ear, "come now." Then he pinched her nipple, hard, and that spun her into the most powerful orgasm of her life. She could actually feel the spasms ripple through her uterus, and the world got dark and fuzzy around the edges for a few moments. Above her he stiffened, and for a moment his grip was painful. "God, my God, Jane!" Then he shuddered all over, and he relaxed as she felt him spurt deeply inside her.

She dozed for a few minutes—it had been a stressful few days. She came all the way awake when she realized he was stroking her lower lip with his thumb. "Get the fuck off me *now*."

"Ah, you're back. I thought you were being uncharacteristically quiet."

"Off. Now. Hate you. Kill you."

He burst out laughing, which did nothing for her temper. She strained mightily and managed to roll him off her. "I'm sorry, love, it's rude to laugh. But most women in your position would be fetal with shock, sobbing into the bedspread. All *you* can think about is how to get your teeth into me."

"And how you might taste," she added silkily.

"Umm . . . well, there are ways to answer *that* question . . ."

"Anything you put in my mouth, you're gonna lose."

He sighed. "I suppose it was too good to last. Pity we're only compatible in bed."

"Compatible in—you *raped* me, asswipe! Do you have any idea what my family is going to *do* to you? What *I'm* going to do to you?"

"I did rape you." He tweaked one of her nipples. "At first."

She blushed with shame. He saw it, and it moved him whereas her death threats did not. "No, you're right—I forced you. None of this was your idea. You're still tied up, for heaven's sake. You don't have anything to feel guilty about."

She was, absurdly, grateful for the lie. Not that she had any intention of showing it. "I feel very guilty that I didn't break your neck in that alley when I had the chance. *Now let me go!*"

"Sorry, Jane. You had your chance to be free, and you chose to stay."

"I did *not*—"

"So stay you will, and just like this, until . . ."

"Oh, what, *what?* Christ, you're driving me crazy!"

". . . until you agree to be my wife."

Long silence, broken by, "You're on drugs."

"Only if you are. Is that why your blood is so rich? God, it was like wine. I don't think I've ever felt better," he said giddily. "I had planned to fuck you and eat you and turn you out into the street in the wee hours of the morning without so much as an 'I'll call you,' but now I'll never, never let you go. You're a rare jewel, Jane. An emerald, a ruby."

"I'm tied to the bed next to a crazy person," she mused aloud. Thinking, *Never drank from a werewolf before, eh, buddy? Interesting. If you become addicted to me, that could be useful.* "And as far as being your wife—you've probably heard this from all your *other* rape victims, but I'd rather be dead."

"Undead," he said brightly. "Well, we've got time for that. You're still in your prime. Although I have no intention of becoming a widower in forty or fifty years."

"*What?*"

"Oh, I won't insist upon it right away, but probably within the next ten years or so, I'll definitely have to turn you into a vampire."

An undead werewolf? What's next, Frankenstein's Monster coming over for dinner? "You're out of your fucking mind."

"Apparently so," he said cheerfully, kissed her, and left her.

Six

Richard knocked modestly—absurd, given what he had just done to her—and opened the door. She was staring at the ceiling and didn't look at him when he came in. He nibbled his lower lip and tried to distract himself from the sight of the lovely Janet, spread-eagled on his bed. It was amazing—he'd just spent over an hour with her, but he could have taken her right this minute. And again. And then again.

He was carrying a tray full of savories. She smelled it and sat up as much as her bonds would allow. "Feeding time at the zoo," Jane said moodily. The spot on her thigh where he'd fed from her was purpling. He stifled an urge to kiss it and beg her forgiveness. *She lied*, he reminded himself. *And you're the monster.*

"Oh, hush. No one in a zoo eats so well. See? Lobster bisque, biscuits, a steak, and milk. And if you eat everything, chocolate ice cream."

"That's a ridiculous amount of food," she said, staring at the tray.

"I've seen you eat, my love. I'm going to let you out of your bonds, but before you hit me over the head with the tray and flee for the hills, I should explain that there are no fewer than three bolted doors—all English oak—between you and the street. You'd never get through them all before being caught. And you must be starving. Surely it's more prudent to eat and plot revenge, right?"

She drummed her fingers on the bedspread and stared up at him. Her eyes went narrow and flinty, but at last she said, "I'm starving."

"Eat, and then a hot bath . . . sound good?"

"And then what?"

"And then agree to be my wife."

"Don't," she practically snarled, "start with that again, dicklick."

"Ah, a blushingly modest bride, how refreshing. I can see you're contemplating homicide—try not to spill the soup."

He set the tray down on the table and unsnapped her ankle bonds. Then he seized the footboard and tugged the bed away from the wall. She could have done the same thing herself, but she couldn't help but be impressed—not bad for an undead monkey. He walked to the headboard, reached behind it, and in a few seconds had her wrists freed. She was off the bed in a bound, pulled off the shreds of her clothes and let them flutter to the floor, and then made a beeline for the tray.

"I brought you a robe—"

"Who cares?" she said with a mouthful of biscuit. "You've already seen me naked."

"Uh—" *You're gorgeous. You're distracting. If you prance around in that sweet little body you'll have your hands full. You have soup on your chin.* "As you wish."

He sat down across from her and watched her eat. She ate like a machine, seeming to take no enjoyment from the meal. *Refueling, the better to kick my ass. Well, so be it.* He deserved that, and more. And he was a fast healer. Let her do her worst. "Why did you break our date?" he asked abruptly and surprised even himself—he had no idea he was going to say such a thing until it was done.

She grunted irritably. "We've been over this."

"Jane . . ." Again, he had no idea what would come out of his mouth, but he plunged ahead anyway. "Jane, if you tell the truth, I'll unlock those three doors and walk you back to your hotel. Just admit that you were afraid of me, that you were only pretending to accept what I am, and—"

Her gaze locked on his like a laser. "My name is Janet Lupo," she said coldly. "I'm not afraid of any man. And. I. Don't. Lie."

He actually felt the chill coming off her. Absurd! She was half his size, even if she had twice the mouth. Her gaze was odd, almost hypnotic. With difficulty, he broke her challenging stare. "Well," he said at last, "perhaps you can understand why I have difficulty believing that your 'boss' would insist on your free time, and why you would have to drop everything and rush to meet him at a moment's notice."

"Pack rules."

"Beg pardon?"

"Pack . . . rules . . . dumb . . . fuck. Am I stuttering? I'm a were-wolf. My boss is the head werewolf."

He laughed and then ducked as her soup bowl sailed over his head. "Oh, come now, Janet! Because you know I am a vampire, you've decided I'll believe you're a werewolf? I'm *that* gullible? There's no such thing, and you know it well."

"Says the bloodsucker!"

He was still chuckling. "Nice try."

"If you could think about something besides your dick for five seconds, you'd see it makes sense. My strength, my speed . . ."

"All well within the range for *Homo sapiens* . . . albeit the high end."

"You've been dead too long, Dick. The average *homo loser* can barely lift the remote control. My rich blood? That's from a diet high in protein. *Raw* protein, during the full moon."

"Ah, the full moon. It's a few days away, but I suppose I had better take care when—"

She slammed her fork down; the table trembled and then was still. "The full moon is eight days away. And when it comes, you're going to get a big fucking surprise. Your little oak doors won't hold me then. I'll be out of here—possibly eating your head on my way out the door—and you'll realize you fucked up, bad. You'll know I was telling the truth the whole time, but you couldn't see past your stupid injured male pride. I'll be gone forever, and you'll have the next hundred years to realize what an asshole you were."

She was so convincing, he actually panicked for a moment. To add drama to her little speech, she stopped eating, walked to the bed, got under the covers, and faced away from him the rest of the night. She never said another word, or looked at him, not even when he tempted her with a brimming bowl of frozen custard.

Seven

He was right. The doors—this one, anyway—were oak. Thick and heavy, with the hinges on the outside where she couldn't get at them. She threw her shoulder a few times—okay, thirty—into the door, but it barely rocked in its frame. "Fucking Brit wood," she mumbled, rubbing her aching shoulder.

She'd prowled around her cage for the last couple hours. It was a gorgeous room with plush, wine-colored carpet, a soft queen-sized bed with about a zillion pillows, and a truly glorious attached bathroom (free of all razors and other sharp things, she was sorry to note). But as far as Janet was concerned, if you couldn't leave, it might as well have a cement floor and bars on the window.

She went through the bureau and found several robes in her size, in various materials. No real clothes. No television, either, but several books. She saw some classics—Shakespeare, Mark Twain, and Tolstoy—as well as—too funny!—the entire collected works of Stephen King. She supposed she might stand half a chance if she threw *Hamlet* at Dick as hard as she could. She'd gotten the drop on him before in the alley, but she wondered if it was possible now. He didn't believe she was a werewolf, the stupid dickhead, but he'd be careful. He thought she was one of the monkeys, but he respected her anyway. If he wasn't such a fuckstick, she could have really liked him.

She wondered what the pack was thinking—what boss man Michael was thinking. Probably that she'd been run over by a train or something. Death was about the only acceptable reason for skipping a meeting with the big dog. Interestingly, that thought—she'd unwillingly disobeyed a command from her pack leader—brought no anxiety. In fact, it was kind of nice, knowing Michael wanted her on the Cape, and here she was, still in Boston.

If only Dick hadn't been such a beast. If only he hadn't been so *nice* about being such a beast—he might have wanted to really hurt her, but he sucked at it. She remembered him pulling out of her when he thought he was too big for her . . . remembered the excellent food, and the large quantities of it. The absurd marriage proposal. Absurd because . . . well, just because.

If he wasn't such a dick, she could start to like him. But nobody—fucking *nobody*—snatched Janet Lupo from the street, tied her down like a dog, and did whatever he wanted. He'd pay. She would have to wait for her chance, but it would eventually present itself. And then he'd better watch out for his guts, because she meant to have them on the floor.

~ • • • ~

The smell of eggs basted in butter woke her up. Before she could open her eyes, she realized Dick was under the blankets with her. Then she felt his mouth on her neck and felt brief pain as his fangs broke the skin. She tried to push him away, but he pinned her down and held her to the bed while he drank. She had no leverage and could only lie beneath him while he took from her.

"You piece of shit," she said directly into his ear.

He laughed against her throat. "That's the problem, Jane m'love. If you screamed or fainted or cried, I'd have no interest in you—I'd want to be rid of you as quickly as possible. But you're fearless, and furious, and it works on me like an aphrodisiac. Which is why you *have* to be my wife."

"I'd rather eat my own heart."

He licked the bite mark on her neck and then nuzzled the tender spot. "That's a rather disturbing visual. Did you sleep well? I admit I was astonished you weren't lying in wait ready to strangle me with the sash from one of your robes."

"I'd rather wait until you dropped your guard. Then you'll be sorry," she said with total confidence.

He rested his forehead against hers. "God, you're delightful."

"I'm going to skin you alive, you fucking undead monkey. Then I'm going to set your skin on fire. Then I'm going to roast your skinless body over the fire I made with your skin."

"And so ladylike, too! Umm . . ." His cool mouth closed over one of her nipples, and she brought her fist down on top of his head, hard. Then she yelped when he bit her. "Sorry," he said, rubbing the top of his head. "That was you, not me. You hit me so hard my teeth nearly clacked together."

"Just you wait," she said ominously.

He kissed her wrist, her pulse point, and then the crook of her elbow. She balled a fist and got ready to sock him again.

"Jane, as delightful as last night was—for me, anyway—I'd rather not tie you up again." She punched him square in the face, a poor blow with her lack of leverage, but his head rocked back, which was gratifying. He went on as if nothing had happened. "So let's make a deal, you and I. I won't tie you up, and you won't fight me. As of now," he amended.

"You won't tie me up?" she asked suspiciously. "But I have to let you fuck me?"

He looked pained. "Yes, you have to let me fuck you."

She pretended to think it over, but it was an easy decision. She could stand almost anything but being tied down. It went against her very nature and made her want to bite somebody. "Okay. I won't punch, and you won't get out the elastic bubble gum."

"And you'll kiss me back."

"Forget it."

"All right, then, I will do all the kissing for both of us." He smiled at her, put a hand on the back of her neck, and pulled her to him.

"What, I can't eat first? This deal blows."

"Later, Jane. I'm begging you." His mouth was slightly warm, and his tongue slipped past her teeth to stroke her own tongue. She felt his hand cup one of her breasts, testing the weight of it, and then his thumb was rubbing her nipple.

She wriggled, pushing more of her breast into his palm. "So the quicker you get off, the quicker I can have eggs?"

He sighed. "You're really killing the mood here."

"What mood? I'm a prisoner, for fuck's sake. And I'm hungry," she whined.

"Oh, for—" But he let go of her and she bounded off the bed. She wolfed down her breakfast—eggs, six strips of bacon, four pieces of toast, and two glasses of milk—in five minutes while he laid on the bed and watched her with his fingers laced behind his head and a mildly disbelieving look on his face. She got up, wiped her mouth with a napkin, tossed it over her shoulder, and climbed back into bed.

"All right, then," she said, infinitely more cheerful.

He smiled at her. "All right, then." He reached out, took her hand, and led her to the bathroom.

Ten minutes later, they were in his giant bathtub and the floor was soaked. Her legs were spread wide and resting on each rim of the tub, and she was gripping the sides so tightly her knuckles ached. Richard was beneath the water, nuzzling and tonguing and fingering her cunt. He'd been down there for five minutes, and she was about ready to lose her fucking mind.

Now his tongue was inside her, and one of his fingers was worming into her ass. She'd never been interested in assplay—the idea had always grossed her out—but the sensation of his long finger sliding up inside her while his tongue darted and stabbed and licked her cunt made her throb. She had no control over her reflexes, she simply started to thrust her hips at his face. Her muffled groans (for her teeth were tightly clenched) bounced off the bathroom tile.

He rose, water dripping down his marble-white skin, and grinned at her. He pulled her up to him and growled, "*Now* you'll kiss me."

She did, without hesitation. He sucked her tongue into his mouth as he pushed her thighs wide, as he took himself in hand and rubbed his cock against her sopping cunt. She moaned into his mouth and strained toward him. He tore his mouth from hers, sought her neck, and she felt him bite her just as his cock thrust inside her. The combination of sensations—slight pain, swamping pleasure—made her come so hard she bucked against him, and another gallon of water sloshed over the side of the tub.

"Ummmm," he said against her throat. "Oh, that's very good. I could do this all day."

"Better . . . not . . ." she managed. "It'll kill me."

He laughed and leaned back. She was still spread up against the sloping end of the tub; they were connected only by his cock. He ran his hands over her soapy breasts, smiling as she groaned again. "Oh, you *are* going to marry me," he said huskily. "Believe it."

"Why don't you . . . stop talking . . . and finish fucking?"

He grinned, flashing fangs, and obliged. When he finished,

she was indecently satisfied, and there were only a few inches of water left in the tub.

~ ◦ ◦ ◦ ~

Later, he brought a second breakfast. "After that half an hour," he explained, "even *I* could eat a few more eggs."

"Not bad for a dead guy," she said casually, pretending she wasn't still throbbing. The man had a fiendish touch between the sheets—or in the tub—and that was a fact. "I'm sure the ladies like you all right, when you're not being such a jerkoff."

He didn't answer, but just sat down across from her and watched her eat. After a few minutes, he started drumming his fingers on the table.

"Yeah, *that's* not gonna get annoying. The kidnapping and the fucking I can take, but not the nervous tics. Cut it out."

"Why only twice?"

"What?"

He was nibbling thoughtfully on his lower lip and watching her. "Why was last night only your second time? You're in your thirties. You should have had hundreds of experiences by now. It can't be a dislike for the act itself—you're sexy, responsive, and open to new experiences. So what's the explanation?"

Her mouth was suddenly dry—weird!—and she gulped some juice. "None of your goddamned business."

"Did he hurt you? Because if he did, I'd be delighted to track him down for you and teach him a richly deserved—"

"Am I speaking a language you don't know? I said it was none of your business." Her hand was shaking. She put down the juice glass with a bang and hid her hands under the table. "And even if it was, I don't want to talk about it. Especially with you."

His eyes were narrow, thoughtful. "Ah . . . *you* hurt *him*. And felt needless guilt ever since—Jane, for heaven's sake. Whatever you did, it was an accident. You didn't mean it."

"Are you deaf? I said I *don't want to talk about it*!" The glass zoomed at his head; he ducked, and it slammed into the far wall. Orange juice and broken glass sprayed everywhere.

"All right," he said calmly. "We won't talk about it."

Her hands weren't the only thing shaking. She grabbed her elbows and squeezed; she clenched her teeth to stop them from chattering. She was morbidly afraid she might puke, and soon.

He got up from his chair, came to her, and scooped her up as if she was a child. For a wonder, she didn't try to pull his eyeballs out of his head. "You're tired," he soothed. "You've had a rotten week. Why don't you take a nap?"

"Why don't you go fuck yourself?"

"Can't we do both?"

She chuckled unwillingly.

Eight

Two nights before the full moon, and she was actually torn.

Torn! It was almost like she was dreading her impending escape. Which only proved a steady diet of rich food and amazing sex lowered IQ points.

Every day, he asked her to tell him the truth, promising to let her go if she did. And every day, she told him the truth . . . a lie would have choked her. She hadn't broken their date by choice. She had wanted to see him again. And she almost didn't hate him.

That one she kept to herself.

He hadn't tied her up since that first night. And she hadn't tried to attack him. Another example of her quickly lowering IQ. When they were between the sheets (or in the bathtub, or on the floor in front of the fireplace), the last thing on her mind was leaving.

But far more disturbing, when they weren't between the sheets, the last thing on her mind was leaving.

And it wasn't that she was thinking with her pussy instead of her brain. Well, it wasn't *just* that. Because to be perfectly honest, what exactly, was she going back to? To be at Mikey's beck and call? To hang out with a group of people who disapproved of her and then go home to her lonely bed? The pack didn't much want her, and she sure as shit didn't want someone who wasn't pack, someone who was fragile—who would break if she really let loose.

Dick fit the bill admirably, and he approved of her—to the hilt! He thought everything she did and said was swell. She could have farted on him, and he would have rhapsodized about it. In fact, she did . . . after a particularly strenuous sexual marathon and when she was relaxing in his embrace. Relaxing a little too well, in fact—she really cut one. Quick as thought, she pulled the blankets over Dick's head, trapping him with the noxious odor. Cursing, he finally freed himself and then they both laughed until they cried.

She rolled over on her back and stared at the ceiling. It was getting rapidly dark in the bedroom; the sun would be down in a few more minutes. She'd adjusted nicely to his schedule and now slept her days away. Frankly, she preferred his schedule—she'd never been much of an early riser.

He'd be here any minute. Any minute. She felt a tightening in her stomach and was disgusted with herself. Just thinking about him—about his long fingers and his mouth and his tongue and his cock—was making her wet. Some prisoner. Now she had Stockholm

Syndrome. Except it was more like Bimbo Hypnotized by Bad Guy's Huge Cock Syndrome.

And then later he would bring amazing food, and they'd talk about everything and anything. And he'd read to her—they were halfway through *Salem's Lot*, which he seemed to think was a comedy—while she paced. She liked books but couldn't stand to sit still for the hours and hours required to read one. Or they'd wrestle, and once she'd thrown the leftover apple pie at him and they'd had a food fight that ruined the drapes.

Jane sighed. If it was *just* his dick, it wouldn't be so bad. She could always buy a vibrator. No, it was *Dick*. She really, really liked him, more than any guy she'd ever known, and she knew a lot of fellas. And she was having a helluva time remembering she was a prisoner. In fact, she didn't think Dick remembered much, either.

~ . . .~

Her vision doubled, trebled . . . and then her knees buckled. Luckily, she was bent over the footboard, so she had some support.

Dick let go of her waist and pulled her back onto the bed. "That was . . . sweaty." Panting lightly, he flopped over on the pillows. "Jane, your stamina knows no bounds. Look at me; I'm actually out of breath. And I don't even need to breathe."

"My stamina? Look who's talking. We've been at it since—holy shit, the sun's gonna be up in another hour. You'd better beat feet back to the coffin, old man."

He snorted. "It's a bed, not a coffin. It's one of the guest beds, in fact. *You're* in my coffin, so to speak."

"So why don't you sleep here?"

"I've been thinking about it." He propped himself up on one elbow, bent to kiss her shoulder, and then said, "More and more, actually. In the beginning, I dared not leave myself at your mercy, but now I wonder."

"What the hell are you talking about? You take longer to say something than anyone I've ever met."

He didn't smile at her bitching like he usually did. "I'd be quite helpless, Janet. If you, ah, decided to be angry, there's nothing I could do until the sun went down. And the tables in here are all made out of wood . . . so are the chairs. It wouldn't be difficult for someone with your determination to fashion a rudimentary stake."

She'd never thought of that. She couldn't believe she'd never thought of that. "Oh." She mulled it over for a minute and then said, "Well, I don't especially want to stake you in the guts."

"The guts I wouldn't mind so much. How about the heart?"

She rolled over and rested her chin on his chest. "There either. I dunno, you're okay. When you're not being a total shit. Stay, go, I don't give a fuck."

"Well, I can hardly turn down such a warm invitation." Still, he glanced nervously at the table in the corner before climbing under the covers. "Ah, well, here goes nothing. Climb in next to me."

"I have chicken grease under my nails," she pointed out.

"So we'll take a nice hot shower together later tonight."

"Sounds like a date." She snuggled in next to him and rested her head on his shoulder. His body was still slightly warm from their earlier exertions and, as she pressed closer to him, remained that way.

"Ahhhhh," he sighed. "You're better than my electric blanket."

"That's the nicest thing anyone's ever said to me. You should write for fuckin' soap operas," she grumbled, but inside she was glowing. He was trusting her with his life. He knew he was easy prey, and he was going to sleep anyway. It spoke volumes about his true feelings for her . . . and her status as his "prisoner."

Well, shit, she thought, drifting into sleep. Her palm rested over his heart, which beat once or twice every minute. *Maybe there's hope for us after all.*

Nine

Richard woke, as he had for the last several decades, just as the sun slipped past the horizon line. He felt Jane's head resting on his shoulder and smiled. A wonderful way to start the evening. And he was *warm*, so delightfully warm. She was better than a hot tub. He'd have to do something really nice for her for not killing him. Like . . . let her go?

He couldn't. He knew it was the right thing to do, knew he had no business keeping her as a sort of mid-sized boy toy, but every time he thought of his condo emptied of her refreshing presence, he wanted to shiver. Hell, he wanted to go for a walk in the sunshine.

He couldn't even pretend it was about revenge anymore. Even if she had lied, they were square after that first night. No, he was keeping her because he was a selfish monster and he couldn't bear to let her go. To be brutally honest, he was thrilled she was sticking to her story, because it gave him the perfect excuse to keep her.

The fact that he wasn't pinned to the bed via a table leg through his rib cage spoke well of her feelings for him. He was as hopeful as he'd been in—what year *was* it? She had her chance for vengeance and hadn't taken it. And he doubted his lovely Jane was in the habit of passing up a chance to avenge herself. Was it possible she'd forgiven him? That was too unrealistic to believe, but perhaps there was hope. Perhaps—

"No! No, God, no . . . aw, jeez, Bobby!"

She was screaming. Screaming in her sleep. He was so startled he nearly jumped off the bed. Never had he heard his Janet so terrified, and so young. She sounded like a teenager.

"I didn't—Bobby, don't move, I'll get an ambulance, oh, God, don't die, please don't die!"

She was clawing at him in her sleep. He caught her hands and squeezed. "Jane, love. It's a dream. It's not real." *Anymore*, he added silently. His chest and throat felt tight. Whatever had happened, it had been horrible. Awful enough to scare her away from love-making for years and years.

Her eyes flew open. He was shocked to see them filling and then her tears spilled over and ran down her cheeks. "I didn't mean to," she sobbed.

"Of course you didn't."

"They told me it wasn't a good idea—that monkeys are fragile—but I didn't listen." She made a small fist and thumped it against his chest. "Why didn't I listen? Oh, we were having such fun—it didn't even hurt, and I thought it was supposed to hurt the first time. And then I started to come and I wrapped my legs around his waist and squeezed and—and—"

"Janet, it was an accident." *Monkeys?* Odd slang—he had never been able to keep up with it. Had she broken the boy's ribs? Had they been in a precarious position and fallen, and perhaps the boy had . . . ? Well, whatever had happened, he was thoroughly certain of one thing. "You didn't mean to hurt him, Jane. You never would have hurt him. You've got to let this go." He was stroking her back while he soothed her, and she finally relaxed against him. He added jokingly, hoping to see a scowl, "Besides, you don't need to worry about such things with me. You could set me on fire while you were having your way with me, and I'd be fine the next day. Before you ask, though, I'm really not into that."

She jerked up on one elbow and stared at him. Her eyes were smudged with tears, bloodshot, and enormous. He thought she'd never looked so pretty. "That's right," she said slowly. "I was thinking about that last night and you . . . I can't hurt you. You can take whatever I dish out."

"And have been," he added, "for several days now. See, look!" He showed her his arm where, in her agitation, she'd clawed off ribbons of skin. It was nearly healed.

Oddly, she was still staring at him as if she'd never seen him before. "I don't know why I didn't think of it before, Dick."

"You've had other things on your mind. Now, that's enough crying over a fifteen-year-old accident you couldn't help," he said briskly, hoping she agreed. He couldn't bear to see her cry. He rolled out of bed and stood up, casting about for a way to distract her. "How about sushi and maybe some vegetable tempura for breakfast?"

She perked up immediately. "I like raw fish," she said. "I like steak tartare, too, but I like it better with steak, not hamburger."

"Sounds like we have lunch figured out, too, m'love."

"But first we have to shower," she said, almost shyly.

He laughed, bent to her, picked her up, and kissed her. "Yes indeed. You are *filthy*. And so am I. I foresee lots of scrubbing in our future."

"Fucking pervert," she snorted, and he cheered inwardly, knowing she was back to herself.

~ * * * ~

For the second night in a row, Richard woke up warm and content. He had made up his mind as dawn broke in the wee hours of the morning, as Janet cuddled up to him and snored softly in his ear. Today they would go out. He'd take her shopping and buy her a ridiculous amount of clothes. Clothes, lingerie, priceless paintings, pounds of steak tartare—whatever she wanted. He knew in his heart she wouldn't run away from him, and it was past time he let her out of his bedroom. She had been admirably patient, and it was time for a reward.

He stretched. He didn't really need to—he always woke energized and hungry and raring to go—but he enjoyed the sensation. Yes, they would go shopping, she would bully the sales clerks, and it would be delightful. Then back to his place for a light lunch and some energetic lovemaking, and possibly a nap, or more of *Salem's Lot*. Yes, it was all—

Where the hell was Janet?

He'd been groping absently for her while he'd been thinking, but she wasn't in his bed, and the bathroom light was off. He could hear her on the floor, gasping in—pain? Was that pain?

In the second before he looked, it seemed like every malady mortals were prone to raced through his brain. She had appendicitis. He'd knocked her up (it was supposed to be impossible, but who really knew?) and she was having a miscarriage. She was having a heart attack. A brain embolism. A kidney shutdown. God help him, he was as afraid to look as he was afraid not to.

He looked. Janet was on her knees beside the bed, panting harshly, and her back—it almost looked like the knobs of her spine were *moving*. Her hair was hanging in her face in sweaty tangles, and her nails were sunk into the carpet. His feet hit the floor with a double thud, and he reached for her. "Janet, I'm getting a doctor. I'll be right—"

A low, ripping growl froze his hand in mid-reach. And then—so fast, it was so quick, he blinked and it was done—she sprouted hair, her nose turned into a long snout, her eyes went wild, and she was leaping for the door.

She bounced off it, but he was alarmed to see it actually shudder in its frame. She coiled and leapt again. And again. He remained sitting on the bed—he was afraid if he stood he would fall—and stared at her. Janet was a dun-colored wolf with silver streaks running down her back. Her eyes were the same color as when she was a biped, but now they were glittery and homicidal. He remembered how she paced when he read, how she couldn't seem to sit still for long, and realized that in this form she was claustrophobic.

Chunks of the door were leaping off the frame and falling to the carpet each time her body hit the door, but at this rate it would take at least ten minutes and she was likely to damage herself. He got up and walked to the door on legs stiff with shock, fumbled with the lock, dropped his key twice (all the while dodging her small wolf's body—she never stopped, she completely ignored him, he doubted he was even a cipher to her now), and finally swung open the door.

He ran after her to do it again, and again. Then she spotted the bank of windows facing west and lunged toward them. He dived and managed to catch her back left leg just as she was coiling for a leap that would take her through the window. She spun, and he had a dizzying glimpse of what looked like a thousand sharp teeth as she growled.

"We're three stories up," he panted, clutching her while at the same time trying not to break her leg. "You'll never survive the fall. Well, you might but—Janet, don't go!"

She snapped at his fingers. Wrathful growls bubbled up out of her without pause or breath.

"Please don't leave! I was wrong and you were right—God, you were so right, I was a blind fool not to see it. *Please* don't leave me."

She snapped again, her jaws closing about a centimeter from his flesh. A warning. Probably her last warning.

"I can't bear it without you. I swear I can't. I thought I was content before, but it was a lie, everything was a lie, even why I was keeping you was a lie—"

His grip was slipping. He talked faster.

"—but you were right, and you never lied, not once, not even to get away, and Janet, I will spend the rest of your life making it up to you—"

She was almost free, and he was afraid if he let go to get a better grip, he wouldn't be fast enough.

"—but please . . . don't . . . go!"

She went.

He lay on the floor in his study a very long time. It seemed too much work to get up, find the broom, and start sweeping up the broken glass. He owned the building anyway, so who cared? Who cared about anything?

He couldn't believe she was gone. He couldn't believe he—who prided himself on possessing at least a modicum of intelligence—had let this happen.

My name is Janet Lupo.

Had done such things, and to such a woman.

I'm not afraid of any man, and I don't lie.

What had he been thinking?

My name is Janet Lupo.

How could he have been so blind?

My name is Janet Lupo.

So stupid and arrogant?

The full moon is eight days away. And when it comes, you're going to get a big fucking surprise.

Oh, if there was a God this was a fine joke indeed. He had finally found the one woman he could spend eternity with . . .

Your little oak doors won't hold me then.

. . . and he had kidnapped her and raped her and kept her and ignored her when she spoke the truth.

You'll realize you fucked up, bad.

He'd demanded she admit to being afraid of him, and when she wouldn't, he assumed it was a lie.

You'll know I was telling the truth the whole time, but you couldn't see past your stupid injured male pride.

His stupid injured male pride.

I'll be gone forever, and you'll have the next hundred years to realize what an asshole you were.

He would have cried, but he had no tears.

Ten

Three days later

Jane rolled over and stretched. Then shrieked in anger as she fell three feet and hit the cement with a *smack*. She'd curled up on the base of the statue in Park Square, promptly gone to sleep, and then forgotten about the drop when she woke up. *Why don't I ever remember this shit until it's too late?* she thought, rubbing her skinned elbow.

She was pleasantly tired and would be for the next couple of days. It was always like that when she chased the moon. She also felt very new, almost husked out. Purified. Whatever.

She stood and shivered. Step one: find clothes. Spring in Boston was like spring in Siberia.

She marched up to an early morning commuter, a businessman obviously cutting through the park to get to the subway. He stared at her appreciatively as she approached, but she had eyes only for his cashmere topcoat. "How—" was all he had time for before she belted him in the jaw and mugged him.

She had made her choice as a wolf and would carry it out as a woman. She didn't have to wake up in the park, naked and alone. Or yesterday, in an alley. Or the night before that, beneath the docks by the harbor—ugh. She didn't think she'd ever get the smell out of her hair.

There were only a hundred safe houses in Boston, as well as acres and acres of woods owned by pack members. She could have romped there and woken to clean clothes and a hearty breakfast. But as a wolf, she had avoided all those places and her kind. The beast knew what she wanted. Now it was time to get it.

Of course, she didn't know where Dick lived exactly. It's not like she scribbled down the address with her paw on her way out the window. Luckily, there were ways and ways. She might not have a super nose like some of her kind, but the day she couldn't sniff up her own backtrail to a den was the day she'd jump off a fucking bridge.

It didn't take long, but her feet were freezing by the time she got there. Dick lived in a dignified brownstone condo that was probably built the year the *Mayflower* landed. She shifted her weight back and forth, stuck her hands in her stolen pockets, and looked up at his window. The glass hadn't been replaced; there was a large piece of cardboard taped into the frame instead. Guess it took time to order that fancy old-fashioned stuff. Except for the rumble of an early morning delivery truck, the street was quiet.

"'Scuse me. D'you live here?"

She looked. The delivery boy was holding three brimming grocery bags, and looking glum. "Yeah. Why?"

"Well, thank God. 'Cause I've been making deliveries for two weeks, but the last couple days nobody ever takes the food in, and it goes bad or gets swiped, and it's just a waste, is all."

Ah, so that's where all the sumptuous feasts came from! Dick had the food delivered and cooked the meals for her. *Yum.* "I was gone for a while," she told him, "but now I'm back."

"Who are you?"

"I'm the owner's fiancée." She shook her head. It sounded just as weird out loud as it did in her head. "Do I have to sign something?"

"No. He's got an account with us."

"Then get lost."

"Nice!" He set down the bags, slouched back to his truck, and pulled into traffic without looking, in typical Boston fashion. Which was good, because it wouldn't do for him to watch her break into the house.

"Well, shit." That had been considerably easier said than done! Dick's front door wouldn't budge, and she was reluctant to break more of that expensive glass. He might not be so thrilled she came back. She had a vague memory of him grabbing her and begging her not to go, but it was more like a dream. She didn't trust her wolf-brain to factually interpret human emotions.

She smacked herself on the forehead. Dummy! Why was she trying to see him in the *daytime*? Even if she got in, he wouldn't exactly be a thrilling conversationalist. He'd be holed up in his bedroom, dead to the world—literally. Until then, she might as well chat with a rock. Still, it would have been nice to swipe some clothes.

Oh, well. The coat was plenty warm enough, and she didn't give a fuck how many people stared at her feet. At least she was in a big city instead of some rinky-dink small town. The yokels always loved something new to gawp at. She just had to kill another ten hours until the sun set. Thank God for the Barnes & Noble café.

Eleven

Richard slumped in the chair beside the fireplace. He'd been sitting in this room every evening since Jane had left. It had been the last place he'd seen her.

He was starving, and he didn't care. He deserved to go hungry. And the thought of leaving—of perhaps missing her if she came back—was unbearable. What if she was hurt? What if she needed something and he was out assuaging his thirst?

Who are you kidding? She's gone, fool. You did everything but toss her out the window yourself.

True enough. Still, he waited. It was the only thing he could do. He'd never insult her by trying to find her and convince her to return. Return to what? An unnatural existence with a monster? And what in the world could he ever say to her? "Janet, dear, sorry about kidnapping you and raping you and keeping you and all but calling you a liar to your face, kiss-kiss, let's go home." As the lady herself might say, "In a fuckin' pig's eye."

"Dick! Stop with the fucking sulking and open the front door!"

Oh, Christ, now his inner voice sounded like *her*. Bad enough he was starving, but it appeared he was slowly going insane as well.

"You son of a bitch! You piece of shit! I trot my ass all the way back down here—twice!—and you keep me standing out here on this freezing sidewalk?"

He buried his face in his hands. How he missed her!

"I am going to rip your heart out and pin it to the bedroom wall with a swizzle stick! I'm going to yank the fixtures out of that stupid bathroom you're so proud of and shove them up your ass!" *Wham! Wham! Wham!* "Now let me in before I lose my temper!"

That's no inner voice, Richard. I ought to know . . . I'm your inner voice.

He jumped up so quickly his head actually banged into the ceiling. He barely felt it. He clawed for the doorway, raced through it and down the hall, down three flights of stairs, fumbled for the bolts and locks, and flung the door open.

Janet stood on his front step, flushed and out of breath. Her little fists were red from the cold and from banging his door. She was wearing a man's overcoat roughly six sizes too big for her, and three large grocery bags were at her feet. She was scowling. "Well, *finally*. Don't sulk on my time, all right, pal?" She stomped past him.

Like a zombie, he picked up the groceries and then slowly

turned and followed her. She shrugged out of the coat and headed straight for their—for his room. He watched her naked form sway back and forth as she went up the stairs like she owned them. "Food," she said over her shoulder on her way up. "I could eat a cow. In fact, I think I did, night before last."

By the time he brought her tray to the bedroom, she had showered and toweled off. She strolled out of the bathroom and sniffed appreciatively. "Oooh, yeah, that's the stuff. I could eat *two* steaks."

"They're both for you," he said automatically. "Why . . . how . . . why . . . ?"

"You sounded a lot brighter when you thought I was a liar." She brushed past him and jumped for the bed, landing in the middle, lolling like a queen, and favoring him with a smirk. "Ah, the mileage I'm gonna get out of this. Let's start with your whole smug speech about how just because you're a vampire, there's no such thing as werewolves. That sound like a good place to you?"

"Janet—"

"Or we could touch on why it's not a good idea to kidnap people when they're on their way to an important meeting."

"Janet—"

"Or we could go into all the times you asked me to tell the truth, and I did, and then you didn't believe me, and then you—"

He fell to his knees beside the bed. He had to grit his teeth for a few seconds to keep his jaw from trembling. "Janet, why are you here? Why aren't you with your family?" His voice was rising, but he was helpless to stop it. "Why didn't you head for the road and keep going? Why are you back?"

She frowned. "You're taking the fun all out of this. I've been looking forward to it for days. I need to see some major-ass groveling, pal."

He didn't speak.

She sighed. "What, I gotta get out the hand puppets? You haven't figured it out? Dick, *you're* my family now. I never want to go back there. Cape Cod in the summer—yech! Tourists cluttering up the roads, the beaches, and the mall—and you get in trouble if you eat them. Can't even take a little bite to discourage them from coming back—"

"Janet."

"I'm serious! Anyway, if I stay with you, I don't have to go back. I didn't realize how unhappy I was with them until I fell in with you. I'm not pack anymore, I'm yours. I mean—if you want."

"Is this a joke?" he almost whispered. "Is it a trick to get even? Because while I wouldn't blame you—"

"Oh, hey, I'm a bitch, but I'm not, like, a sociopath! That'd be a rotten thing to do. I love you, you stupid fuck. I'm not going anywhere. Except, of course, for a few days a month. Think you can put up with that, you undead dope?"

"I've been waiting almost a hundred years to hear those words. Well, not those exact words." He reached out and pulled her down onto his lap. They sat on the floor while she cuddled into him like a bad-tempered doll. "Oh, Janet. I missed you so much. And I was such a fool."

"Yeah, a real arrogant asshole."

"Yes."

"Completely unreasonable and jerkish."

"And then some."

"And you're really, *really* sorry."

"So unbelievably sorry."

"And totally unworthy of me."

"In a thousand ways."

"And you're gonna buy lots of food and get a house in the country so I don't have to hunt in the city."

"The refrigerator is full, and I already have a house in the Berkshires."

"Then that's all right," she said, sounding quite satisfied. She stretched out her legs and wiggled her toes. "Um . . . the steaks are getting cold."

"So am I."

She giggled and turned so she was straddling him and then hooked her ankles behind his waist and kissed him on the mouth. Slowly, she cupped the back of his neck and brought his mouth to her throat. "Hungry?" she purred.

He thought he would have a seizure. She had come back—she loved him—she would stay—and now she was freely offering him her blood. Soon the Palestinians and the Israelis would make peace, and Janet would willingly enroll in charm school.

He sank his fangs into her throat without hesitation—he couldn't have held back if he tried. He could feel her breasts pressing against his chest while her blood warmed him from the inside out. She was wriggling against him—now her fingers were at his zipper—now her warm little hand was inside his trousers, clasping him, stroking him. He groaned against her throat.

"You *did* miss me!" She shoved him back and he was happy enough to lie down for her. He stopped feeding and licked the bite mark. Her glorious breasts were jiggling in his face, and he couldn't recall ever being happier, not once in his long, long life.

She seized his cock with delightful firmness and raised herself above him. His arms went around her waist as he guided her to him.

Entering her was like slipping into luxurious oil. Her head tipped back, and she said "Ummmmm . . . that's good. I missed that," to the ceiling.

He stroked her breasts, running his fingers over her firm nipples, marveling at the softness of her skin in contrast with her strength and stamina. She'd jumped three stories, and there wasn't a mark on her—and he was certainly looking! Not a bruise, not a scratch. She healed almost as quickly as he did.

"You're gorgeous," he said.

"You're just saying that to get laid," she teased.

"In case you haven't noticed, I *am* getting laid."

She snorted and then began to rock back and forth. He noticed an odd, sudden reticence about her and wondered about it—then suddenly realized she had likely been on top when she crippled her first lover.

"For heaven's sakes," he said with mock disgust, "can't you go any faster than that? Any harder? I'm about to fall asleep down here."

She was so astonished she nearly fell off him. Then she made the connection and smirked. "Okey-dokey, dead guy. Here we go."

They ruined the carpet. They didn't care. Toward the end, she was screaming at the ceiling and he could feel his spine cracking—and didn't care. Her legs were around his waist in a crushing grip, her arms around his neck, cutting off his air—and he wanted more. He told her so, insisted on it, demanded it, and then bit her ear. He could actually feel the temperature change within her as she reached orgasm, felt her uterus tightening around his shaft. That was enough to tip him dizzily over the edge.

They weren't able to speak for several minutes until Janet finally managed, "Oh, cripes, I think that should be against the law."

"It probably is, in at least three states."

"My supper's cold," she complained, making no move to stand up and get the tray.

"So I've got a microwave. Why did I even cook it? I doubt you'd have minded it raw. A werewolf," he mused, stroking her thigh. "Even after I saw the truth with my own eyes, I could hardly believe it."

"That's because you're kind of a dumb-ass sometimes."

"I have to take this from a foul-mouthed tart like you?"

She pounced on him and nibbled his throat. "I'm *your* foul-mouthed tart, so there."

"Excellent." He kissed her nose. "So . . . how do you feel about being an undead werewolf?"

She groaned. "Let's talk about it in ten years, all right? Let me get used to the idea of not being pack anymore first."

"It's a date. Will they come after you?"

"I have no idea. No one's ever voluntarily left before. I doubt the boss would really mind—he's softened up since he got hitched—but I s'pose I should tell them I'm not dead."

"Tomorrow."

"Yeah. Tomorrow."

"We've made our own pack, Jane. We're two monsters who do as they like, when they like. Everyone else had best stay out of our way."

"Ooooh, God, I love it when you talk like that . . ."

"How about when I do this?" He leaned down and nibbled on her impudent nipple, running his tongue over the velvety bumps of her areola.

"Oh, God."

"Or this?" He sucked hard and nipped her very, very lightly.

"Ummmmm . . ."

"I love you."

"Ummmm. Me, too. Don't stop."

He laughed and bent to her warm, lush flesh. "Not for a hundred years, at least."

"We'll figure something out."

Epilogue

From the private papers of Richard Will, Ten Beacon Hill, Boston, Massachusetts

"I'm in love! No entries of late—too busy. Too much to do just to keep up with my lovely monster. She's everything I ever wanted and, even better, I appear to be everything she ever wanted.

"No more time to write today—we're breaking in a new chef. He's used to catering large office functions, so he should be able to keep Janet satisfied.

"I suppose I'll give up this journal very soon. I realize now I wrote in it as a way to stave off my loneliness. No need for such distracting tricks any longer.

"Must go—my bride has just playfully tossed a marble bust at my head to get my attention. I think I'll chase her down and spank her."

Turn the page for a sneak peek at

Wolf at the Door

by MaryJanice Davidson.
Available October 2011 from Berkley Sensation!

Prologue

The werewolves were holding hands. They did not share kinship by blood or bond; their relationship was more like a protective secretary looking out for her clueless boss. Her extremely clueless boss.

The female leaned over and spoke softly in his ear. She wasn't trying to be secretive. The werewolves across the table could hear every word. "We've been through this before."

His nostrils flared. "*You* have."

"And I'm still here."

He seemed to take courage from that, from her neat designer suit, her unmarked face, her unchewed ears and dark eyes. "You're still here. And so am I." He glared across the table and she caught an unpleasant whiff . . . a cactus catching fire, maybe. Strong and sharp, enough to make the eyes water.

"Remember the rules," she reminded him. Her hand was beneath the table, so the other werewolves couldn't see her nails digging into him.

He swallowed a gasp and nodded. The rules. Right. Show no fear. Ideally, *feel* no fear. If you do, don't show it. If you absolutely can't help showing it, make the fear about something else. Anything else.

"Ow, my suit!" he yelped, and showily yanked her hand away from his lap. "My wife'll kill me."

"Nah," one of the wolves across the table said. "She won't."

"Be worth it, though," his partner said, leering at her blunt, small hand and unpolished fingernails. Rachael resisted the urge to make an obscene gesture, or put one of his eyes out with her thumb.

"Won't be anything left to kill, anyways," his partner added, and they wee-hawed together like two of the three little pigs. *Wee wee weeeee-haw!*

"Quit that. Anyways is wrong, just like towards is wrong." Oh, boy, she hated towards. More than plague, she hated towards. "Don't get me started. Now, if you two are through chortling," Rachael snapped, "maybe we could get some work done?"

The werewolves, a little taken aback by the feisty tone, had a quick huddle at their end of the table ("She's so little!" "Chortling? Who says chortling?"). Then they manned up ("Shouldn't it be wolfmanned up?" "Why are you asking me these things? What's wrong with you?") and slammed down several thick folders bristling with Post-it flags. The least jarring color was a queasy pale green.

The burning cactus smell intensified, and her client slapped his hand on the table, hard; the *crack!* got everyone's attention. "You need to understand . . . this is vital. Do you hear me, boys? I'm talking life-or-death here. Critical shit." Their ears pricked forward. "Our records are one hundred . . . percent . . . accurate."

"Balls."

"What he said. This audit's been coming a long time," the older werewolf said, jabbing his thumbs at (weirdly) himself. "You've had years to get your shit together, years of half-assing it, but now time's up. Now you gotta fight or flight." He smiled. "And everyone in the room knows you're not so good at the fight part."

As one of the people in the room who knew that, Rachael said nothing. Her client spoke instead. "I'm ready. We're prepped, we can go anytime."

"Oh-umm?" The younger werewolf paused, and Rachael smiled at the sight of him sifting scents and trying to match them to the wrong sounds. "You are? I mean, you can?"

"Sure." It was amazing, she thought, how someone could smell so utterly different from one second to the next. The smallest boost to his confidence, and burnt cactus changed to orange bubble gum! "I just thought . . . I mean, I thought Michael . . ."

At the name of the Pack Leader, all four werewolves eyeballed each other while pretending they weren't. Rachael Velvela was in the room because she was Michael Wyndham's cousin by marriage.

That was bad news for Tom Fritzi of Fritzi's Fried Funnel Cakes (FunCakes™), who had been audited with a vengeance yet at first had no idea who she was. He'd hired her because he thought her last name was Velveeta, and was so fond of fake cheese he kept her on after he realized the mistake.

The toads across the table, lesser beta-males, had audited Fritzi for the chance to get close to a relative of the Pack Leader, and also because they hated FunCakes™. (They were neutral on the issue of processed cheese food.)

So here they all were.

"I can't stand suspense, and maybe you can't, either, so I'll just come out with it. My cousin isn't popping in for a cameo." Rachael was already bored with the proceedings. She had been hip-deep in Fritzi's finances for the last month, and could actually smell FunCakes™ coming off the files. "He's busy running the (were) world. And since there's no point in waiting for him, we might as well get started."

So the blood-soaked nightmare that was the audit of Fritzi's Fried Funnel Cakes, Inc. (seventeen locations nationwide) began.

One

"There's no easy way to say this. There's not even a cool, clever way to say this. So I'll just come out with it. I need you move to St. Paul indefinitely and keep an eye on the vampire queen."

Rachael had suspected nothing when the summons came. In fact, she had assumed the Pack Leader, Michael Wyndham, was wishing her a belated Happy Thirtieth. He was notorious for remembering significant dates about seventy-two hours too late. It was possible to time him. Sometimes he would round up all the cousins for a big b-day blowout that left the little ones in sugar comas and the adults reaching for sunglasses long before the sun rose high. Could a werewolf get a hangover? Sure. How much booze did it take? Gallons.

But he'd had his hands full with the newly discovered vampire issue (Vampires! In Minnesota! Thousands! Controlled by a moron who loved designer shoes!), so she thought nothing of never hearing from him three days after her birthday. She loved her cousin, but he had many responsibilities. As, of course, did she. Tax season was nearly upon them.

So she had suspected nothing when she drove to Wyndham Manor (how too, too aristocratic East Coast!), once a monastery, now the seat of North American werewolf power and home to several generations of Pack Leaders.

The monks must have had a keen eye for both architecture, mood, and luxury, for the pile of deep red bricks they had abandoned (or had they been turned out of and devoured . . . history was not Rachael's gift) was truly castle-like.

It was built of enormous red bricks and stones, with a dazzling number of windows on all sides, sweeping porches, turrets, multileveled decks, swimming pools (idiotic, given that the Atlantic was right behind the mansion), miles of private beach, and even a golf course. Not that she played; it seemed too much like Fetch.

She herself liked to drive out here in her blue Kia Rio when her Change was upon her. She liked to park in the private lot on the beach below the bluffs, Change, then race up the cliff until she was looking at the back of the mansion, nearly always abandoned because her Pack had all Changed and gone away.

Then she would trot around to the immense green lawn in front of the manor, a lawn so wide and deep it was like a dark green lake, one that would take her a while to swim across. She'd flop on her back, wriggle to work out some kinks (human form to wolf form left a nagging ache in her vertebrae), and look up at the bright stars while the wind groaned in her ears and everywhere there was the smell of the ocean, so salty and strong and alive it was almost like the smell of fresh blood.

Now here she was, being packed off like an embarrassing relative ("Away to the sanitarium with you, crazed aunt!"), and who knew when she'd be able to roll around on that green lawn, that lake of grass? The stars in Minnesota couldn't be as big, or as bright, or as clear. No oceans. The Land of 10,000 Lakes had no oceans.

Lakes often smelled like dead fish.

And *he* wouldn't be there. Michael, her Pack Leader and, always more important, her cousin and friend. Her protector. Sending her away when he had many stronger and rougher and smarter—all right, maybe not smarter—but there were literally hundreds of werewolves who would *leap* at the chance. But Michael wanted her to go . . . and for what?

She opened her mouth and coughed; for the moment her throat had been too dry to speak. She tried again. "Spy on the vampire queen?"

Michael winced a bit at *spy*, and from his furtive manner, he was clearly hoping his mate, Jeannie, couldn't overhear any of this. It was also probably why the door was closed. Jeannie Wyndham hated intrigue, or as she sometimes called it, "werewolf sneakiness." Also, from what Rachael had seen and heard, Jeannie *liked* the vampire queen.

"Keep an eye on," he said again. "Okay? Keep an eye on. That's all. I've already arranged for you to rent a house in her neighborhood—"

"Rent?" She tried, but not very hard, to keep the sharp tone out of her voice. She hated renting. Land was the only thing they could not make more of; owning property was the way to go. It had been true a thousand years ago, it had been true five hundred years ago, it was simply that the masses teeming over the planet knew that, now.

Her *cousin* knew that, now.

"Rachael, I'm sorry." He spread his hands and gave her a wry smile, no teeth. Werewolves were terrible at deceiving each other, and she and her cousin had grown up together. She knew he was sorry.

She didn't care. Because she knew what he was sorry for, and it left her unmoved.

I'm sorry I'm sending you away from your home and everything you've known. I'm sorry you have to leave your lands. I'm sorry I'm making you uproot your life for my whim du jour. Sorry, sorry, so sorry. Hey, you want to go play with my kids while I explain that to keep their way of life safe, I have to uproot yours? No? Maybe another time.

Or maybe never.

"Rachael, your house here on the Cape will always be yours. It passed to you when your mother died; it will be yours, and your children's, and their children's (assuming that part of the Cape doesn't drop into the Bay) forever."

Well. That was something, at least. She restrained herself from sniffing.

"While you're away we'll take care of maintenance, send someone out to shovel and mow, get in there for some light cleaning every month or so, pay your utilities, keep the lights and phone going . . . things like that."

"That's the least of it," she replied, and he nodded. It was. He was a billionaire. He could keep a thousand houses going with electricity and garbage service. "What if I can't get established in Minnesota? All my clients are from around here, and I'm only licensed on the East Coast."

Her mother's insistence, years ago, before she died. Probably died. They'd never found the body. "Why limit yourself to Massachusetts? What, because most of the weres in this country are here? What, you'll never need to help the family in, say, New Hampshire?"

Sound advice, but it hadn't covered the Midwestern states, so right now, she couldn't, either.

"We'll get you licensed for Minnesota. Paperwork's already in motion."

"No doubt," she said dryly.

He shrugged, and kept his expression neutral. They were close kin, but he *was* still her Pack Leader. Just because he had never, ever asked her to jump before did not mean he never would.

She studied him while he droned on about licensing and software and boys who mow. It was funny how the older he got, the lighter and denser he got. When they were kids, his hair was jet black, long and curly. He started getting gold streaks in his teens, streaks that exactly matched his startling yellow eyes.

Now, in his thirties, his hair was the dark gold of an autumn sunset; he remained one of the few men on the planet who could pull off a mullet. (Perhaps the only . . . ?) The older he got, the less like one of *them* he looked. Funny how the humans never noticed. But then, as a species, they weren't known for such things.

Lucky for us.

". . . and your laptop goes everywhere. What's the difference between a living room ten blocks from here, and a living room in a rented house in St. Paul?"

Oh, let's see. Ambience, lighting, wallpaper, smell, windows, carpeting . . .

"Same laptop, same software, right? You've been telling me for years you hardly have to visit your clients face-to-face anymore. You get everything electronically."

"Mmmm." This was Rachael's way of saying, "Dammit, I know there's a flaw in your stupid plan and when I figure it out I'm giving you a ground glass suppository."

"And you won't be on 24/7."

"On the vampire queen?" Ugh.

He nodded, jerking a gold wave out of his eyes. "If you need to fly back here to meet a client or see one of us or, I dunno, pick apples or something—"

"Pick *apples*?" When in the blue hell would she ever turn to tourist agriculture?

"—someone will keep watch on the queen while you're gone."

The flaw! Not only was she being sent away, there would occasionally be a blundering werewolf she didn't know and probably didn't want to know, stumbling through her rental house, making messes and generally being a pain in her hindquarters. When she returned to St. Paul, it would doubtless be to clean up whatever mess he or she left.

Wherever you are, Mother, you're laughing, aren't you? Even as an infant, Rachael had disliked having her things moved around. Her only weapons had been poop, pee, and drool, and she had heartlessly wielded them.

"The economy's still pretty bad," she added with more than a little warning. "You might not have noticed, O mightily wealthy Pack Leader who never once worried about a meal in his spoiled-silly life—"

He started to grin, then his gold brows rushed together and he did a credible job of looking stern. Too bad he didn't *smell* stern. He could fool the *sapiens*, he could even fool werewolves who didn't know him very well. He couldn't fool family, ever.

She was trying to stay annoyed, but the truth was, she loved Michael Wyndham and would do what he asked, no matter how annoying or time-consuming or stupid or dangerous or irritating or inconvenient.

Her earliest memory was of falling through the ice of a cranberry bog not even two miles from where they were both standing. It would have been her last memory, but her tall cousin leaned down with his yellow eyes blazing and, with a mittened hand that held hers so hard he broke two of her fingers, yanked her from the awful cold water and the dreadful, freezing, sucking mud.

She scowled, hoping to cover her out-of-character sentimental journey. She would do as he asked, but had no interest in making the asking part easier for him.

He saw her look and again held up placating hands. "Aw, Rache, give me a break. Can't help it that the Wyndhams have never missed a meal. It's not my fault they went into lumber at the exact right time in the exact right part of the country. You remember Aunt Forcia?"

Rachael made a determined effort not to giggle. *Must . . . remain . . . a stone . . .*

Aunt Forcia had loved sheep. Loooooved them. During full moons, she'd pull down as many as she could and just gorge. Then she'd pass out for a week or so. The cousins had all thought it was hilarious. (The sheep, less so, but it was a werewolf-gobble-sheep world. At least it was on Cape Cod.)

"You know perfectly well you'll inherit a chunk of our ill-gotten gains in another generation or so. Your mom asked me to keep most of it in a trust for you until—"

She knew the parameters of the will, and waved that away. Being wealthy was complex and annoying, caused too many questions and created too much paperwork. She supported herself very well as a CPA. Let the money remain in trust for another decade; she truly did not care. Perhaps if she had cubs someday she would change her mind, but it wasn't likely: either changing her mind or having cubs.

"Look, even if you weren't a blood relative, we wouldn't let your house crumble into ruin, no matter where you are in the world doing your duty for the family, and no matter how long it takes."

"My duty for the family." She said it in a flat tone. She, like her cousin standing before her, was a werewolf: *lupi viri* (strictly translated to "men of wolves" . . . when was Latin going to get with the program with their female tenses?).

And the *lupi viri* gave their habits no more thought than the *sapiens* pondered their humanity. When *sapiens* pondered anything, and weren't dreaming up more excuses for global devastation. A less potty-trained species she had never met in her life. There was a perfectly good reason most werewolves stayed in Massachusetts, and it had nothing to do with all the beaches. Or the Freedom Trail. Or the New England Aquarium.

"So that's what this is, Michael? My duty?"

"It's not just that I need someone to go out there. I need someone who wouldn't go solely out of duty. Rache, you're one of the smartest people I've ever met. You're blood, too. But you're a better choice because . . ."

"Because . . ." His scent, which had been a mild and unwarlike vanilla, suddenly shifted, and now she could smell dry sea grass, a lot of it, ablaze.

Ah. Here came the precautionary tale.

"Rache, I can't lie to you." It was true. He was a dreadful, laughable liar. "The last person I sent out there died in the vampire queen's service."

Two

She had known that, had been expecting that, so it wasn't the shock Michael had feared.

Rachael nodded. She remembered the incident well, and the memorial afterward, on the occasion where they'd had the chance to meet the queen and her consort. Rachael hadn't gotten more than a glimpse, or much chance to hear the trial—Wyndham Manor had been crawling with thousands—but regardless of what little she saw, she still found Betsy Taylor silly beyond belief.

No one had especially liked the late Antonia Wolfton (except Derik, Michael's best friend), but they'd all been angry that a werewolf had died on a vampire's watch. And what the hell kind of a name was Betsy for a monarch?

"I need someone smart, someone I can trust, who can take care of herself—they don't have any cranberry bogs out there for you to fall in—"

"Ha, ha, O Rotund Pack Leader."

"Back off, I've only gained a couple pounds since Lara started all that ruckus. Do you know how many boys have been following her home? She's in goddamned elementary school and the boys are already trotting after her! I'm gonna have to start beating them off with sticks!"

"The terrible trials of our magnificently round Pack Leader."

"That's all sheathed in sculpted muscle, Rache." He patted his (to be fair, reasonably flat) stomach. In fact, Rachael was pleased to see evidence that he was able to relax enough to indulge now and then. Before his mating, before his cubs came, he had the lean look of a man always too close to a bad mistake. Jeannie—and their cubs—had changed all that.

It occurred to her, again, that he had changed in other ways. Usually when she saw him, there were dozens of others around, usually the cousins and their kin. She couldn't remember the last time she had been alone with him. So things she normally never thought of were not only occurring to her, she was thinking of them again and again. Things that had changed . . . and things that never changed.

His looks, for instance. When they had played together as kids, his wavy hair had been nearly black. And he'd been narrow and lean until adulthood—all gawky elbows and long legs. Maturity had helped him grow into his powerful body.

His eyes, though. . . .

His eyes had always been a savage gold, rare and striking even among their kind. From the moment he pulled her from the bog, she knew this boy would be the greatest Pack Leader in the history of the *lupi viri*. And no matter what had happened to the Pack since then, no matter the deaths and births and matings and Challenges, his eyes had *never* changed.

No, Michael Wyndham was in the right place, the right Pack, and she knew it, and nearly everyone else did, too.

Oh, sure, there were scuffles now and again, mostly in the early years. Jeannie Wyndham, mother of Lara, the future Pack Leader, was involved with at least one. *That* had been humbling for all of them. A *human* coming to Michael's rescue . . . Ah, the shame of it . . .

Now, years later, as an adult male in his prime (to be fair, the males tended to be bigger and stronger, though she disliked distinctions by gender), his no-longer-black, no-longer-long, now-shoulder-length dark gold hair had a ripple of a wave through it, and when he stepped into sunshine it often looked to her as though he was blessed by the sun god; their Pack Leader was dazzling, which was annoying.

He had no idea. At all. No idea that to her, to the Pack, he really did seem as something of a living god. And that was annoying, too. She could hear herself thinking such nonsense, and wanted to roll her eyes. Unfortunately, knowing it was a cliché (and a silly one, at that) did not make it untrue.

He snarled at her, showing a lot of teeth, but it was more show than substance. He was still trying to articulate what he needed from her. Her! One of his least fiery, passionate, ferocious pack members. One who had never married. One who kept to herself, had never left the state of Massachusetts except for one ill-fated trip to New York City. One who didn't seek people out.

Come to think of it, she would go because Michael knew all her flaws, knew she disliked fights and intrigues, knew she was more *sapiens* than any other Pack member, knew she was happy at spreadsheets. She would go because Michael *knew* all those things about her . . . and loved and valued her not in spite of her odd habits, but because of them.

Her father and Michael's father had been brothers born a generation apart. Her father loved to read, loved to figure things out, loved to learn, loved to teach.

Michael's father loved to fight.

So here they were, two branches of the same tree, but for all they had in common, there were many differences, too.

"Listen, I don't think they mean trouble for us. Specifically, I don't think Queen Betsy does. I don't know what her consort wants . . . that fucker's harder to read than my own dad had been."

Yow. Not a lightly made comparison. Michael's father—her uncle—had been famous for sitting quietly one moment with a cub in his lap, then exploding into a fight to the death after tossing said cub to a bystander.

Her irritation at the rude uprooting of her business and personal life—

What personal life, you silly bitch?

Shut up, inner voice.

—began to fade, and interest began to take its place. The

interest wasn't necessary, but it was a bonus she was grateful for. Because the two people in this room knew she would leave at once for Minnesota, despite the dreadful seven-month winters.

Of course she would go; there had never been a doubt. If it meant her death, fine. If it meant permanent banishment from her homeland, as it had for Antonia, fine. If it meant tedious meetings and bad food and shrill vampires and dreadful weather and frostbite and a thousand tornadoes (they had all sorts of them in Minnesota, right?) and having to eat lutefisk and lefse so as to blend in, and to march through the monument to consumerism that was (drum roll, please, or maybe a cow bell?) THE MALL OF AMERICA . . . so be it.

But she was a family member first, a werewolf second, and an accountant third. Aw, nuts. If her mom was still alive, she would have given Rachael a smack. Mom had always thought her only daughter's priorities should be different.

But! Mother was (probably) dead. So Rachael's priorities were her own.

And it suited her fine.

She would go. He was family; more, she loved him like a brother and was bound, not only by their blood, but by her heart, to do as he asked.

But it would never do for Michael to know too much of that, so she fumed and scowled and insulted him and let herself be placated and pretended this thing was a terrible inconvenience.

Oh, wait. It *was*.

Dammit!